A LISTING

OF THE WORKS OF

ROBERT NATHAN

WILL BE FOUND AT THE END

OF THIS VOLUME

A STAR IN THE WIND

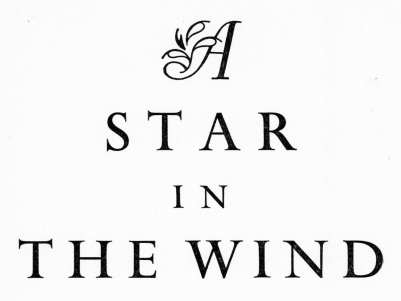

A
STAR
IN
THE WIND

Robert Nathan

New York · Alfred·A·Knopf

1962

L. C. catalog card number: 61–17085

THIS IS A BORZOI BOOK,

PUBLISHED BY ALFRED A. KNOPF, INC.

FIRST EDITION

"To Shirley,

also known as Minnie:

strictest critic, gayest companion,

and best friend."

This is the story of my friend

Josef Shaftel

—as he told it to me—

and the things he did

in that spring of the year 1948

ROBERT NATHAN

A STAR IN THE WIND

CHAPTER

I

MORNING rose above the hills of Moab, swept across
the sea to Cyprus, and lifted the shadows from the ruins of
Berlin and Nuremberg. It touched the faces of Jews behind the barbed wire of the detention camps at Bremen
and Wilhelmshaven, on board old, lumbering freighters in
the Mediterranean, and outside the stifling tents of Cyprus,
where they waited and brooded in bitter patience, barred
from Palestine, the promised land.

Nevertheless, time after time these obstinate remnants of Israel, survivors of Belsen, of Auschwitz, and of
Buchenwald, slipped through the barbed wire, eluded their
guards, and with their few possessions on their backs stole
across frontiers, hid in ditches, and made their way to the
waiting steamers in Marseilles, in Villeneuve, in Genoa—
only to be seized at Haifa by the British and sent back to
Cyprus or to Germany again.

England, which was already preparing to give up

3

*Suez, Asia, Africa, India, Malaya, Singapore, and Ceylon,
hoped in this way to ensure the friendship of King Farouk,
the Grand Mufti, Ibn Saud, and King Abdullah of Trans-
Jordan. The Jews on Cyprus comforted themselves with
songs and dreams and mocking jokes, and tried to forget
the past which was tattooed in numbers on their forearms
below the elbow.*

It was the spring of the year 1948. In England, the
Labour party was in power; on the Continent, defeated
Rome lay in peace upon her hills. The Italian elections
were over, the Communists had been put off, and all America rejoiced.

Rome was quiet under the warm Italian sky. The cries
of children, sharper than birds which were singing in the
parks and gardens and in cages hanging from the balconies, rose above the ancient, mossy walls—lion-colored in
the sun or blue in shadow—the baroque palaces, the obe-
lisks and spires. From the boulevards, the piazzas, the narrow cobbled streets, came the explosion of motorcycles, the
bleating of horns, the falling of water, the splashing of
fountains, the shouts of women leaning from their windows, and the sound of radios playing "Luna Capresi,"
"Buttons and Bows," and "Mañana."

Near the railroad terminus, a young man came out of
his hotel into the clear, golden, morning light of the Via
Cavour. His name was Joseph Victor; he was from Cleveland, Ohio, and he had arrived a few days earlier to cover
the Italian elections for a Canadian news service.

At almost the same moment, from a *pensione* on the
Via Margutta, Priscilla Greene, of Boston, Massachusetts,
started for her desk in the *Herald Tribune* offices in the

Foreign Press Building, where she ran an information service and contributed articles from time to time to the Paris edition. She had been in Rome for more than two years.

There are few meetings without some effect somewhere; the tunnel-like burrowings of human beings through time, like the underground passages of insects, meet, collide, take strange, roundabout patterns, and go off in unexpected directions. From the Hotel Mediterraneo or the Pensione Flora to the Via della Mercede was not very far; but behind this one short journey were many others, and if the road from Boston had been, on the whole, a simple one, the road from Cleveland had not.

These two, Joseph Victor and Priscilla Greene, met in the most direct way possible: they bumped into each other. Priscilla was coming out of the building, Joseph was going in. Each recoiled as from a blow, which it was. "*Prego*," said Priscilla. "Excuse me," said Joseph.

"Oh," said Priscilla, smiling, "I'm sorry!" at the same moment that Joseph muttered in elegant Italian:

"*Per piacere!*"

They both laughed, and stood back and looked at each other. Joseph saw a tall girl, fine-boned and slender, with corn-silk hair and golden-brown eyes; and he had taken her for an Italian. Young, he thought, not more than twenty-three or twenty-four. There was fragrance in the air: a perfume, a little musky, not of flowers. . . . He felt suddenly very gay.

Priscilla saw a short, dark man in his late twenties or early thirties—wiry, quick, and eager, with warm, alight, sorrowing eyes. A sensitive face, she thought, intense, proud, and anxious. But American; it definitely had that look about it.

5

"You are an American, aren't you?" she said, and held out her hand. "I'm Priscilla Greene."

That was the way she was, always—direct and sudden and assured. His fingers, thin and hard, touched hers for a moment, and then let go. "Joseph Victor," he said awkwardly. "I'm . . . I'm a correspondent."

She smiled, and turned away. "Have fun," she said, and got into a little car and drove off. Joseph stood looking after her; at one point he thought she looked back, and he lifted his hand shyly in a salute. But he couldn't see that she answered it, and after a while he turned into the building and went upstairs to the *Herald Tribune*.

His business didn't keep him long. He didn't know any of the correspondents or the photographers well enough to more than pass the time of day, but when he came out again he had at least found out who she was and where she lived. "Pat Greene?" the A.P. man had said. "Sure, look her up in the directory. Lives somewhere out near the Borghese."

Joseph walked through the city and along the Via del Tritone in the bright spring sunshine. The sky overhead was a soft blue, fleeced with cloud, and life bloomed and blossomed around him. The little tables in front of the cafés under the striped awnings were already crowded for the morning *apéritif*: the Campari, or the white vermouth from the north. Everywhere the dark-eyed whistling men gazed boldly at the women, and the women paraded past without a glance, wonderfully aware. Everywhere voices rose in a surf of sound: the sound of life being lived, being enjoyed.

It was a concert for a lonely man who had once been a musician. Joseph felt excited; he felt free, and about to do

6

something—anything—altogether unlike himself. Have fun, he thought; she told me to have fun.

And coming to the Trevi Fountain, with its sound of mountain streams, he stopped to watch some old men resting themselves upon the steps. The fountains of Rome, he thought, and heard in his mind the music of Respighi. He tossed a coin into the fountain for luck, or for happiness, or to return again to Rome, and only realized by the surprised expressions on the faces of the old men that he had declared himself by this gesture to be a foreigner, whereas they had taken him to be a Roman like themselves. Blushing a little, he turned and walked away with an air of unconcern.

That night, after dining on *fetuccini* at the restaurant at his hotel, Joseph Victor sat in his high-ceilinged, old-fashioned room typing out an article for Toronto. "We cannot accept the premise," he wrote, "that an anti-Communist vote is necessarily a vote for democracy; one is struck not by the democratic majority achieved by the Democratic Christians, but by the forces attaching themselves to the Christian Democrats as the only means of registering their anti-Communist sentiments."

He was busy, thoughtful, and content. He heard the shrill scream of the trains as they entered the Terminal Depot, not far away; they had none of the sorrowful ululation of the trains at home, rolling across the lonely countryside over the prairies and along the river bottoms. There was none of the solemn bell-tolling of the Cleveland yards, or the air-shattering klaxons of the great diesels coming into Los Angeles from the deserts and the orange groves. Here there were only impatient whistles and high, shrill blasts; the locals, the expresses, the *wagons-lits*, rolled in from

Heaven-knows-where; he had no picture of the land itself
the way he had at home, seeing in memory the empty plains
and lonely prairies, the small towns lying out under the dark
night sky with its stars, the far-off coasts with moonlight on
the sea. . . .

". . . the forces attaching themselves to the Christian
Democrats . . ."

He stopped and stared at the fingers of his left hand,
the tips still calloused from biting down on the strings of
his Guadagnini. His mother's sister had bought it for him,
the one with money; but that was when they still expected
him to be another Mischa Elman, another Heifetz, and the
glory of his family. "A man of distinction," his mother
used to say tearfully, as he struggled with his scales. "A
genius."

How strange, then, that he should be where he was.
He closed his eyes for a moment; and for that moment he
was in the little room back of the butcher shop again, and
his mother was urging him to work—to practice, to give
more time to his music, to work even harder. . . . He
could hear her voice, gentle and complaining.

"Yonnie"—she used to call him Yonnie—"where are
you going?"

"I don't know, Ma. I'm going out. I'll be back."

"Don't go, Yonnie. Stay and practice. Only great you
have to be!"

"Why?" he said to her in his mind. "Why do I have to
be great, Ma?"

"Don't ask," she said. "Don't talk; play. Look how
Elman earns! A gift from God to his family. His mother
could be proud.

"Play, Joseph, play!"

"Not Joseph . . . Josef." It was his aunt's voice, the one who paid for everything: for the lessons, for the fiddle, even for his clothes. . . .

He shook his head and turned back to his typewriter again. ". . . Running adjacent to the Italian problem," he wrote, "is the struggle of East and West. America's fears . . ."

It had been such a struggle between the two women to see who could do the most for him. Each was good to him in her way, each gave him what she could. They wanted him to be great, to work hard, to be an important man, to be a credit to them. They tore each other to pieces with what they wanted for him.

Well, he was free of them now. And with a sudden feeling of audacity, he picked up the telephone and asked to be put through to the number opposite Priscilla Greene's name in the directory. He thought he'd say something amusing to her; he'd say: "This is the man you bumped into today. How are you?"

There was no answer to the phone, and he turned back to his article again. The question was—what was to become of Italy's colonies?

But the excitement was gone, and some of the feeling of freedom. He felt lonely, the sounds of the city outside his high-ceilinged room were strange to him. He hummed a little of the G minor Bruch and let his fingers dance for a moment on the table.

Priscilla Greene, meanwhile, was perched on a hard couch in the even more high-ceilinged studio of the sculptor Ezio Monteverdi, in the Via dei Greci, off the Via Babuino. The studio, a made-over stable dating from the fifteenth century, was full of Monteverdi's friends who stood or sat where they could between the great statues made of bolts, flattened tin cans, welded iron bars, and scraps of steel, which bore such titles as "Motherhood," "Patriotism," "Birds in Flight," and "Figures 1 to 7." There was no particular reason for the party; it was given out of exuberance and the joy of living and Ezio's desire to drink as much wine as possible in the company of his friends.

He was a successful man, and had already had one showing of his works in the Galleria La Medusa on the Via Babuino, as a result of which he had sold several of his pieces to Americans who were able to appreciate a nice bit of welding. Bearded, his bare, dusty feet in leather sandals, he gazed happily around him, and held up his glass in a toast to Priscilla Greene, to whom he attributed most of his success. It was Priscilla who had brought his work to the attention of the Galleria La Medusa.

"You are the friend and mother of man," he said in his own language.

"She is the Little Corporal of all the world," agreed young Antonio Ariano, gazing at her with ardent eyes. His family, the Counts of Ariano, still owned a small farm in Campania, and he was related, though distantly, to the Caraccioli. When he had first met Priscilla, a year before, he had at once asked her to become his mistress, an offer which—like several before and since—she had refused, not without a feeling of gratitude; and six weeks later he had found himself, without quite knowing how, engaged in the business of exporting Venetian leatherware and making, for the first time in his life, a small but adequate living.

"*E'vero*," said Fabrizio Pertile, a great barrel of a man whose delicate but cruel cartoons delighted the readers of the *Popolo d'Italia*; "without her we would doubtless also have lost the peace." And he dipped his great head into his mug of beer. "Like Fiume," he said.

Priscilla smiled back at him; she was accustomed to these remarks, in which she saw no bitterness, for it was her nature to take charge and to help people. This was due as much to a warm heart as to her Boston upbringing, which had taught her to regard the rest of the world as underprivileged and in need of light.

Only Kevin O'Connor, of the *Irish Times*, failed to appreciate her properly. He came across the room now, from where he'd been talking to Clelia Bellochio, and stood looking down at her. He had a long brown beard and the appearance of a young George Bernard Shaw. "Well, Pat," he said genially, "what devilish good have you been up to lately?"

"Kevin!" she exclaimed happily, and held out her hand. She was fond of this rough, keen man in his heavy, brown-green, heathery tweeds that looked as though they'd been made for his grandfather. "Come sit with me," she said.

"What's going on in the world?"

"Nothing good," said O'Connor, "beyond the dismemberment of the British Empire. There's been no empire fallen with such a thump since the fifth century. It's a joy to watch, from a safe distance . . . like yourself, now, the way you'd run the whole world if you were let, and looking like innocence itself!"

Priscilla opened her wide, golden eyes at him. "Why, Kevin," she cried, "what do you think women were put into the world for?"

"Ah," said the young Count Ariano, "this I can tell you, if you wish to know." And he licked his full red lips in a knowing way. But Priscilla brushed him aside. *"That,"* she declared severely, "we have always with us, like the poor."

"She has never loved," said Monteverdi; "therefore she is strong with influence, like the Virgin."

"Nevertheless, we are stuck with De Gasperi," said Fabrizio Pertile, "who does not resemble a virgin."

As the conversation veered inevitably toward politics, Priscilla leaned back and let her mind drift off onto other matters. There were her articles for the Sunday papers; there was one, for instance, begging to be written, about the new school of Abstractionists which had sprung into being some four years earlier, after the Liberation, when a sergeant in General Anders's Polish Army, ordered to paint black crosses on the off-limits sections of the city, decided to become a painter, and founded a school. Or was it too silly to be believed? Yet it was the truth. And the beatings that still went on at night in the old Jewish Quarter—but did people want to hear the truth? That was the question. What should she tell her *Tribune* readers?

"The saintly face of Pope Pius XII, gazing down from the balcony of the Vatican . . ."

That was always safe.

Certainly, the face of that young man she'd all but knocked down on the Via della Mercede had been anything but saintly. Or had it? It was strange: she had only seen him for a moment, but his face was quite clear in her mind. Angelic, perhaps—but on the dark side of the seraphim, along with Lucifer. And, like that great archangel, forever sorrowful.

She had no idea who he was. Joseph Victor, a correspondent. . . . He had stood there, staring at her, like somebody looking in through a doorway . . . the lonely

Lucifer gazing in out of the darkness. He must have thought her Italian, for the first moment, anyway; what a surprise it must have been. She smiled a little, remembering their formal manner to each other.

Prego.

Piacere.

She found—somewhat to her surprise—that she was thinking of what she'd say to him when they met again— that is, supposing they bumped into each other somewhere . . . something light and amusing. Her lips curved in a smile, delicate as a shiver of air on a leaf. "You are dreaming?" queried Ariano softly in her ear. "Possibly of me?"

"No," she said, sitting up, "not of you, Tony. Be a good boy and fetch me another drink, will you?"

"Of course," he said, rising gracefully to his feet. "I am delighted to be of service.

"But afterwards I will tell you *my* dream. It is altogether full of love. In it we are transported to an island . . ."

"Please, Tony—my drink?"

"*Subito.*"

There was no message for her when she got home that night, dismissing both Antonio and Fabrizio at her door. Not that she had expected any, but still . . . She looked at her silent telephone with a strange feeling of unfriendliness, as though in some way it had disappointed her. She undressed slowly, almost as though she were waiting for something to happen. Afterwards she lay in bed for a longer time than usual before falling asleep. She thought about her home; she had a vision of Marlborough Street, and angels riding on enormous wings, sailing above the Charles, high over Boston, over the Common, over Copley Square. . . .

One of them was Lucifer. The face of the great arch-angel was sorrowful and proud.

Joseph Victor also slept. He dreamed that he was seated once more in the first desk of the violin section of the Los Angeles Philharmonic. Around him were the un-heard, crashing chords of *The Firebird;* the conductor was orthodox, but the concertmaster was an old woman, and he was afraid.

Always, at home, he seemed to wake in a hostile world; he didn't know why this was so, but it was. But this time he awoke with a cheerful feeling, and a sense of happiness and freedom. There was something exciting about waking in a strange city, listening to foreign sounds, seeing a different light, feeling a different air . . . and at the same time knowing that there was a special face some-where in that city, in those humming streets, in that morn-ing light—one special form in whom the whole city was personified, embodied, reflected, like the sky in a drop of water.

He had no business downtown that morning, but at eleven o'clock he was on his way to the Foreign Press Building, stopping off at a flower stall on the Via Cavour to buy a dozen carnations. What he meant to do with them, he didn't know; but if he did bump into Miss Greene again, he would at least—he thought—be prepared.

Miss Greene was not in her office; the door of 14 Via della Mercede didn't open and waft her out into the street and the waiting carnations. But it didn't matter; there was no sinking of his spirits, no clouding of his day. After a while, when no young woman with hair the color of corn silk appeared, he gently deposited the flowers in the arms of a little girl with a torn frock and enormous eyes, who had been watching him from the shadows of an archway.

14

Taken aback by such an unexpected gift, frightened, enchanted, disbelieving, and ready to flee, she could only
stare at him in silence. But when he had gone, she dipped
her dark, hungry, shrewd little face into the blooms and took
a deep breath of their fragrance. What an escape, she
thought; anything could have happened.

Joseph walked through the city under the cerulean
sky with its clouds all the color of old tapestries. He walked
in the gardens of the Borghese, and in the Piazza San
Pietro. He was in no hurry; on the Monte Gianicolo he
sat for a while beneath the pines and the wisteria, watching the nuns and seminarians parading along the Passegi-
ata, seeing the Tiber flowing below him, and the blue cloud-
shadows on the city across the river; he ate his lunch in the
middle of the afternoon in the garden of a *trattoria* below
the moss-covered steps. The day flowed gently over him,
sights and sounds, sun-warmed stone and ancient marble,
churches, palaces, and fountains all making a sound of
peace around him, through which the harsher noises of
the streets barely seemed to penetrate. Something—he
didn't know what—rested and comforted him: there's no
hurry, it seemed to say; we have been here a long time.

At six o'clock he returned to his hotel by taxi and immediately telephoned Priscilla Greene. The speed with
which the call was answered might have suggested to a
cooler mind that Miss Greene had been sitting very near
the phone—even waiting, perhaps, for just such a call. But
Joseph's heart was beating too heavily for him to do more
than say, in a strangled voice:

"Hello?"

"*Pronto,*" said Priscilla warily.

"Miss Greene?"

"Yes?" asked the cool, silvery voice.

"Oh," he said. "Well . . . this is . . . this is Joseph Victor."

At her end of the line, Priscilla smiled a little to herself and settled back comfortably in her chair. I know, she thought; I know very well. But she said, instead:

"*Prego?*"

"No," he said earnestly. "I mean . . . I'm the one who bumped into you . . . remember? We talked Italian to each other."

"Yes," she said. "I remember."

"Well," he said, "I thought—that is—are you doing anything? I mean . . . would you have dinner with me, or something . . . sometime?"

His voice trailed away into a hoarse whisper. He felt awkward, defenseless, uncertain, frightened, audacious, ashamed; it was all there in his voice, and Priscilla's heart went out to it.

"Why, of course," she said. "I'd love to. When?"

"Whenever you say!" Life flowed back into him again, all warmth and happiness. "Tonight?"

"Well, no," she said, considering, "not tonight." One should have a day or two, she thought, to savor things like this. "Perhaps later in the week?"

"Tomorrow?" he asked, so eagerly that she had to smile again.

"Well, then," she said, "tomorrow."

"That's wonderful," he said. "Tomorrow." He seemed to think of something. "*Grazie,*" he said happily.

"*Non ce di che.*"

"At what time?" he asked.

"At eight?"

"Great!" he said. "I'll pick you up at eight."

"Do you have a car?" she asked.

"No . . . I'll take a taxi."

She was silent for a moment. "Look," she said in a matter-of-fact, no-nonsense voice, "I have a car. Suppose I call for you instead."

CHAPTER

2

THEY SAT on the terrace of the restaurant on the Pincio and looked down over the evening city, in which lights were already beginning to appear. To the south, across the Tiber, the dome of St. Peter's floated up like a great sea-bubble in the fading sea-green evening air, above the blue shadowed streets and houses of the Quarter.

She was looking even lovelier, he thought, than he had remembered, in the blue light of evening, with the yellow candlelight reflected in her eyes and in her hair. "You're not a correspondent, really," she said, "are you, Mr. Victor?"

And she looked at him with a smile in which he thought he could see a touch of mockery, not unsympathetic.

"Well, yes," he said soberly, "I am, in a way. I wasn't always, of course. I mean . . . I was something else, before."

"Naturally," she said. "Most people are." She nodded her head, and for a moment the candlelight sparkled on tiny sequins caught in a cobweb of lace she wore around her throat. "You're a musician, aren't you?"

Joseph felt a sudden sagging of his spirit; was it as apparent as all that? "I was," he said shortly, and looked out, frowning, at the deepening sky.

"Well," she said gaily, "that's nothing to be ashamed of, is it? Or is it?"

It isn't that, he thought bitterly; it isn't being ashamed of what I was—but of what I wasn't. "How did you know about the music?" he asked.

"From little things," she said. "The way your fingers drum on the tablecloth, fast and strong, like little trip hammers. But only the left hand. You were a violinist, weren't you?"

"Yes," he said unwillingly. "A child violinist. A prodigy."

"And you gave it up?"

"I gave it up."

"But why?"

He didn't want to think about it, and at the same time he felt a need to tell her, to tell somebody.

"It was my family," he said. "My mother wanted me to be a musician."

Priscilla smiled, and he noticed that there were little shadows on her cheeks, almost like dimples. "She might have wanted you to be President," she said. "I think she was very modest, considering."

"That would never have occurred to her," he said. "A rabbi, perhaps; but not a President."

"Oh," she said, and was silent. So that was it: he was a Jew. She had known only a few Jews in her life, and none of them well. They were strange, dark, mysterious people from far back in time . . . Jerusalem, the Psalms, and the Prophets . . . hated and beaten, exiled, driven out, herded to the gas ovens, killed like starlings . . . poets and bankers, fiddlers and peddlers, martyrs, proud women, men of fear and courage . . . the incredible beauty and obstinacy, the ferocity of a race that refused to die. . . .

"Does it matter?" he asked bitterly.

"Yes," she said simply. "I like it; it makes you more of a person."

Joseph shrugged his shoulders; he found such a remark almost incomprehensible. Why should being a Jew make him more of a person? Besides, he had left all that behind him when he had broken away from his family, from his career, from all things Jewish . . . that night in New York City, in the rain.

"My aunt wanted me to be called Josef," he said, "with the *f*, like a virtuoso. So for that I had to work while the other kids were out playing shinny or one-o'-cat."

"I played field hockey at Marlborough," said Priscilla. "All you get is a cracked shin."

"Yes," he said. He sounded angry and unhappy. "A person is what he is," he said. "I don't think about being a Jew."

She stared at him in surprise. She wanted to ask: How can you not? but refrained, from a feeling of delicacy. As for Joseph, the whole thing depressed him; he didn't want to talk about it. "The war's over," he said. "Hitler's dead; Mussolini, too."

She looked around hastily. "Careful," she murmured. "I wouldn't mention that."

He stared at her stupidly. "Why not?" he asked. "Who's listening?"

"Who knows?" she answered. And she added coolly: "A snake never dies before sunset. No matter how you chop him up."

He continued to stare at her for a moment or two, like someone who has just received some unwelcome news from far away and hasn't yet understood it or accepted it. And then suddenly his mood changed, and with a warm, almost boyish smile, he asked quickly and at the same time a little shyly:

"What about you?"

The abrupt change took her by surprise, and she straightened almost instinctively in her chair, for a brief moment on the defensive, before she let her hands flutter in a helpless gesture in front of her. "Do you mean . . . do I die at sunset?" she asked, to gain time.

He waved it away. "No," he said. "Who are you? I mean—where do you come from?"

"From Boston," she answered, "and Marlborough and Wellesley. What do you want to know about me? I didn't make Phi Beta. My father sells rope."

"You mean little bits of it over the counter?"

"He's Boston Hemp and Cordage," she said simply.

"Oh," said Joseph. "Big business." He raised his glass and looked at her through the clear, cool yellow-green wine. "*L'chayim!*" he said.

She questioned him with her eyes, and he flushed uncomfortably. "I didn't know I remembered it," he said. "It means 'to life.' "

"Oh," she said. "Well—*Salut!*" She lifted her glass in turn, and smiled at him across the rim of it.

"I didn't really care about your father's business," he said. "What I meant was—are you happy and kind? The way you look?"

Priscilla was amused, not so much at the question as at herself for trying, in that single moment, to look as kind and happy as possible. It was an old trick of hers, to try to be all things to all men—to want to appear to every man the image of what he wanted to see in a woman. It was instinctive with her, and dated from her childhood, when she had watched her rigid, unimaginative mother splinter herself against her father's unyielding granite. She herself had charmed him, and then, just in time, had fled to boarding school.

Of course, one had to have a knowledge of men; to know, for instance, that when a young fellow like Tony Ariano asked you to be his mistress, what he really wanted was a mother-image (one that he could first worship and later detest) and a nice position in a bank.

Well, she thought, she always meant to be kind, and at the moment she felt quite happy.

"I suppose so," she said. "I never had much reason not to be. I mean, I've never had any reason to dislike people."

He nodded solemnly. "It's easier to like people," he said, "if they like you."

"People like you for what you are," she said. "Don't you think?"

"I suppose so," he said. "But what are you? I mean—in the long run?"

"What are you . . . ?"

"I was going to be a child prodigy," he said. "Now I'm a newspaper correspondent, on my way to Russia."

"You didn't tell me that," she said.

"I haven't told you anything yet." He leaned forward suddenly and laid his thin, hard fingers on her wrist. It felt deliciously soft, and for a moment it stopped him, and he just sat looking at her. "I haven't told you that you make me feel that I'm in Rome," he said at last.

She laughed, and drew her wrist away. "That's strange," she said lightly. "Why me? I'm a stranger here myself."

"Maybe that's it," he said. "Only—you're at home here, and that makes a kind of home for me too."

He ran out of words, and sat staring at her. He was so in earnest that for a moment it completely stopped her. Could I really like him? she thought. I wonder. In some way he managed to trouble her; she had been troubled before, of course, and more than once, but it hadn't been quite the same; she had always known that she could slide out from under, evade, slip away . . . turn into a tree, perhaps. This time she wasn't sure. His need was so naked—not, she assured herself quickly, that she herself, Priscilla Greene, was the only, the unique, and particular answer.

To turn into a tree, like Daphne chased by Phoebus Apollo—or a fountain, like Arethusa. But Joseph wasn't Apollo, and there were enough fountains in Rome . . . and, anyway, she wasn't actually being chased, as far as she could see. Certainly not the way she had been by the young Romans; they made a gallant view-haloo of it. There was something morose about Joseph, something that might be hard to handle. She was always able to handle people; it was one of the things she liked about herself. "The women of antiquity," her teacher Miss Bates used to say to her class, "had no vote, but their influence was by no means inconsiderable. They, too, were Movers and Shakers; and I am not merely talking about the hetaerae, women of a certain professional competence, but of the duly registered wives and consorts of men of affairs."

The opinion of the class was that one didn't necessarily have to be a wife, one could be a consort; and that professional competence was not of itself necessary to an interesting life.

Well, she was competent enough, she guessed, from such experiences as had come her way; but while competence certainly added to one's pleasure, and was nothing to be sneezed at, the solider satisfactions came from being a Mover and a Shaker . . . the way she had moved young Ariano into the export business. It was a game, a shining, May-morning sort of game, to be played with energy and charm and beauty and youth, and the full resources of Marlborough School for Young Ladies behind her.

What sort of game was Joseph playing? With a little shiver of pleasant apprehension, she decided that it was something very dark and ancient, that she would have to find out for herself, and that it would certainly be an Interesting Experience.

She looked up at him from under her eyelids, her eyes, fringed with their dark lashes, like sudden flowers; and he trembled; it was like a golden goddess of the Greeks appearing in the Negev to Isaac or Jacob. "Have another cup of coffee," he asked, "or an ice, or something? . . . A semifreddo, it says here—whatever that is."

"No, thank you," she said contentedly. She had caught the quickly covered tremor in his voice; perhaps, for a change, if there was any hunting to be done, it would be the man who fled.

"Have you been to Tivoli yet?" she asked. "To Hadrian's Villa? There isn't much left of it, of course, but it's quite magical at dusk, if you squinch your eyes up and imagine. . . . And the Villa d'Este with its water-gardens?

All dancing uphill and down like those silver thingummies on a Christmas tree!"

"I haven't been anywhere," he said. "I wouldn't even know where to go."

She gazed at him thoughtfully, pleased, her shining head cocked a little to one side like a bird. She had a way of watching and listening, with what appeared to be intense interest, which was very flattering to him. "Well," she said comfortably, "we can attend to that part of it, anyway."

"I don't know if I care about water-gardens dancing downhill," he said; "it makes me think of 'Jill came tumbling after.'"

She looked up at him, puzzled, wrinkling her nose. "Does it, Mr. Victor?" she asked. "Why?"

"Joe," he said. "For Joseph. With the *p-h*."

"Joe, then," she said. "I don't see the analogy. . . ."

"Jack fell down," said Joseph. "And Jill came tumbling after. The whole world, if you ask me."

"I see," she said. Oh please, she thought to herself, don't let him turn out to be tiresome after all.

"There's another one," he said. "'When the wind blows—'"

"I know," she said. "The cradle will fall."

Down will come cradle, baby, and all. It was depressing.

He smiled across the table at her, so suddenly and warmly that her heart gave a startled skip. Oh Lord, she thought uncomfortably, who's chasing who? It was not exactly grammatical, and she corrected it in her mind, but the correction didn't have the appeal, somehow of the earlier remark.

"I'll have a semi-freddo," she said.

.   .   .

Far off to the northeast, a woman and her child waited in a forest meadow near the Czech frontier, huddled in the shadows. She was not alone; she was one of a small group, of many such groups of refugees making their way to Palestine, like hares, like foxes, from the D.P. camps of mid-Europe, over and under and through the barbed wire, past the guards and the sentries, shot at sometimes, turned back often, carrying with them their few belongings left over from the burning and the beating. "Anna," said someone in a low voice; and she slipped out of the shadows for the swift, short run across the night-dark, still half-frozen field. The child beside her stumbled, and let out a cry. "Hush, Mia," she whispered; "hush, my darling."

Joseph and Priscilla drove down the lighted, busy, echoing Corso to the Piazza Venezia. They said little, and she left him at his hotel; he wanted to escort her back to the *pensione* in the Via Margutta, but she wouldn't let him. "I'm perfectly safe," she said. "I'm used to this sort of thing. Don't forget—I'm a newspaperwoman. Where would I be if I had to be escorted everywhere? Good night; and thanks for the dinner. It was fun."

Fun? he thought dimly; it hadn't seemed exactly like fun to him—rather like something exciting, and foreboding. "When shall I see you again?" he asked.

She looked at him with a mockingbird air. "Why," she said, considering, "when indeed? When would you like to?"

He gave an inward snort of impatience, but only to himself. What was the sense of all that? She knew as well as he did that the answer was tomorrow, or why would he have asked? Still, to say so was to stretch his neck out for the ax. "I'll ring you," he said.

She nodded, and smiled, and put the car into gear,

and waited a moment; but he didn't lean forward to kiss her, and after a moment or two she drove off. She felt obscurely irritated. So he'd ring her; well, perhaps she wouldn't be in.

As she stepped in through her doorway, the phone was already ringing. "*Pronto*," she said. "Yes?"

"It's me," he said. He sounded young and lonely and somehow vulnerable. She took a deep breath, and kicked her shoes off. "Oh," she said, "hello."

"I just wanted to say good night again," he said. "And thank you. I mean instead of you saying it to me."

It was strange how amused and cheerful she suddenly felt. "Not at all," she said. And again: "It was fun."

"Really?"

"Of course, really!"

"It seems like such a strange word."

"It's the nicest word there is," she said. "Anyway, to begin with."

"Oh," he said, and hesitated a moment. "Priscilla," he said. "Miss Greene . . ."

"I'm called Pat, usually."

"Pat . . ."

"Yes?"

"Would . . . tomorrow . . . ?"

She could feel her heart beating a little faster. It was one of those Moments, when whatever one said . . . What was it Caesar crossed? The Rubicon? She could hear the voice of Miss Bates, talking to the class of '45 at Wellesley: "A woman need not be a Passive Object, simply because she is a woman." Oh—what was the use of fooling around with it? Did she want to, or didn't she?

"Yes," she said.

CHAPTER

❧❧❧❧❧❧❧❧❧❧❧❧❧❧❧❧❧❧

3

IN THE DAYS which followed, while the countryside
blossomed through the Roman spring, the friendship of
these two—so unlike, and so unlikely—blossomed too, at
least from bud to early leaf. It was quite true that Priscilla
was at home in Rome, that she knew everyone and went
everywhere. And she took Joseph with her: to her favorite
restaurants, from Cecci's Trattoria in the working-class section, to the original Alfredo's, and even—on one fabulous
occasion, after Jospeh had sold an article—to the Osteria
dell' Orso itself. Not that Priscilla was in any sense a gour-
met; she was as happy with fried clams and a bottle of
Valpolicella as she was with filet of sole flamed in old
scotch, and a Château Gruaud Larose Sarget, '37.

At Galeassi's in Trastevere they dined on *scampi* and
gnocchi with Kevin O'Connor, enjoying a long discussion
of the Marshall Plan, about which said O'Connor: "If Ireland had had any sense, she'd have declared war on Amer-

ica, instead of England, and lost it, by God, and been re-
habilitated to the tune of millions; and if there isn't a
story in that for some Irishman to write, I'll eat it!"

Flowers were blooming everywhere: in the gardens, in
the parks, banked high in the street-corner flower stalls.
They rarely came home from an evening without their
arms full of blossoms for Priscilla's room, or sometimes for
Joseph's. The cypress and the pine, in fresher green, stood
outlined against the sky, above the old stone walls and on
the hills—the age-old pines of Rome, which, like her fountains, made their own music. The little Topolino threaded
its way through cascades and whirlpools of traffic: buses
and trams, small darting Vespas, horse carts and carriages,
bicycles, motorcycles, and scooters, all competing for space
between the narrow noisy sidewalks.

They went together to the Borghese Gardens, to the
puppet shows; one dreamy, cloud-flecked afternoon they
watched the play of the fountains at the Villa d'Este; hand
in hand they wandered through the ruins of Hadrian's
Villa at dusk, and squinched their eyes.

And they worked together on Joseph's stories. It was
Priscilla who arranged for him to visit Togliatti, whom she
knew—and Priscilla who arranged for him to interview the
sculptor Pericles Fazzini.

They were Joe and Pat to each other, but that was all.
They weren't lovers. Not yet.

She was in no hurry. Something—she didn't quite
know what—held her back. She was still a little puzzled by
him, although she knew him, she thought, very well: he
had told her about his childhood—about the little butcher
shop where his parents struggled for their lives, the shul in
the synagogue where he had studied Hebrew and where
he had been beaten over the head with a cane when he

didn't pay attention. She knew about his Orthodox grand-father who ruled his family like Abraham, which was so easy in Ur, and so difficult in Cleveland, and the tragic, long, long battle between his mother and his aunt to see who could do more for him, for his career—to make him into the virtuoso he never wanted to be; his mother with her anxious love, the other with her money. There was such a drive, such a compulsion for him to be a success. . . . It had to be one or the other, he explained, success or failure; there wasn't anything between.

And yet, there was something missing, something she didn't know, something he hadn't told her—some darkness and bitterness from which he turned away, which kept him always poised to strike, if only at himself. As though some-where in the past there was something he couldn't bear to remember. It fascinated her; she felt that she wasn't quite, altogether, able to manage him, and that disturbed her. She wasn't exactly in love with him, but she could be, she thought, if she let herself. It was like flirting with danger; once you'd gone too far, once you were over the line, it was too late to draw back. Then you'd better be in love with whatever you were doing—or else!

She had always been able to control things. That was what it was to be a lady; a lady allowed only those things to happen to her over which she could exercise control. A lady could have a heart as big as a circus tent, but she had to be the ringmaster. To be whirled around on a fly-ing trapeze could be frightening. Joe's dark bitterness troubled her; it had a feeling of strength about it. She'd have been more comfortable if he'd been a little weaker.

It didn't feel like strength to Joe, it felt like longing. It didn't even feel like bitterness; because, now, for the first time that he could remember, he was happy. He was in

love with a city, a dream, a season, a golden girl, and they
were all mixed up together in his mind. Even his loneliness
was different.

He knew of no way to express it, this dream; it would
have embarrassed him even to mention it. He had been
in love only once before, with a girl in Cleveland; like himself, she was a student at the Conservatory. One night he
had taken her for a ride in an old battered Hupmobile; he
drove her into the woods, and sat for a long time just looking at her. He couldn't think of anything to say; his heart
was full of beauty and the Brahms D major Concerto. The
next day she complained about him to the head of the
music school. He was never able to understand what it was
she had complained about; neither, as a matter of fact, was
she.

And now, simply to walk with Priscilla along the green
hills, through the busy, noisy street, to sit with her on the
Pincio, or at some little sidewalk table at Rosati's, or at
Angelino's; to meet her in the bright morning sunshine on
the Spanish Steps; to drive with her sometimes through the
countryside, along the dusty, cypress-gated roads, past the
small farms with their tumble-haired children and wandering goats. . . . It would have been enough just to look at
her, to feel the beauty and the longing—for what, he didn't
know; for something with the sweep and comfort of a
solemn service.

And with his hand on her shoulder, he hummed that
part of the Brahms where the violin comes in at the 206th
bar, in the sixth theme, or D in the score. . . . His
thoughts trailed away. Her shoulder was soft under the silk,
soft and disturbing. He drew his hand back slowly, confused and almost frightened by the sudden feeling—in the
hand, in the arm—in his heart?—made suddenly aware of

31

another world, of Priscilla in an unknown guise, of flesh, of woman . . . a stranger to him, alien, secret, troubling . . . a stranger to his flesh. . . .

And Priscilla, too, for a moment was aware of her shoulder, of Joseph's hand on it, warm and dry; and moving smoothly out from under his grasp like a wary bird or insect, she said lightly, and quickly and with a little gasp:

"You told me once your aunt gave you a violin?"

"Yes," he said, relieved, "a Guadagnini. Red and gold, with a one-piece spruce back and a maple top. I had a Vorin bow, too, a French bow, octagonal—a real beauty."

It seemed to him that he was chattering—and all about what? A bow and a fiddle. He felt suddenly very sad; so much time lost, so much time wasted. "I got to be pretty good, as a matter of fact," he said dully. "But the more the family quarreled, the more I grew to hate it. I was a moody kid; I used to hide in the attic, and dream."

"What about?" she asked. "Girls?"

"No," he said, He was shocked. "I used to read a lot," he said, remembering.

"Did they really beat you on the head in school?"

"Of course," he said matter-of-factly. "We had an old teacher named Itzak: we used to call him Hitchkock." He laughed mirthlessly. "He had a cane like a shillelagh," he said.

He shrugged his shoulders. "I can still speak a little Hebrew," he said. "I'd have done better to learn Italian."

"After all," she said, "you didn't know where you'd be."

"That's what I mean," he said. "You never do."

Near the fountain in the Piazza Santa Maria in Trastevere they were surrounded by ragged children begging for coppers. They looked very small and dark and fierce.

"Got a nickel, Joe? Got a nickel?" They chanted the shrill, monkeylike, mocking phrases, left over from the war, from the G.I.'s with their gum and their nickels and their cigarettes. But they fell back before Priscilla's unmistakable authority.

"*Vergogna! Ma vattene—via!*"

He looked at her out of the corner of his eyes. She's a hard girl, he thought; under that softness, there are hard bones. He felt a little fearful and at the same time elated. She could have handled the aunt, he thought. The grandfather, too.

And Rome itself delighted him: Rome, too, had its hard bones underneath the softness, the baroque curves, the Renaissance splendor. He wrote a story about the Tomb of Augustus in the moonlight and sent it back to Davies in Toronto. He received the following reply:

"What the hell, Joe!"

When he told her about it, Priscilla pursed her lips. "I guess there's too much about death in it," she said. "Maybe you'd better write about something else."

Joseph was surprised; he hadn't been thinking about death, he had been thinking about greatness, and power. "I used to think about dying," he said; "at night particularly, I'd think about how everybody has to die sooner or later, and me too; and I'd feel trapped. Did you ever feel like that? Like a rat in a trap?"

"Certainly not," said Priscilla.

"Well, anyway," he said, "I'd lie there sweating, and think there was no way out, no way at all. I still do, sometimes. Why is that, do you think?"

She made a gesture of dismissal; she didn't know. As a matter of fact, she herself went to bed every night and woke in the morning with a feeling of health and of being well situated in the world, which was full of unexpected pleasures, accidents, and triumphs.

The truth was, she enjoyed being alive, and being a young woman, which seemed to her the most satisfactory condition possible. She also, in her own way, had power and used it; and her tomb, smaller than that of Augustus, would be somewhere in her grandmother's plot in St. Michael's at Marblehead, but not for a long time yet. Not that she actually—at twenty-three—thought of herself as "young"; rather, she felt immortal, and free, and remembered with pleasure Ariano's unabashed desire for her, and other successes.

One day they drove to Frascati for lunch, and to taste the white Frascati wine. Coming home they went by way of Rocca di Papa, and Monte Cavo, from which they could see rolled out before them the whole of Rome, the surrounding hill towns, and the sea. The gentle Italian sky, flecked with its Roman clouds, rose like a bowl above them and threw blue and umber shadows over the green hills and the dreaming Tyrrhenian Sea. The whole day felt free and fine.

"Here," said Priscilla, looking about her like an eagle, "is the whole ancient world. From here I can see all that was known of the world in Caesar's time. Out there, beyond the horizon, across the water—if you could see that far—would be the Pillars of Hercules, the ruins of Tarshish, and the ends of the earth. Behind us—just over the hill— lies Parthia, and to the south, Egypt. Look out across the city, to the north; do you see beyond those hills, the Gauls? —and beyond them the Teuton forests? I do! It all centers here, like the spokes of a wheel, here in this spot of earth, these hills, this sea, this shining city, Rome. Mistress of all the world."

It pleased her, it had a sound of poetry; what were the lines? "This royal throne of kings, this scepter'd isle, This precious stone set in the silver sea . . ." Richard the Second and the dying Gaunt; she was amused at herself. But Joseph found himself obscurely irritated; and standing near her, beside a low stone wall, kicked moodily at a pebble. I never had a mistress, he thought.

He meant that he had never had a lover. He had had women—a few, and of a certain kind; but what he had done with them had not been done in love. The mere idea of such a thing in connection with Priscilla embarrassed him: this fair, springlike girl, this stranger, this woman of a different race, to whom the butcher shop, the shul, the Sabbath candles, the Passover, were pieces in an unknown game . . . this maiden who lived in sun, blossoming, welcome and assured, with her fair hair and her skin the color and feel of apricots.

"What's the matter?" she asked. "Did a cat walk over your grave?"

He smiled weakly, and with a slow, heavy-beating heart put out his hand to touch hers. She grasped it firmly, like a friend, a companion; there was nothing yielding about her. He didn't dare to draw her closer.

"So much for the world," he said. It was irrelevant; but the day didn't feel fine and free any longer. "We'd better go back," he said. "I've got a piece to file before the office closes."

"We should go to the Lido someday," said Priscilla, looking westward to the sea. The sun shone in her eyes, and the strong wind blew over her and ruffled her hair. "Always when I see the ocean, I want to go and put my feet in it."

"It isn't summer yet," said Joseph sulkily.

"Tomorrow," said Priscilla. "We'll go tomorrow."

When they got back to town, there was a letter from his mother waiting for him at the American Express office, along with a card from his friend Bert Aaronson in New York, and a prospectus from the Hollywood Bowl Association. He read his mother's letter hurriedly, and with a feeling of impatience, skipping about in the spidery handwriting; he felt it as an intrusion, almost an appeal, to which he had no answer. There was nothing about his present life that he could tell her or that she could possibly understand.

It threw a momentary shadow over his spirits; he didn't know why: he guessed it was irritation at having to listen once again to the family opinions and the neighborhood gossip. Or perhaps it was knowing that she *wouldn't* understand—that no one in his family would. Why can't they leave me alone? he thought dully, and crumpled the letter in his pocket. He hadn't written home since he'd reached Italy, and he had no intention of doing so.

They sat together on the sand at Fregene, with their backs to the dunes and the little forest of pines over which the moon, rounding to the three-quarters, had already risen, golden in the night-blue sky. A few lights burned in the houses further down the beach, and occasional faint sounds of music seemed to steal out across the water and die away at sea. Priscilla had gone wading, they had run up and down the beach together, and now they sat, wrapped in sweaters, on a blanket she had brought with her from the car, and shared a crusty loaf of bread, sausage, cheese, and a flask of red Chianti. There was a night-smell from the sea, damp and fresh and sad, and a faint fragrance of pines, and a little smell of wood-smoke now and then from the houses down the beach.

They talked for a while about the political situation; they tried to sound interested and eager about what was going on in the world, while the moon rode over their heads and the waves lapped at the shore at their feet. Surrounded by darkness and stars, by mystery and by the night, they discussed art and literature, between longer and longer pauses.

Joseph was vexed with himself; why was he talking about socialism? He wanted to talk about happiness, but he didn't know how. He was like a child at a birthday party; it was all too much for him—the night, the moonlight on the water, the faint music. He wanted to say: "I am happy." It is all here, he thought—beauty, everything, and a longing which is liable to make me burst; I am blowing up like a balloon.

This was the way he wanted to be, this was the way he wanted the world to be, forever on the brink of beauty and joy—taking him always further and further away from the past, from guilt and shame. He would have liked to say something memorable, or to be able to say nothing at all, but the silence made him uncomfortable. The girl at his side was quiet; she was so near him, he could smell the faint perfume she used. So near, and so quiet; and so many worlds away.

"Are you warm enough?" he asked, with a slight croaking sound.

Priscilla didn't answer; she, too, was waiting—for what, she didn't know. But where Joseph was tense and over-eager, she was relaxed and withdrawn into herself. The night, the water, the stars, the small breaking waves, all made her think of home, reminded her of other nights —at Quisset, or at the Hole, with the moon going down over Buzzards Bay—the summer nights of childhood, of

37

scrub pine and sweet fern and dune grass, and the clam-and-seaweed smell of the flats.

"You never know what's going to happen to you," said Joseph. "A month ago I was in Ottawa—or in New York; I've forgotten—it all seems about the same, far away and long ago. And before that . . ." He paused for a moment, and then went on with an air of mild surprise. "I was in California. It didn't mean a thing to me."

He half turned toward her; his fingers played for a moment with the soft suede of her walking shoes. "Where were you, a year ago?" he asked.

"Here," she said.

"I know. But—with whom?"

She felt a sudden sense of grievance; what business was it of his? Besides, she couldn't remember: a year ago? Was that when she had gotten Tony that job with the export house?

"Oh," she said lightly, "dozens."

She couldn't see the bleak look he turned to the dark ocean. "Well, of course," he said heavily. "But I meant . . ."

"Why ask questions?" she countered. "I didn't ask you whom you were in California with."

"I was with the whole Los Angeles Philharmonic," he said simply. "For eight weeks."

"Well, anyway," she consoled him, "you weren't lonely."

Joseph looked at her blankly. But I was, he thought; I was lonely all the time.

"I wish you could have been there when I was there," he said wistfully. "We could have sat on the beach like this at Malibu."

"It wouldn't have been the same," she said.

"No," he agreed. He paused for a moment, frowning. "As a matter of fact," he said, "it was longer ago than I thought."

"A year?" she asked. "Two years?"

"Two," he said slowly, remembering.

"I was a green girl then," she said, "just out of Wellesley. We wouldn't have been good for each other."

Joseph's fingers moved from her ankles to her legs, and something inside her sat up suddenly like an alert rabbit. "Joe," she said.

"Are we good for each other?" he asked. Her legs were silk-and-satin-soft and velvet-firm; something electric traveled along the nerves of his hand, up his arm, and in the direction of his heart. "Are we?" he asked uncertainly. "Are we, Pat?"

"I don't know," she said. She wanted to sit up, to draw herself away; but for a moment she seemed unable to move; she felt weak, lying there, feeling the warmth of his hand on her leg, waiting to feel more—or less?—wanting, willing him to be more—or was it less?—ardent; not knowing what she wanted.

But when his hand moved higher, she pushed him away firmly. "No, please," she said.

He drew his hand back at once, as though it had been burned. He was ashamed, and frightened—like a child, frightened at his own audacity, and ashamed at being caught at it and scolded. Ought he to apologize? Or act as though nothing had happened?

"I guess maybe we aren't," he said at last in a low voice, choosing a child's way of self-pity.

"Aren't what?"

"Good for each other."

She put her hand out and touched his cheek; hand

and cheek were cold in the night air. "I think we are," she said.

He turned to her with such sadness that on impulse she drew his head down against her shoulder. In the fragrant warmth of her sweater, with her arms around his head, he scarcely breathed; he closed his eyes and lay still, feeling an overwhelming happiness and a sorrow. He was truly transported, and could have wept from relief and unaccustomed delight, and wonder for himself, and pity for the lonely child in the butcher shop practicing his fiddle for whom there was this comfort, late, and not—perhaps—forever. . . .

And Priscilla, with the dark face pressed against her breast, felt a moment of bewilderment: who was this stranger cradled in her arms? And by what mysterious passages had she arrived at this place? Was it too late now to turn . . . into a tree, or a fountain?

She bent her head and kissed him. It was a cool, firm kiss, without any nonsense. "Come along," she said. "It's time we got back to the city."

CHAPTER

4

THE PASSOVER was celebrated in Jerusalem, and elsewhere among the homeless refugees who gathered in their huts and tents and told the story and drank the wine. In Cleveland, Ohio, Mrs. Victor murmured a prayer for her son. "Live in good health, Yonnie," she said under her breath. "*L'chayim.*"

Easter was over. In the churches the altars were massed with flowers; the bells rang again over Rome. The Pope had blessed his people.

In the Via della Croce, the old Marchese del Ascoli-Prieto gazed about him at the guests at the party in the apartment of Fabrizio Pertile, the successful cartoonist. The Marchese was eighty, and still in his way handsome; one could understand his reputation as a lover of many women, the youngest of whom was already a grandmother. This did not, of course, include the young actresses from the Cinecitta, for whom the attentions of the Marchese were always good for mention in some newspaper or other, or ladies of uneasy virtue, for whom the Marchese had never had much appetite. He had seen a great deal, and experienced a great deal; he had enjoyed the life of an Italian nobleman during the flowery exuberance of Savoy and—rather less so—during the black magnificence of Mussolini; he had been a guest of Edward the Seventh on the royal yacht in the harbor of Naples and of Isadora Duncan at Capri. He had lived through two large wars and several small ones; he had heard Patti herself, Tamagno, Battistini; he had had his own box at the Opera for Verdi and Rossini; he had seen D'Annunzio and Duse. And he had lived to admire Anna Magnani, the cinema, Roberto Rossellini, and the music of Respighi and George Gershwin.

He was too old now for the serious business of love, but not for gallantry; beauty appealed to him, and so did youth, for which he felt a certain sympathy.

And catching sight of Priscilla and Joseph in the crowd around the famous sculptor Pericles Fazzini, he said to his friend Fabrizio Pertile: "There is the little Greene, looking like a delicate peach. It is to these downy young creatures with their hard pits that we must entrust the future of mankind."

As Priscilla and Joseph, drifting through the room, came abreast of him, the Marchese stopped them by placing his finger under Priscilla's chin and tilting her face up at him. "My child," he remarked, "you are even more enchanting than usual. From the heart."

And he looked curiously at Joseph. "You are the friend of this lovely young lady," he said. "You are fortunate. I have known Miss Greene of Boston since at least eighteen months."

Priscilla introduced Joseph, and the old man shook hands with him. "If I were younger," he declared, "I would be one of Miss Greene's friends, like yourself."

"If you were younger," said Priscilla, sparkling, "I would have no other friend than you."

The Marchese sighed lustily. "Ah," he exclaimed, "the missed opportunities! One is too old—or one is in the wrong place. Had I been in Milan when the divine Sarah visited there in eighty-three, who knows what might have been the result of that meeting? But I was in Calabria. I was fifteen at the time, but well formed, and already a man of experience.

"But love," he said meditatively, "today—what is it? Who sees anywhere nowadays the glance between a man and a woman like a thunderclap, like a discharge of electricity, lighting up a whole room? There are too many distractions; when women became politicians, Olympic runners, and university professors, the grand manner of love flew out the window."

"That is why," said Fabrizio Pertile happily, "in matters of this sort, one always lands on one's head."

Since most of this conversation had been conducted in Italian, Joseph, who understood very little of it, had nothing to say, which was quite satisfactory to the Marchese, who preferred to do the talking himself. But out of politeness to the young foreigner, who seemed ill at ease, and also for the pleasure of being able to communicate his ideas to a larger circle than to his friend Fabrizio, who had already heard them, the Marchese changed to English, which he spoke very well. "It is the weakness of men," he declared, "that they have allowed women to take over so many of the bureaus. No woman now is willing to sit at home with her eye on the door waiting for the return of a husband or a lover—not when she can be seated behind a desk, dipping her pen in green ink, and using a rubber stamp."

"It cannot be helped," said Pertile with a shrug of his massive shoulders. "We have lost too many men, in too many wars. Women have become a necessity."

"They have always been a necessity," agreed the Marchese, "in the boudoir, but since when are they necessary in the office? Is it possible to sweep off her feet an Amazon who is a lieutenant commander in the American Navy? Or the president of an aircraft company? No, my friend; to be a woman now is a considerable business."

"Perhaps that's why so many men are turning womanish," said Kevin O'Connor, coming up to them with a glass in his hand.

The Marchese glanced at him with mild distaste. "Do not make fun of a tragedy, my friend," he said. "It is these womanish men who have persuaded the ladies to diet, in order to resemble as much as possible a bean pole. To a man of spirit who remembers the voluptuous figures of his youth, made like an hourglass, this is a development outside of nature. Is it possible to be carried away by love for a clothespin?"

"Must one be carried away?" asked Priscilla. "I think of it more as a coming together."

"Ah, yes," said the Marchese, "in a sense, it is a coming together. What I am speaking of is the grand passion."

"Isn't it always grand?" she asked, her golden eyes wide and mischievous.

44

The Marchese gazed at her with a sweet smile, for which he was famous. "Dear Miss Greene," he said, "there are many moments of love in a man's life, but love itself, which I have called the grand passion, is something which comes not so often, and is of great beauty. Also it comes with sorrow, it being the nature of man to be jealous of all other men, and to grieve for the passing of the seasons. I have reason to be grateful to women, having in my time enjoyed the favors of many, and even the affection of some; but I have had few great loves in my life. Of the two—of woman's favor or woman's love —the one least to be sought after is love, except to some-one of strength and spirit, because beauty and sorrow are terrible things to have inside the heart, and often burst the heart that holds them."

So saying, the old Marchese patted Priscilla on the cheek, bowed courteously to Joseph, and went off with Fabrizio Pertile toward the bar which had been set up in the corner. "Ah, Fabrizio," he said, "if I were but ten years younger, that is one whose favors I would seek." "Alas, my friend," replied Fabrizio, "you would end up running little errands."

It was the first time that Priscilla had taken Joseph to a party given by one of her friends, and he was beginning to wish she hadn't. He found himself defensive and ill at ease; he felt himself alien to all these people, who seemed to know one another so well and who appeared to float about on top of the world with gaiety and malice. That Marchese, for instance . . . what did a man like that know about love? Or sorrow, either?

"Pat here tells me you're going into the Iron Curtain countries," said Kevin O'Connor. "Will they let you in, do you think?"

"I don't know," Joseph answered. "My people in Toronto are trying to arrange it."

"Whatever for, then?" asked O'Connor. "Once you're in, they'll only give you the old runaround."

"I'm supposed to do a series of cultural articles," Joseph explained. "Music, and that."

"Do you talk Russian?"

"A little. Enough."

"I should think you'd be for Palestine," said O'Connor. "With all that's going on there—the Jews trying to get in, and the bloody British throwing them back out again like shuttlecocks."

A feeling of rage swept Joseph; where it came from, he didn't know. What business was it of this Irishman to tell him where to go? "I have no interest in Palestine," he said coldly, and turned away. But the bearded O'Connor wasn't to be put off so easily.

"No interest," he said gravely. "Well now! It's history, d'you see: it's the thirty-seventh chapter of Second Chronicles being written this very minute. I should think you'd want to see it for yourself."

"History is being written in Russia, too," said Joseph.

"It is," agreed O'Connor enthusiastically, "it is! But not in the same fine, Machiavellian style. What with your President promising one thing to the Jews, and your State Department whispering to the Arabs to pay no attention to him at all, because he doesn't mean it—and the Foreign Office and the Colonial Office changing their minds every minute—it'll be a wonder if the little country ever gains any kind of independence at all!"

Suddenly Joseph wanted to talk, to talk quickly, and with violence. "Look," he burst out, "I've never had a country. My ancestors didn't fight for independence. They fought for bread."

"Ah, now," said O'Connor soothingly, "mine fought for praties. Potatoes," he explained to Priscilla. "And for a bit of sod."

"My grandfather came from Russia," Joseph went on in a rush. "From the Ukraine. Is that my country?"

"Well, I don't know," said O'Connor. "It's a terrible great country indeed. The point is—he left it. But take Palestine, now; I hear they've made the desert bloom like the rose. That should be a beautiful thing. You say you're for music, and like that?"

"Yes," said Joseph.

"Music is beyond me," said O'Connor, "though I can do a bit of 'Danny Boy' when the mood is on me.

"But I'll tell you this," he said, dry and sudden and sharp, "if it was the Irish the English were throwing out of their own bit of country like so many forkfuls of hay, I'd be there on the next boat to decry the proceedings and maybe throw a brick or two myself for the sake of my feelings."

Joseph turned away. How could he tell this Irishman that Israel meant nothing to him? That Jews were small, dark, restless people who fought for the world's scraps, and prayed for a son with talent on the violin? And that he—Joseph—was a man, not a Jew. A single human being. . . .

But he knew in his heart that he was being disagreeable and, feeling that Priscilla was displeased with him, sought to hide his own discomfort in an appearance of indifference. "I guess I'm not a brick thrower," he said; and to Priscilla, reaching for the empty glass in her hand: "Let me get you a refill at the bar."

When he came back to her, holding both glasses full of the sweet, strong punch, he found the young Count Ariano at her side, his dark eyes melting over her like cheese, and purring away in his own language. "Tony," said Priscilla—and Joseph thought that her cheeks were a little pinker than usual—"you'll have to talk English now. This is Joseph Victor.

"Joe—Count Antonio Ariano."

"Here's your drink," said Joseph.

Ariano barely glanced at him, and turned away. "Why is it necessary to speak English," he asked sulkily, "when I am already speaking the language of the heart?"

"You know you have no heart, Tony," she said lightly. But she took a quick, anxious look at Joseph. They weren't going to like each other, she thought.

"Truly, my heart is very full," said Ariano. "It expresses itself without reserve."

"He always talks like that," she said to Joseph. "It's his way." And bending her head so as to avoid Ariano's moist and hungry gaze, she took a sip from her glass. At once her eyes flew open in shocked surprise. "Heavenly days," she gasped. "What on earth is that?"

Joseph shrugged helplessly. "It's some kind of punch," he said. "It's what they gave me."

"Oh Lord," murmured Priscilla. "Wasn't there any scotch?"

"I will get the scotch for you," declared Ariano. "If necessary, I will defy everybody."

"Look," said Joseph, "I'll get Miss Greene's drink myself."

Ariano's eyes narrowed; he gave Joseph a flickering glance like a knife in the ribs. "Allow me," he said. And turning his back, he inquired in Italian: "Who is this man?"

Joseph walked around in front of him and took up a position at Priscilla's side. "I understood that," he said. "He wants to know who I am. So tell him."

Priscilla's chin went up in an obstinate way, and she hesitated; she resented being pushed. Things were getting a little sticky, she thought; it was time to establish some authority.

"I already told you his name, Tony," she said quietly. "He's a friend of mine, from America. He came with me; I brought him here with me."

Ariano bowed. "Then when it is time to go," he said, "you will leave with me. I will escort you."

Whenever Joseph grew angry, he felt cold and shook a little. "I am taking Miss Greene home," he said, "when she is ready." And he added: "That is the custom in my country."

"You are in Rome," said Antonio. "An Ariano takes a back seat for nobody; not even for an Orsini. Maybe for a Colonna."

It was a mistake for Joseph to put his hand on Priscilla's arm; he could feel her stiffen in his grasp. "Whenever you're ready," he said.

"The lady stays," declared Ariano. "I have said so."

I ought to poke him right in the nose, Joseph thought; but he felt uneasy, and outnumbered, the way he used to feel at home sometimes, when he was small, and outside his own territory. He looked at Priscilla. "Do you let people talk to you like that?" he asked unhappily.

Ariano flushed darkly, and his eyes sparkled. He was a man of spirit, quick to take offense, and accustomed to quarrels, which he rather enjoyed, with insults loudly exchanged, a certain amount of pulling and shoving, perhaps a slap, and defiant attitudes. His father had fought a duel in the twenties and sustained a wound on the thumb; his son would have been quite willing to go that far.

"You have succeeded in insulting me," he announced.

At the same time Priscilla, annoyed and a little worried, exclaimed: "Really, Joe! I am not a child!"

The sharpness with which she spoke entered Joseph's heart like an icicle. This was succeeded by a plummet of grief, and a sick feeling of having been abandoned.

He turned away. After a while, he left the party, and went home.

He felt miserable and betrayed and angry—at himself, and at Priscilla, who had betrayed him. His heart was bitter and heavy; it was a deep well of anguish. The very air weighed on him, the night-blue Roman sky pressed down on him; he felt lonely and humiliated. It was unbearable. "*Stay*," the black-haired bully had said; and she had stayed.

On the other hand—why should he have expected anything else? He had simply let himself be taken in. Women were all alike: in the end, they went with the whip. "*You will go home with me.*" It had been a command; and Priscilla, the cool goddess, the self-assured, the strong, firm girl, had meekly acquiesced.

He stopped at a small *trattoria* off the Via Cavour for a drink, either beer or brandy, he didn't care which; he didn't want to go back to his room yet, to be alone in those four walls. Sitting at the bar in the rear, brooding, with his chin on his hands, he was aware of the woman beside him. She was enveloped in the scent of cheap perfume; her hair was dyed a brittle yellow and hung down over her shoulders. She had large hands and feet; and her evening gown, slightly soiled, of a shade of electric blue, was draped low over her large but sagging breasts. " 'Allo," she said in a strong German accent, smiling at him with her mouth, but watching him warily with greedy, cash-register eyes.

"Cigarette?"

Without a word, he held out a package of American cigarettes to her. "*Ach*," she said. "So."

She leaned a little closer to him. "A light?" she said.

Joseph looked at her; he saw the imitation jewelry, the sly, worn face, the flabby flesh underneath the make-up, the half-defiant, half-frightened, businesslike look she gave him; and he felt sorry for her. He wondered what her life had been like. "You give me?" she asked, reaching for the package.

"Be my guest," said Joseph indifferently.

"You were G.I.?" she asked, tucking the cigarettes into her bag.

And leaning still closer, she whispered confidentially: "You would like some company?"

Suddenly—for no reason that he could see—all the rage and the humiliation, the betrayal, the self-contempt, boiled over; and in a cold, level voice, he declared: "I was burned to death at Buchenwald."

The woman turned pale; the cigarette in her fingers shook a little, and her eyes glittered like a snake. "*Judenschwein*," she muttered, and moved to another seat further away. Joseph looked after her with indifference, paid for his drink, and went out.

As soon as he got back to his hotel, he went upstairs to his room, and went to bed. There were no messages for him.

51

At two o'clock the phone rang. "Hello," he said, still half-asleep.

"Joe . . . are you all right?"

He was awake instantly. "Of course," he said coolly. "Why not?"

But he couldn't keep it up; the sense of injustice and his own self-pity were too strong. "Besides," he said, "what difference does it make?"

"A lot," she said. "It makes a lot of difference. Joe, why did you run off like that?"

"What was I supposed to do?" he asked bitterly. "You stayed, didn't you? That was what you wanted."

"I didn't stay," said Priscilla. "I went home too."

"Oh," said Joseph. "With—with him, I suppose."

"I went home with the sales manager of a linen factory in Milan," said Priscilla. "I phoned you, but there wasn't any answer."

He felt suddenly very happy. While he'd been talking to a whore in a bar, she'd been trying to reach him.

"Well, look," he said. "I thought you were mad at me."

"I was," said Priscilla. "Don't you know why?"

"No. How would I? Just because some man tells you to stay—you know, like a poodle or something."

"Oh, Joe," she sighed, "don't you see? If I'd cared about *him*, it would have been him I scolded."

"Oh," he said again. He felt extraordinarily light and free; he wanted to listen, to hear her saying it, to take it in, to understand it.

"Good night," she said. "Sleep well, Joe dear. Call me in the morning. *Ciao*."

Joseph put the receiver down slowly and gently. He

didn't say anything; he lay there, smiling a little, listening to the Brahms again.

The train, having dragged itself through the mountain passes, unwound itself slowly across the plain. It was made up entirely of third-class carriages; the wooden benches, compartments, and aisles were overflowing with humanity, refugees of every age and condition, in every stage of weariness, sleeping huddled against one another, clutching their small belongings or sitting in numb stillness, staring out of the dusty windows at the foreign darkness. Somewhere ahead of them lay Eretz Israel, the promised country, the homeland—through many days and nights, across yet other frontiers—long voyages, by land and sea, the bright, dangerous, suspicious land, the dark, secret sea.

In one carriage a group of young chalutzim, *pioneers bound for the kibbutzim, the farm-communes of Palestine, were singing in low voices songs of Poland. Out of the burned forests and trampled earth they had crept like rabbits, starved and frozen, wary, frightened, with only one thought: to find a home in Zion, and perhaps a parent or a child or even a cousin left over from the massacres.*

Near them a woman cradled a child in her arms, whispering to it in Hungarian. "Little green pig," she whispered, "come into the farm house, and we will give you tea with sugar. Little green pig, everyone loves you because of your expression."

It was a nursery rhyme out of her own childhood, but she had never seen a pig, and she had never lived on a farm. Her father had been the owner of a large business in Buda Pesth and a respected member of the Jewish community.

There was nothing left, only herself and her child. Father, mother, brothers, husband, parents-in-law . . . all lost—forever lost—

She sighed wearily, and closed her eyes, clasping the child still closer to her breast. Ahead lay yet another frontier, another country to cross. And then . . . ?

"Go to sleep, Mia," she murmured. "Sleep, my dove."

CHAPTER

5

CLOUDS were massed over the Alban Hills, spring storms swept the Apennines. The sky above St. Peter's was gray, the wind blew; the first drops of rain fell on Rome.

In the concert hall, the Argentina, a young violinist was making his debut; pale but composed, he was standing with his manager and his mother and father in the musician's room behind the stage in the rear of the auditorium. His name was Tedeschi, and he was going to play the Vieuxtemps D minor after the intermission.

The concert was actually a charitable affair organized by the Little Ladies of San Vincenza, and therefore unusually well attended by Roman society. Mr. Tedeschi's fee was modest; in fact, he was playing for nothing, and making a small donation besides; and the usual hour of starting, five o'clock, had been moved to five-thirty, to accommodate the British Ambassador, who had taken a box.

The concert itself had not yet commenced; while the

air hummed with sound—the rustle of late arrivals, people looking for their seats, voices and conversations, the tuning of strings and little runs on the flute and clarinet—the musicians of the orchestra looked placidly out over the ancient and somewhat dingy baroque of the auditorium. The conductor was Pedrotti; they had nothing to be afraid of. In the stalls, men stood up in front of their seats or in the aisles, boldly surveying the boxes above them, from which the ladies gazed down at them through lorgnettes and small opera glasses. The appearance of the Princess Ruspoli, accompanied by the Spanish Ambassador, caused a murmur of respect to ripple through the audience, as did the arrival of Miss Elsa Maxwell in the party of Sir Charles Mendl. "She is the De Sévigné of her time," said the Marchese del Ascoli-Prieto to his companion, a young lady from the Cinecitta. "It is a fact that her writings do not have the wit, the warmth, or the charm of the original, but she describes our age as it is, for which we have no one to blame but ourselves."

Joseph, sitting with Priscilla in the rear of the orchestra stalls, thought that he had never been happier. The lights, the bustle and animation all around him, the perfume of women, the sound of the orchestra tuning up, and Priscilla's soft, smooth, golden presence at his side, all combined to give him a feeling of excitement and joy, a sense of the richness of life, and an anticipation of still greater delights to come. At the same time, he felt a slight uneasiness, without being able to explain why. Small, nagging, and obscure, it seemed to belong to the past and to remind him of grief. He put it resolutely behind him; and taking Priscilla's hand in his, he whispered:

"This moment is my whole life."

Priscilla returned his handclasp with a firm, even pressure. She had heard such remarks before, and had paid no attention to them. No one lived out his whole life in a moment, unless he was a bee. On the other hand, she felt more than a little fondness for Joseph; she was even in love with him in a way—though she wasn't sure how much; and she allowed herself to think about it during the first part of the program, and to hold his hand during the Leonore Overture and the Haffner Symphony of Mozart.

If only, she thought, she were a little more certain of him; certain, that is, of what she could only think of as the balance of power between them: if she knew, for instance, where his strength faltered, and where hers could take over, where his bitterness stopped, where his salt could be sweetened by her caring. She wasn't going to use the word "love"—not yet; caring was enough to begin with. But without knowing all that, without, in fact, knowing any of it, a woman could easily let herself in for more than she could handle: sow the wind and reap the whirlwind. One of the girls from her class at Marlborough had had an affair in Greenwich Village with a poet—at least they said he was a poet. The poor girl hadn't been able to handle the situation at all.

Well . . . Joseph. There was no doubt that he attracted her—but how serious ought she to let herself get? He was a dear person, and she believed that he loved her, and thought that it made him happy. It was a moving thought, to know that his happiness was so bound up in her. And he excited her, too, in a troubling way—his darkness and his strangeness. If only she could be sure; if only she could be sure of his kindness and his gentleness, of his understanding; if only she could be sure that she understood him, that she could handle him . . . sure of not getting into too deep water. . . .

She gave his hand a little pat and drew her fingers out of his. During the last movement of the Mozart, she sat with her hands folded in her own lap.

And Joseph, dreaming in the music, with his eyes closed, felt again that sense of uneasiness—perhaps because she had taken her hand away from him?—and felt troubled by it. Was it, perhaps, a feeling of unreality, as though he didn't quite know where he was or what he was doing there? In Rome, of all places!—and with a girl like Priscilla. How did it all happen? There seemed to be an empty space between the boy he'd been and what he was now—a void, a desert like the Mojave or the Great Salt Lake, with nothing to fill it, to fill the emptiness, nothing to comfort him except that hand, so soft, so pliant.

During the intermission the foyers, the salons, and the upstairs bar were crowded; many women were dressed in old-fashioned, formal gowns of rose and gold and green and lavender, with bare, powdered bosoms, and long white gloves, while their escorts wore black and white, the white fresh from the *lavanderia,* the black often moth-faded from the long years of the war. There were a few uniforms and ready-to-wear dresses and ordinary business suits, such as the one Joseph was wearing, a suit he had bought at Coulter's Men's Shop in Chicago. Monsignors and an occasional bishop, to whom the music of Beethoven, Mozart, and Vieuxtemps was not forbidden, stood about conversing gravely, watched with respect by young seminarians from the academies. Everywhere the chatter of voices, wafts of perfume, the fall of velvet and the rustle of silk, filled the air, along with the smoke of cigars and cigarettes, the aroma of wine, and the sweet stab of peppermint.

Priscilla and Joseph stood in the foyer near the entrance. It was already night and it was raining; the pavement was black and wet and gleaming with reflected lights. The rain drove steadily down, deepening Joseph's vague feeling of sorrow. Almost with indifference he watched Count Antonio Ariano make his way through the crowd toward them.

Priscilla saw him too, and looked troubled for a moment. "Joe," she said, "please . . ." But he only shrugged his shoulders.

Ariano bowed to him soberly, and then turned with a delighted expression to Priscilla. "It is so nice to find you!" he exclaimed. "What have you been doing?"

He didn't wait to find out; he had other things to say. "I have been busy with important business affairs," he told her. "We have just sent a thousand gross of the small leathers of Venezia and the Lakes to your United States. Imagine that; are you pleased? This Venetian work is more fashionable now than the Firenze. I would offer to see you safely home in the rain, but I am in the box with Dolly Caracciolo, and we are going afterwards to the Rugantino. So"—he lifted his shoulders expressively—"another time."

"I have missed you," he added ardently, by way of second thought.

The rain, beating on the pavement, was already depressing Joseph. He imagined young Tedeschi warming his hands in the artist's room back of the stage, flexing his fingers, tuning and retuning his instrument . . . the mother and the father probably sitting mute and anxious in a corner, the teacher too, perhaps, the manager very cheerful, very businesslike. He could imagine it. It hadn't been that way with him, but it might have been. The way it actually was . . .

He realized that Ariano was talking to him, that he must have asked him some sort of question. "I'm sorry," he said. "I wasn't listening."

The young Italian gave him a look of surprise; then he turned back to Priscilla with a gesture of helplessness. "Your friend," he said, "is elsewhere. He is not here; he does not stay with us."

The two bells rang: the intermission was over, and people thronged back to their seats; the foyers emptied of voices, and filled with the sound of rain. Priscilla, sitting beside Joseph as before, slipped her hand into his, but he scarcely felt it. The dream had changed; as Ariano had said, he wasn't there, he hadn't stayed. . . .

He was back in the artist's room, waiting to come out, waiting to walk across the stage and lift his bow in the first bars of the Vieuxtemps. It had been the Vieuxtemps in which he, too, had planned his debut. But not in Rome, not in the Argentina, not in spring; it was to have been at Carnegie Hall in New York, in winter. It was raining then, too: a cold, drenching rain from the northeast. He was back in that bare, dusty room off the stage, across the corridor, flexing his fingers, rubbing his hands, freezing one moment and sweating the next, tuning and retuning his violin, his Guadagnini, which his aunt had given him, hearing the rain, his ears filled with the sound of rain, knowing that he couldn't go on.

He didn't hear the applause as young Tedeschi walked out onto the stage—pale, erect, and sure of himself. Joseph's eyes were closed; he heard only the sound of rain, and an orchestra tuning. Priscilla cast a quick glance at him; he looked angry and far away, and she withdrew her hand. She thought that he was probably still jealous of Ariano; it vexed her, but it made her smile. Such childishness! Men were like that, she supposed: childish and violent. She considered putting her hand back in his, but decided against it; he might take it for an act of contrition, or appeasement; one could lose control that way.

What she didn't know—what she couldn't know—was that Joseph was already out of control, even of himself. What controlled him now was the dream, and it was a bad dream. The sorrow, the weight of grief, had risen over him in a wave, too strong, too heavy; it carried him down. It wasn't some stranger up there on the stage—it was himself, Josef Victor with the *f*, and he couldn't stand it. Because he, Joseph Victor, had never made that debut; he had run away from it.

That was ten years ago. And he had to run away from it again, here and now—away from the audience, from the night and the rain, from the feeling of fright that was turning into panic—or let himself be carried down, down and away, to live the whole thing over again, the wild coatless flight through the winter-dark streets, drenched and freezing, with the tears running down his face, not knowing where he was, not wanting to know. . . .

As he was running now, down a narrow street, down the steep steps of a cobbled hill, while the rain pelted him.

He had left the Argentina and Priscilla without a word; he had simply risen from his seat and hurried out. All he knew was that he had to get to safety somewhere, anywhere—back to his room at the hotel, back to the clinic in New York, back to the butcher shop in Cleveland. To get back, to get back . . . He was lost, as he had been lost that night ten years ago, in his own darkness, in strange ways, in avenues that didn't go anywhere. . . .

Priscilla saw him get up and go out, without even a word of explanation or apology, and felt a quick rush of indignation—how could he? And then, just as suddenly, she was taken with an inexplicable feeling that something was wrong, very wrong, and that it wasn't because of Ariano at all, it was something much deeper, more important, something that had been building—now that she thought of it—for a long time. Ariano, she knew all at once, as she rose to her feet, hearing people hissing at her, had been no more than a fuse; the explosion was in Joseph himself.

He needed her; she was quite sure of it.

She found him holding himself upright against the rim of a small wall-fountain in the Botteghe Oscura, wet to the skin, his eyes closed, and a look of utter anguish on his face. He let her put him into a taxi; it was almost as though he had expected someone to find him and take him home. She got in beside him and gave the driver the address of his hotel. "Hurry," she said unnecessarily, "*presto!*"

Joseph said nothing; he huddled shivering in his corner as they careened through the wet, noisy streets. Priscilla also said nothing; tight-lipped, her golden eyes dark with uncertainty, she sat fiercely erect, looking straight ahead of her. Was it still some kind of game? She didn't know. She thought it wasn't a game.

He let her pay the driver, and bundle him into the lift. In front of his room, she took the key from him and opened the door. "Get into bed," she ordered. "Get undressed." And when he hesitated, looking at her in confusion, she snapped: "You're wet through."

The bed had already been made up for the night. While he undressed in the bathroom, she ordered a bottle of brandy sent up from the bar. Then she lit a cigarette and sat down to wait.

After a while Joseph came out of the bathroom in his pajamas and an old dressing gown. He was pale; he looked tired and confused—surprised, almost, to find Priscilla there. He didn't seem to know what to say. It was Priscilla who broke the silence.

"Here," she said. "Drink this brandy and get into bed."

He took the brandy and shook himself like a dog. "I'm all right," he muttered. "I'm all right now. I know where I am."

"Joseph," she said, "what's the matter?"

He turned away, almost angry, she thought; and then he turned back to her helplessly. "I don't know," he said. "It was the way it was before. I had this feeling that it was I up there on the stage, and that I couldn't do it, that I had to get away."

"Before?" she asked slowly. "Before what?"

"Before my debut."

"Oh," she said.

"I just ran," he said. "I went out into the streets and ran. I didn't know where I was. A friend of mine went after me, and found me. He was a wonderful friend— Bert Aaronson. He was a musician, too. He'd been to Harvard."

He looked at her in a kind of dull surprise. "You're

from Boston," he said. "That's strange, isn't it?"

"No," she said. "What happened after that? After he found you?"

He lay down on the bed and put his hands under his head and stared at the ceiling. "Nothing," he said. "They had a doctor talk to me, a psychiatrist. I guess he helped me. He was wonderful, too. Everybody was wonderful. My aunt kept saying: 'Don't worry, everything will be all right.' I was in the hospital for a while. But nothing was ever all right after that.

"Why do I hate all those wonderful people?" He said it helplessly, like a child. "It never was all right," he said. "It never will be."

Priscilla came over and sat down on the bed beside him. She didn't know what to do with her hands; she kept them folded in her lap and stared down at them. "Don't say that," she said. "That's all long ago."

She felt moved, and uncertain, and a little breathless; she felt as though she were waiting, poised in the moment like a bird in the air. She raised her eyes to look at him, and they stared at each other, and the room filled with silence and with the beating of their hearts, which neither heard. The silence between them was full of power; it was a force, drawing them together in longing, in confusion, in tenderness, in a sweet terror. . . .

Slowly, questioningly, he held out his arms to her, encircled her, drew her gently down to him. "Pat!" he whispered. "Pat!"

Her lips were like nothing he had ever imagined; his own drowned on them, they were so soft, so warm, so gentle, and like a trumpet call to his blood: a surrender and a victory, a ripeness, a promise.

She undressed slowly, keeping her eyes on him

gravely, yet smiling a little self-consciously, feeling very far from the assured young woman she wanted to be and which she wanted him to believe her. The moment was one of great importance, in which time moved very slowly; it stood behind her like a giant angel, its vast wings unfolded on either side—Lucifer, perhaps? She had a moment of doubt, but it was too late; a moment of delicious fear. . . .

She lay down in the bed beside him without speaking, and in silence they flowed into each other like two rivers, long pent up, and freed at last; they rose together like waves, battering each other, and went down together. His hands were all over her; how cool she was and yet how glowing, how firm and fragrant! She was his; a sense of triumph rose in him like wild music, carrying him beyond himself, outside himself. He was filled with laughter and strength and enormous sorrow; he rode the wind. . . .

They lay quiet at last, side by side . . . ebbing away, leaving each other little by little, slowly going back into the aloneness of self. There was a sadness about it. She must try to rally herself, she thought, put herself together again; but it was a delicious sadness. And Joseph, filled with a sense of wonder and surprise at his victory —if it was a victory—over this poised and golden girl so unlike himself, so unlike any woman he had ever known, felt for an instant, for a single drowsy moment, a mingled stab of guilt and triumph, a triumph secret and bitter, over his own people, who with their love and worry had made him what he was.

The Roman night rolled through the heavens, noisy and sweet-smelling; water falling, fountains playing, flowers and bushes sending out their fragrance on the air; voices calling, lovers bending over one another along the parapet above the Tiber, in the deep shadows of the trees; cats squawling, motors roaring, thieves in the shadows, and neon signs blazing along the Via Veneto. Around the rim of the city the hills rose pale and cold into the moonlight which shone alike on St. Peter's and on the broken columns of Hadrian's Villa, and on the Hotel Mediterraneo, where Joseph and Priscilla slept, and woke, and made love again, and sat up in bed and smoked cigarettes and drank the brandy, and fell asleep in the gray dawn, smiling and secret, with a taste of kisses on their mouths, and the nightingales singing.

It was late in the morning when Joseph finally awoke and, turning his head, saw Priscilla unbelievably beside him, her light, silky hair spread like a frame around her face, pure and sweet in sleep, untroubled and secure. Leaning on his elbow, he looked down at her with wonder and pity—wonder at her beauty, and pity for her mortality: that she should ever grow old or die, or ever be anything other than what she was then, at that moment, with whatever dreams there were behind those marigold-shadowed eyes, was something he couldn't bear.

He rose and, tiptoeing to the window, peered out at the bright, shining day. Behind him, Priscilla woke startled, wondering for a moment where she was; and then, seeing him standing there, naked against the light, remembered with a mixture of ruefulness and mirth, satisfaction, and a motherly feeling toward the thin and not very large body of her lover.

"What," she asked, "are you doing?"

Joseph gave a start, and glanced back at her sitting up in the bed, the sheet held in front of her. "I was wondering," he said, "if I could see the Forum from here."

66

"The Forum?" she asked, surprised.
"Titus' Arch," he said.
"Why that, of all things?"
"I don't know," he said. "I just wanted to see it."

CHAPTER

6

SUDDENLY Rome was filled with lovers. It had always been filled with lovers, but Joseph hadn't been aware of it before. An air of sensuality pervaded the city; unlike the delicate and practical French, who, meeting in the streets at the close of the working day, exchange affectionate embraces before hurrying home to cook the evening meal, the Romans made love their main business, applying themselves to it with an ardor in which there was not the slightest trace of embarrassment or reticence.

Joseph and Priscilla moved through the city in a sensuous dream, tasting the air perfumed with flowers, breathing the scent of cypress and pine, laurel, ilex, and box, the delicate melancholy of the mimosa. They, too, leaned on the parapet above the Tiber near Sant'Angelo in the deep shadows of the plane trees and sought each other with endless kisses. In a horse-drawn *carozza*, they drove through echoing, narrow streets where the walls of old, rust-colored palaces rose from the cobblestones, past iron-barred windows and little open shops where in the lamplight mattress makers were still at work, to the cobbled Square of Santa Maria in Trastevere. There on the terrace in front of the restaurant, a sloe-eyed, sly-faced guitar player sang his songs for them—Neapolitan songs, with sighs and dying glances for Priscilla, while a glum-faced fiddler played in the background. Coming home they passed a line of Campanian wine carts with great red wheels and the drivers seated at one side under their awnings. In the dark and narrow lanes between the old walls, to the clop-clop of horses' hoofs and the creak of the *carozza*, they lost themselves in each other's arms, in whispers and fondling. The Triton Fountain, naked in the moonlight, seemed to them no more than the expression of their own unself-consciousness.

During the day there was usually work to do for one or the other: Joseph would have a report to file at the post office or the cable office, Priscilla an interview or an article to prepare for Paris or New York. But when sunset turned the streets to rose, they were together again, racing across the city to each other; and later, drowsy and dreamy, to make the evening rounds, the cocktail or Campari at a sidewalk table in front of Rosati's, dinner at Beppone's, or Nino's, and finally "Tartufo" at the Tre Scalini, before Bernini's great fountain in the Piazza Navona. There, toward midnight, Carolina with her bundle of newspapers would stop at their table to give them advice, and the benefit of her philosophy. "My friends," she would say, her small, round, leathery face wise and wrinkled with the woe of human affairs, "my poor little ones, be happy."

She believed in happiness, and she believed in marriage. "To be happily married," she insisted, "is the ideal

way of life. I myself, with four husbands and many
lovers, have never despaired. I have never found the ideal
one; but that is a solitary misfortune. *Non io mai trovato
l'idèale.*"

They would look at each other and smile, touching
hands across the table. They were not thinking of anything; Carolina's voice came to them from another world,
a world of middle-aged sorrow; their world was no wider
than their arms could reach, stretched out to each other;
no more distant than their fingertips, each to each.

The old Marchese of Arcoli-Prieto came across them
one day as they were walking hand in hand under the
chestnuts of the Via Veneto. He needed no more than a
glance to tell him what had happened. That night he said
to his friend Fabrizio Pertile, the cartoonist: "The little
Greene has a lover."

"Ariano?"

"No—the American."

Pertile was shocked. "Did she have to come to Rome
for that?" he demanded. "She could have stayed at home.
It is an insult to the country."

But the Marchese disagreed with him. "Believe me,"
he said, "the American is as foreign to her as Ariano. She
is having an affair of the heart; she is enjoying her salad
days, out of sight of her family."

"Then you believe that she will marry Ariano in the
end?" asked Pertile.

"Whom she will marry," said the Marchese calmly,
"I do not know. But I will tell you this: it will not be
until after the salad!"

Kevin O'Connor also ran across the lovers at the
Market in the Piazza Vittorio, where he had gone to buy
a fish for his landlady's supper. He approached them

where they sat at a sidewalk table in front of a small *trattoria,* holding his fish wrapped in newspaper, his brown beard shining in the sun. "Kevin!" cried Priscilla gaily. "Come sit with us and catch us up on world affairs."

"Well, now," said O'Connor, sitting down contentedly and placing his fish on the table in front of him, "it all depends on which world you mean, doesn't it? If it's the world of the cinema, then Rossellini and Bergman have taken a house together at Santa Marinella. And if it's art, then Clelia Bellochio is having a show at one of the galleries on the Via Babuino—I've forgotten the name. And, if it's literature you're after, the Existentialists are meeting at Il Baretto. But if it's politics, all I've got to say is the world is in a bloody mess."

Joseph looked about him at the busy Market with its double row of stalls, and then out at the great view across the city, which was clear and fine in the bright April weather. He felt the warm sun on his cheeks; he looked at the pretty young girls selling vegetables, at the countless cats drowsing in the light, and listened to the din all around him, which sounded happy to him because he was happy.

"I don't think it's in such a mess," he said, looking across the table at Priscilla. "Not in Rome, in this season of the year."

O'Connor saw the look, and smiled to himself. Ah, he thought, the poor loon. But what he said was: "It's the blessed St. Peter's own city. But there's a world of the homeless beyond the Sabine hills."

A fortuneteller came up to the table with dolls in a jar of water, and white mice running up and down on a string, and offered to tell their fortunes. "Very good," he said. "Very inter-est-ing. No?"

71

"No," said O'Connor.

Presently he was talking about Palestine again. "The British will be out of there by August," he said, "with the Mandate coming to an end."

"October," said Priscilla.

"As to that," said O'Connor, "the Colonial Secretary said May. They're figuring the Arabs will bloody the noses of the Jews—with a little bit of help, of course—and then they'll be in again, by the back door. Ah, the cleverness of it—the poor deluded sods!

"It's they that can't make up their minds who their friends are until it's too late; but then, they never could."

Joseph's warm, contented feeling left him abruptly; he was aware of a feeling of irritation and an obscure sorrow. Why can't they leave me alone? he thought; but whom he meant by "they," he didn't know. From somewhere out of his childhood, the verse of Amos came to mind: "And I will bring again the captivity of my people, and they shall build the waste cities and inhabit them; and they shall plant vineyards . . . and they shall make gardens. . . ."

With a sudden, swift presentiment, Priscilla put her hand on his. "Kevin," she said, "where would you go if you had a few days' holiday?"

O'Connor considered gravely. "In the country," he asked, "and not too far?"

She nodded, not looking at Joseph.

"Then," said O'Connor, "I'd choose Santa Marinella, for the joy of being by the sea."

"With Rossellini and Bergman?"

"You couldn't have better company," said O'Connor.

He had an appointment at the Irish Consulate, and so the three of them got into Priscilla's Topolino, fish and

all, and they let O'Connor off near the Planetarium and
went on up to the Borghese Gardens to walk a while under the magnolias. It was a favorite spot of Priscilla's:
she loved to watch the little girls, their faces little moons
of innocence and secrets, marching two by two behind
the grave, peaceful-looking nuns; the couples seated on the
grass or under the stone pines, offering each other kisses
and other sweets. As the afternoon waned and the shadows
grew longer, the statues peering out at them from groves
of laurel or ilex took on a curious air of attention; they
seemed to be watching them from far off and ages away,
stealing through the leaves to peer at today.

They came down onto the Pincian terrace as the An-
gelus bells were ringing, and stood for a while gazing out
across the city. It was almost the same view as that first
night they'd dined together at the Valadier. The sun was
setting behind St. Peter's; they could see the aerials of the
Radio Vatican against the light, and the sound of bells
swept across the rooftops like swallows. To their right, cars
rushed in and out of the Porto del Popolo, and below them
men and women hurried across the Piazza in the pink
flush of evening. The sun went down, and a golden light
spread across the city; on the other side of the river, St.
Peter's, Sant'Angelo, and the Janiculum glowed in the sunset light. Orange and crimson stained the west, fading upward into rose and green, toward the darker blue of the
evening sky.

One star appeared low in the southwest: the planet
Venus, the evening star.

"Darling," whispered Priscilla. "My darling. So
many thousands of years. It goes so far back."

"I know," he said. "That's what you said, the first
night."

"Here, where we're standing, Lucullus had his palace and his gardens. Messalina was murdered here. Messalina."

She shivered suddenly, and moved closer to him. "It's all around us," she said. "The world and all its history."

She thought he sighed a little, and looked up at him anxiously. But he was staring out over the darkening city; and suddenly her heart gave a queer little turn; there was something in his dark, aquiline face that made her think of a caged hawk. That was the way they must have looked, she thought—the barbarians from Parthia, from Londinium, from Gaul. That was the way they must have looked after the destruction of Jerusalem. The Jews, marching in chains under the Arch of Titus.

He stirred, and looked down at her, and smiled, and nuzzled her hair, and the moment passed. "What did you say?" he asked, and she answered:

"Nothing."

After a little while, she said: "It's so beautiful, with the lights coming on in the city, and the sound of bells. And the evening star. Make a wish, Joe. Wish for something happy."

"Yes," said Joseph. But he couldn't think of anything to wish, except something he didn't really want at all—a sudden, ridiculous longing, confused and mocking. I wish I were a kid again, he thought, and immediately dismissed it; nothing could be more untrue. All he wanted was for life to go on always, forever, just the way it was.

Troubled, he followed Priscilla to the Square.

They drove to Santa Marinella the next day, and took a room in a *pensione* run by Signora Barbetti. From the little balcony outside their windows, they could see the Mediterranean stretching away to the horizon, blue as the sky near shore and darker farther out and shining in the sun. Joseph had brought his camera with him, and took pictures of the shore, and of Priscilla standing on the balcony.

It was still too early in the year to swim, though there were a few hardy bathers already in the water; their cries floated up to them through the open window. They found a little grocery not far from the *pensione,* and bought salami and cheese and crusty bread and Parma ham and a flask of wine, and ate their supper in the room, watching the sun go down across the water, the colors fade, the blue deepen and darken. They felt far away from everything and everybody, together, by themselves, alone—wonderfully secure, hidden from the world, comforted and safe. It's like being married, thought Joseph; but Priscilla thought: It's like playing house.

They loved each other very tenderly that first night and very passionately, and with deep gratitude and wonder; and slept, and woke in the bright morning, and had their hot chocolate and rolls and honey sent up to them by the Signora, and ate what was left of the salami, sitting out on their balcony in the sun-glowing, ice-shadowed air fresh and salt from the sea, and smelling a little of salt-grass and pines. Later they went for a long walk on the beach with its sand-and-seaweed smell, and picked up seashells and dried-out starfish and strangely shaped stones. Priscilla took off her shoes and stockings and went wading in the sea. "It's cold!" she cried; and he took some pictures of her, laughing, with her feet in the water.

A kind of wild joy possessed him; he kept looking at her and marveling at so much beauty and grace and delicacy and gaiety, all delivered into his hands like some incredible golden treasure. He felt beyond himself, as though he could sing like the greatest singers and dance like a great dancer . . . fly, leap, soar with the eagle, dive with the porpoise. . . .

On the way back to Signora Barbetti's *pensione*, he thought he saw Ariano at a distance—or a figure which reminded him of Ariano. In the faded, dusky light he couldn't be sure. "What's the matter?" Priscilla asked him when he stopped, and after a moment he answered:

"Nothing."

But that night he slept badly. He woke in the early dawn, while the birds were singing, and leaned over her, looking down at her in the cool, gray light. The pure young face, closed in sleep, far off in spirit, touched his heart. Slumbering, she looked like a happy child; yet he knew that back of those blue-veined eyelids, whose dark lashes rested so lightly on the peach-skin cheek, was a loneliness, an apartness, as deep as his own. And in the grip of a sudden fear for which he was not prepared, he woke her up and exclaimed:

"Do you love me?"

She looked up at him drowsily through eyes which saw him only mistily and with surprise. "Really, Joe!" she murmured.

"Promise me," he said to her urgently; "promise me . . ."

She closed her eyes and sank back on the pillow. "What?" she murmured. "Promise you what?"

"That you will never love anyone else."

"That I will never . . . Oh, Joe!" she said, opening her eyes. "Did you wake me up just for that?"

"I feel as though we were married," he said solemnly.

She didn't look at him. Presently she turned over on her side. "I'm sleepy, Joe," she said, and closed her eyes.

After a while he fell asleep; he dreamed of the woman

concertmaster again. The orchestra was playing the Brahms, but there was no soloist, only great, green, moving hills of water; and then, at his feet, a snake sliced into pieces which wouldn't die.

But Priscilla didn't sleep; she lay awake, staring at the dawn. She was troubled; the bells of Santa Marinella, ringing for Matins, rang in her heart for the first time with the sound of an alarm. She felt like a swimmer who has been happily splashing about in shallow water, and puts one foot down to touch bottom, and finds no bottom there, only an unknown deep.

Something had gone wrong somewhere. Something or other, something she hadn't expected, or thought about, had been happening . . . something had slipped out of her hands, had gone out of control. . . .

She tried to stand back, to think, to see herself and Joseph, to look ahead. . . . All the things she hadn't done. Where was she being taken, so swiftly, so desperately?

She was in love: that was true, she didn't deny it. And it was wonderful, it was a dream of happiness. . . .

But—marriage?

She felt a slow unfolding of panic. Had she been playing, then, with such serious things? Marriage meant a family, and a family was a dynasty. Marriage was a walk down the aisle of a church, in white satin and lace—something old, something new, something borrowed, and something blue—with someone (someone suitable) waiting for her at the altar. And after that, a home, and children, and being a member of the community, and a Mover and Shaker.

That was the way it was done; that was the way life was managed. But this thing with Joseph: somehow or other—somewhere—she had let it get away from her.

They'd been like children, playing house; or, at least,

it had seemed like that. They hadn't worried about a future, about a tomorrow, about what was going to happen when . . . when what? When Joe left? For where? Was he going to Russia? He'd be going somewhere surely: he couldn't stay in Rome forever. For that matter, neither could she. But when she left, it would be to go home; and long before that . . .

She had a sudden picture of herself in Rome without Joe—missing him, missing him much too much; and her heart contracted in fear. It mustn't be like that, she thought; it mustn't ever be like that.

She wasn't used to such thoughts, but she was honest, or reasonably so, and for a moment in the cool gray sea-side dawn, she faced herself squarely. She was never meant to die for love—she knew that; or to lose the whole world for its sake. I've got to think about this, she told herself soberly. I've got to think a little beyond my nose.

It wasn't just that Joseph wasn't suitable. There was a strangeness in him, and a darkness, which she knew in her heart would never yield to her. She didn't know how she knew it, but she knew it . . . neither to her love nor to her will. Lucifer . . . Perhaps in Lucifer she had found too strong an Antagonist.

The thought sobered her like a plunge of icy water. We've gone too deep, she told herself; we've lost something, some innocence. . . . A strange word, she thought, considering everything!—and she smiled a little wryly. But it was the only word that would do. Falling in love was always innocent, for a while, at least; it was like an early morning in summer. Dimly as yet, but nevertheless surely, she could sense the presence of pain ahead; for one of them, or both: she didn't know which.

And it didn't matter which; for either one, it was bad enough. But she didn't want it for herself at all. If it had to be anyone . . .

They were quiet with each other at breakfast. Joseph's dream hung over him, but he didn't think that was what was troubling him; it was something else, something he couldn't put his finger on. For some reason, he kept thinking of Ariano; it bothered him, and he didn't know why. He kept glancing at Priscilla, and thinking: Something has happened. But what could have happened? Could the heart shift suddenly, like a slipping of the earth . . . ? He had no experience.

They went for a short walk along the beach, but it didn't help, it wasn't the way it had been the day before. They tried to be gay and happy, but it was easier to be silent, and after a while they turned back to the *pensione* and got into the car and went back to Rome. Priscilla was quiet and thoughtful; and Joseph was uneasy and dispirited. He tried to think of something to say, something casual and light, to make conversation. "For what it costs in gasoline," he said, "we could have had dinner at any *trattoria* in town." But Priscilla didn't answer.

In the later afternoon they stopped at the studio of Ezio Monteverdi. The sculptor of iron figures took one look at them and brought out his best—and only—bottle of brandy. "When in Rome," he said cheerfully, "do as the Romans do." But to himself, he added: More than the flesh is tired here, I think.

He tilted Priscilla's chin up and walked around studying her face. "How do you feel, my little one?" he inquired gravely.

"Why?" asked Priscilla. "Don't I look well?"

79

"You both of you," said Monteverdi, "could make a little visit to the Bambino in the Church of Santa Maria in Aracoeli."

"Good heavens!" cried Priscilla. "That's for the dying!"

Monteverdi shrugged his shoulders and ran a rough hand through his beard. "It is also good for other things," he said, "such as the spirit. It is said to be good for lovers, to give them the strength they need for one another, although that is not the opinion of the Church."

"Does *everybody* know about us?" cried Priscilla.

"But naturally!" exclaimed Monteverdi. "However, only in Rome. Not in Paris, or Palermo."

She laughed a little shakily. "That's frightening," she said.

That evening she excused herself from dining with Joseph: she pleaded a headache. She wanted to be alone, to be free, for a little while, of pressure, of emotion, free of the demands of loving, or being loved. She needed time to breathe, to put herself together again, to see things with her mind, not only with her heart. "I'm sorry, Joe," she said; "I'm just no good tonight. It's been a long day. See you tomorrow."

A long day? he thought. That's strange. It had seemed almost too short. He had thought that after a weekend like that, they'd be even closer than before.

He walked home in the rosy evening with a sense of bewilderment and dismay. Something was wrong—somewhere; he didn't know what it was. He felt suddenly as though he were on the outside again. . . .

But an outsider was someone who was kept out, who didn't belong. And he belonged to Pat.

Or did he? He tried to tell himself that he did, he

tried to think of them together, as one—but other thoughts came crowding into his mind, unbidden and unwelcome. Cleveland, the butcher shop . . . Boston Hemp and Cordage, Marlborough, Wellesley . . . Ariano. . . .

For the first time, he felt a little homesick. Everything had been so light, so filled with happiness; and now there was a shadow. He didn't know what the shadow was; he only knew that it was there.

All right, he said to her in his mind, trying to be resigned and hopeful, tomorrow will be fine.

He phoned her when he got back to the hotel, wanting to be reassured; but she was quiet and cool and contained. "Pat," he said, "I want to talk to you. Please. I want to see you. There's something . . ."

"I'm tired, Joe," she said. "I'd rather not, tonight."

"But that's just it. I mean . . . why . . . ?"

"Please, Joe; I just want to be alone. Tomorrow . . ."

"Well," he said, "all right—tomorrow. But . . ."

"Good night, Joe. Sleep well."

He hung up, and sat staring at the phone. He felt like a fly that had blundered into a spider web; what was it, and why was it there? But look, he said to her in his mind, I love you!

The words seemed to go out into the silence and lose themselves. She's tired, he told himself; it doesn't mean anything. But something told him that wasn't true, not altogether. Something had happened; he didn't know what it was.

He went to bed that night with a heavy heart.

And Pat, in her room in the Via Margutta, unconsciously echoing the Marchese, said to herself: Face it, Greene—you're scared. What's that song about a love affair that's too hot not to cool down?

Daphne, she thought; was it too late to turn into a tree, or a fountain?

They climbed the long steps from the Capitol to Santa Maria in Aracoeli; and there, in company with a group of women and a Franciscan friar, knelt in front of a lighted, glass-enclosed, rosy-faced statue of a child, decked and crowned with jewels. Priscilla gazed up at the Bambino reverently. She felt a little confused; she wasn't sure why she was there, or what to pray for: happiness?—or should she pray for peace—and for a quiet heart? She remembered what Monteverdi had said: ". . . to give them the strength they need for one another." She would pray for strength.

But there was such a heavy feeling of guilt in her heart. She ought to pray for Joseph's happiness; she ought to ask forgiveness for herself. Instead she found herself repeating a prayer out of her childhood: "Now I lay me . . ." It was hardly proper, and certainly not called for, but there was something about the Child. . . . She had been a child, too, once long ago. And someday she would have a child of her own.

But not by Joseph.

And with head bent beneath the scarf covering her fair hair, she thought to herself: I have sinned against another's heart. What now, Pat? she thought. And for how long? While he grows always more desperate, and you less so . . .

It was then, kneeling before the Bambino, sorrowfully, but with a feeling of peace, that Priscilla made up her mind what to do about Joseph.

And he, in the echoing, icy church, with its smell of incense and old stones, felt a dark tide flow over him from the past; the marble columns, rising to the roof, had been there a long time, had been standing on the Capitol in temples to other gods when Jerusalem fell, had seen Vespasian and Titus and Josephus. . . .

How many hopeless tears had washed those ancient pillars?

The Bambino . . . the little King, covered and crowned with jewels. To accept, to adore, to pray, to move like a branch of seaweed in the tide. Moving, swaying in concert—clinging, safe, secure, part of the whole, belonging . . .

Except that he didn't belong. It seemed to him that some enormous figure stood behind him with folded arms and shadowy wings, dark and inscrutable, and unforgiving. He felt a sudden chill of dismay; what was he doing there, in that strange and alien church, before an image that was anathema to his people? He was only there because of a woman—not as a worshipper; he was cheating the Child, he was cheating that other, shadowy figure behind him. . . . But the figure refused to be cheated.

Coming down the steps from the church, Joseph said to Priscilla: "What were you thinking, there in the chapel?"

"Nothing," she lied. "And you?"

"Nothing."

In a refugee training camp in a little fishing settlement outside of Genoa, Anna fed her daughter bread, cheese, goat's milk, and a soup made of fishheads and other remnants. Now for the first time she was able to borrow a needle and thread to mend their few bits of clothing. There were many rumors going about: the ex-Mufti, escaped from France, was back in Jerusalem; the British were firing on the ships which were ferrying the illegal immigrants across the Mediterranean; the Exodus *had been rammed and sent back to Marseilles; another little steamer, the* Teti, *would be sailing soon* . . .

The Italians were not unkind—not as kind, she heard, as the French, but still, a little money (from the Haganah) into the right hands . . .

Perhaps they would be able to get onto the Teti *when it sailed. In the meanwhile, they were alive—though she wondered sometimes to what purpose.*

But then she would look at Mia, and her expression would grow firm again. Her own life was over; but Mia . . . Mia at least must live.

CHAPTER

7

"IT WOULD be a mistake," wrote Joseph, "to imagine that Fascismo is dead. Just as a snake, with its head cut off, lives until after sunset . . ." He crossed it out and started over. "Fascism in Italy is still alive," he wrote. "The M.S.I., the Movimento Sociale Italiano, is by no means moribund; in certain houses of the Trastevere, strangely enough, and among the old palaces and narrow streets of what was once the Field of Mars, gentlemen like Signor T——, at one time an official in the Ministry of Marine, continue to carry on their small, nostalgic, dangerous affairs. It would not take very much to bring the marching men out again, the rubber hoses, and the bottles of castor oil; perhaps no more than a serious Communist success, in which case one might confidently expect to find the Signor T——s everywhere backed by the hierarchy of the Church, the Catholic party, and the Saragat Socialists.

"The election in Italy has by no means been conclusive. The fact is that eight million of Italy's twenty-six million voters declared themselves in favor of the Communists. Unless De Gasperi can provide jobs for two and a half million unemployed, house and feed the homeless—for more than seven millions of homes were destroyed in the war—and institute economic and political reforms, he is in for a rough time. Then watch out for the marching men: first Togliatti, and then the death-and-glory boys."

He had come back from the Ardeatine Caves, shaken again by an emotion he hardly understood, and whose intensity surprised him. He had stood in front of the great slab of concrete which covers the tomb of 335 persons killed by the Germans in reprisal for the blowing up of an S.S. truck—an act of which they were completely innocent. The Cross and the Star of David stand on the rockledge above the entrance, for among the 335, 100 were Jews. Joseph looked at the Cross and the Star, and felt his heart fill with unexpected tears.

But it was for *people* that he mourned, he told himself fiercely; it wasn't just for the Jews—he was quite certain of that. He tried to picture a hundred men; he set them up in a row in his mind. The row stretched quite a long way. Old and young, he saw them, tall and short, bald, thin, fat, with or without spectacles. . . .

One hundred men; one hundred families. He tried to think of a hundred families in Cleveland, but couldn't; the Victors didn't have that large an acquaintance. Of course, if you counted everybody who came into the butcher shop, or the entire congregation of the synagogue . . . One hundred Jewish families. Roman families, that is.

He sighed, got up from the table he used as a desk, and went over and stared out the window. What's the matter with me? he thought. Why have I such a feeling of unreality?

It was all real enough: the hotel room, the street outside, the trams, the green buses, the rocketing Vespas—the fountains, piazzas, steps, the flowers in the flower stalls and in the window boxes, the olive groves on the hills— the buried and broken ruins overgrown with grass and bushes, and farther out, along the Appian Way, the silent catacombs, the tombs, the Ardeatine . . .

And Priscilla—Pat—waiting for him somewhere— where were they to meet?—with tickets for the Teatro Valle. . . .

He went back to the table again and put a fresh sheet of paper in the typewriter. "Today," he wrote, "I visited the Ardeatine Caves . . ."

The play, a comedy by Giraudoux, was to begin early. They left Priscilla's car near the piazza in charge of one of those innumerable sharp-eyed young men in their "official" caps, who appoint themselves guardians of a street or square and collect "protection" from each car parked within their territory, and descended to the theater.

Priscilla was in a gay mood, though to anyone who knew her she would have seemed to be overdoing it. But Joseph, still struggling with new and obscure emotions, scarcely noticed. "Pat," he said soberly, "I've done a piece on the Ardeatine Caves."

"Have you?" she said quietly. "That's good, Joe."

Seated in the darkened theater, with Priscilla's hand in his, and his ears filled with the swift, musical dialogue, very little of which he understood, he began to relax. Her clasp on his hand was strong and steady. She was already planning to leave Rome by herself before the week was out.

It hadn't been an easy thing to decide; it was costing her more than she liked to think. But there was a hard core to Priscilla: if something had to be done, she could do it. There was a time for everything; as the Preacher said, a time to be born and a time to die, a time to plant and a time to pluck up that which is planted . . . a time to keep and a time to cast away. A time to meet, and a time to part.

It was the only way. If they both stayed in Rome it could only end badly for at least one of them. Sooner or later. She had a job in mind that could take her to Milan.

Outside the theater a crowd was gathered, in the middle of which two *carabinièri* were busily taking down depositions. The crowd was too thick for them to see more than the vague outline of a prone figure, with its arms up, possibly shielding its face. "What is it?" Priscilla asked of the protector of her car. "What has happened?"

The young man drew himself up with dignity, and with a noble expression.

"It is nothing, signora," he said. "Merely a Jew."

"A Jew?"

"He received a beating, signora. From a small group of patriots."

"What did he say?" asked Joseph. Priscilla told him.

He stood quite still, feeling a fierce, slow fury rising up in him like a fire. All of a sudden he wanted to go back, to shoulder his way into the crowd, and knock people aside like ninepins. "God damn," he said softly. "Holy God damn."

She caught his arm as he started, and held him back. "Joe," she said, "there's nothing you can do."

"Why not? I want to know why not."

"It isn't news, Joe. They've been doing it right along."

"I didn't know," he said. "Why didn't I know?"

"You didn't want to know. Remember what you said: 'I don't think about being a Jew . . .'?"

He was silent, feeling angry and confused. "This is different," he said at last.

"Is it?" she asked. "Why? Because you happened to see it yourself?"

It was true; and that made him feel even worse. That was what O'Connor had meant, then, when he'd said that Joseph ought to be off to see things for himself. He could hear the bearded Irishman's voice: "If it was the Irish the English were throwing out of their own country . . . I'd be there on the next boat to decry the proceedings."

He took a deep breath. "If this has been going on," he said slowly, "how come the police haven't done anything about it?"

"What can the police do?" she asked. "A beating here —or there. A single man."

"This is a Catholic city, isn't it?" he demanded. "The Pope . . ."

She smiled, as a woman might smile at her child, with pity and exasperation. "The Pope is a very kindly man," she said. "He would rather not know."

"Can't somebody tell him?"

"He would express regret," said Priscilla calmly; "and he would say that there was nothing he could do about it. Which happens to be the truth."

"A small group of patriots!" said Joseph bitterly. "Heil Hitler!"

"Stop it, Joe!" she said. "After all, you aren't doing anything about it yourself—are you?"

"What do you suggest?" he asked bitterly.

They stood staring at each other, aware, suddenly, of their separateness, of a gulf between them over which there was no bridge. "Well," he said defiantly, "what do you want me to do? What *can* I do, except make myself heard?"

"On a street in Trastevere?" she asked coldly. (How dreadful she sounded . . . but she wanted to sound dreadful.)

"Where else?"

"You don't know what you're talking about. You've never wanted to know! That's been the trouble." He was angry now; he was being unreasonable and that made it easier for her.

"I see," he said. "Well, I guess there isn't anything more to say."

"No," she said. "There isn't, is there?"

She left him in front of his hotel and drove away. He watched the little car disappear down the Via Cavour; and then he turned and went up to his room. It seemed to him that something terrible had occurred. He wasn't angry any more, he was frightened; he felt a heavy weight in his chest; he gave deep sighs and took long breaths. He noticed that his heart was beating rapidly. What had happened to his girl?

She had gone off and left him. There had been a sense of something ending in the way she'd said good-by. Had it been good night, or good-by? He tried to remember. The earth rocked a little under his feet. It had been good-by.

It was over, he told himself; it was over. Something was different, something had changed; it was gone; it was finished. It was true, he was sure of it. She no longer loves me, he thought. The first, the best and only beautiful time of his life was over.

At midnight he phoned her; the line was busy.

For a while he let himself dream in a mournful way: he saw himself going off with his cameras over his shoulder and around his neck, waving good-by carelessly, and smiling, while Priscilla's eyes filled with tears. The thought of it comforted him, but not for long; he imagined that he saw Ariano come forward and stand at her side, and his heart turned over and he felt sick.

A hundred sensuous images, memories, rose up before him: of her drowsy eyes half closed, deeply shadowed, so close to his own; of the downy skin at once so soft and so firm, so cool and so ardent; of the loving, busy hands, the moving, tremulous mouth . . . the whole golden enchanting girl with her swift, delicate, sure motions, the way she stood, and moved, the way she had of smiling . . . her perfume, the scarf she wore at night, the sound of her voice, her low laughter, the page-boy sight of her half undressed. . . . He was tormented by them.

The line was still busy at one o'clock, and at two; he realized finally that she must have taken the receiver off the hook.

When she didn't phone him the next day, he knew that he was right: he had lost her; it was finished. He felt that she owed it to him at least to tell him so; he wanted some sort of scene of sorrow, and a little bitterness, and dignity.

But when he finally reached her at the end of the day and heard her familiar *"Pronto"* over the wire, all he could think of was that he wanted to see her again.

But she was sorry: she had a previous engagement, she couldn't see him. "With whom?" he demanded, having trouble with his voice. There was a great hollow place where his heart should have been.

She knew that he was suffering, and it wasn't easy
for her. "I'm sorry, Joe," she said, "I've got a business engagement." "At night?" he cried. "Can't you put it off?"
"I'm dining with a little man from Milan," she said. "It's
the only time he has."

"Where?" asked Joseph explosively, and after a moment she said: "Rosati's," and hung up.

Joseph went down to the bar and ordered a double
brandy. He sat there for an hour, staring straight ahead of
him, not looking at anybody, not talking to anyone. She
didn't want to see him; she was with a little man from Milan. He could see her in his mind, the golden dark eyes
glowing across the table at her companion, the charming
little gestures; but why Milan? They were probably drinking champagne. The Milanese were tall and fair and rich,
usually. He ordered another double brandy. Well, she'd
seen the last of Joseph Victor.

At nine o'clock he got up and took a cab to Rosati's.

When she saw him come in, her eyes widened for a
moment, and she sat up a little straighter. He thought she
looked tired, and a bit pale. "Hello, Pat," he said.

She was looking at him with a strange expression,
half defiant, half appealing. "This is Mr. Mancini," she
said, "from Milan." And turning to the man at her side,
she explained:

"My friend, Mr. Victor."

"How do you do?" said Mr. Mancini, rising politely.

Joseph paid no attention to him. "Pat," he said, "I've
got to talk to you."

Mr. Mancini sat down again, and Joseph sat down
across the table from him. He saw a plump, amiable-look-
ing little man, sallow and middle-aged, with fat little hands
and square-cut fingernails. And Priscilla with a mask on

her face, chatting away like a stranger, making conversation—too lightly, too easily—and her eyes not meeting his, not looking at him. . . . There was no way to reach her; there was nothing between them, only air, nothing to catch hold of. . . . It was like a bad dream.

"Mr. Mancini has a linen factory in Milan; he's been teaching me about linens."

"We get the woven flax from Germany," said Mr. Mancini. "From Westphalia. We do not weave from our own flax."

"I'm sorry about last night," said Joseph.

"Our embroidered linen is the finest in the world," said Mr. Mancini. "Finer even than the Irish."

"Pat," said Joseph.

"Even the Swiss," said Mr. Mancini.

"He wants me to do a piece about his factory," said Priscilla.

"It is in Milan," said Mr. Mancini.

"I've got to see you," said Joseph.

She threw him a quick, flickering glance. "Of course," she said brightly. "Whenever . . ."

"Tomorrow? Tomorrow night?"

She didn't look at him. "I'm going to Milan tomorrow," she said, and kept her eyes down on the table.

It was true, then: it was over. "I see," he said slowly. "Well," he said, rising to his feet, "I guess I'll be getting along. I've got to see about my visas first thing in the morning."

She looked up quickly, and paled a little, although he didn't see it. "Visas?" she asked. "For where, darling?"

It slipped out; and she bit her lip. But Joseph wasn't even aware of it. What difference did it make where he went?

"Good-by, Pat," he said. "Have a good time in Milan. "Have fun."

He didn't see her face as she looked after him, or how her fingers trembled as she fumbled for a cigarette. But Mr. Mancini did. "Perhaps you would prefer to leave for Milan on a later train?" he asked gently. "In case there is something you would like to attend to."

Priscilla shook her head blindly. She was having trouble with her eyes: they didn't seem to want to focus on anything, and they kept misting over. "No," she said, "we'll keep it the way it is. But I think perhaps I could use another drink."

Mr. Mancini pursed his lips, which he did some- times when he had something to discuss with himself. What use is it, he thought, to be young and free and to have won the war? Even for Americans there are problems.

"*Camerière!* For the young lady another martini; for me, a vermouth."

"Make it a double," said Priscilla.

Joseph was also saying "make it a double," a little later, in a bar in another part of the city. He'd said it several times along the way, to several bartenders, and after a while to various companions he had never seen be- fore, but whom he felt—before they disappeared—he knew quite well. They were nice people, and he was drunk, but it was certainly the right night for it. Because in the morn- ing he was going somewhere . . . somewhere . . . he couldn't remember where, but it didn't matter. The thing was . . . the thing was—to go. "I'm going to pack my tents like the Arabs," he told someone—he wasn't sure whether it was a man, or two men, or a woman—"and silently steal away."

"You are going perhaps to Palestine?" asked the two men or the woman, and he nodded solemnly. "Like an Arab," he intoned. And lurching suddenly to his feet, he shouted:

"They killed a hundred Jews, the bastards!"

"*Via!*" said somebody else; and he found himself outside on the cobbles.

It was a swinging night, all rolling and swirling, with figures coming in and out of a haze, and sounds suddenly loud and then just as suddenly rocketing off into silence. Nothing made any sense, but it didn't matter, because at the same time everything seemed to make the greatest sense in the world.

He was never able to remember it very well afterwards. Except that sometime before dawn, two *carabinièri*, one of them with a Sten gun, found him half lying, half sitting, in the Fountain of the Rivers, soaked to the skin, with a blue bruise on his forehead, and all his money gone. He was just able to tell them who he was; and after a little hesitation, they took him back to his hotel, rather than to the *polizei*. "*Grazie,*" he kept saying, "*grazie.* That's very nice of you. Thanks. I mean . . . The hell with it. *Grazie.*"

But when he was in his room again, and they had left him, and he discovered that he had not only been beaten, but robbed, he suddenly flung himself at the walls, striking them with his fists, and screaming in hysterical rage.

"The bastards! The dirty bastards!"

Then he was sick.

He was sick for a long while, and when it was over he fell onto his bed and slept for fourteen hours.

When he awoke, there was a wire waiting for him from the Canadian News Service. "Cancel Russia," it said. "Want you to cover British withdrawal in Middle East [signed] Davies."

He still felt pretty weak, and his money was gone. He was ashamed, besides, and confused; he couldn't think it through. It all seemed like a muddled nightmare. Priscilla . . .

He stopped instantly, and waited for the pain to begin. He tried not to think about her; he held himself in suspension, as though he were holding his breath. In a minute the pain would begin. . . .

But it didn't. After a while, very gingerly, the way a person with a toothache touches the sore place with the tip of his tongue, he let go the tight hold on his thoughts, and came up, again, with the name:

Priscilla.

There was only a sadness, and tiredness. Perhaps someday there'd be more; but whatever he'd done the night before had acted as some kind of catharsis. He felt dull, and empty. . . . His gaze strayed back to the wire from Davies in Toronto, which lay on the table next to his typewriter.

The Middle East. Israel.

It had been coming at him all along. From that very first night up on the Pincio. Only, he hadn't known it.

Well, now he knew.

He slept that night without dreaming. In the morning, he went to the Foreign Press Building and sold one of his cameras to a man from *Newsweek*. It was a good camera, a Rolleiflex, and he got a good price for it. After that he went to a barbershop off the Piazza Barberini and gave himself the full treatment.

Then he sent off a wire to Davies and went to see about visas for Palestine.

CHAPTER

8

THE HIGH OFFICIAL at the British Consulate was polite, but immovable. "It is impossible," he said.

He went on to point out that there were no planes and no boats. "Even if I gave you a visa," he said, "it wouldn't do you the least good. There's really no way of your getting there, you see."

His clear, frosty eyes regarded Joseph without animation. You can always tell an American, he was thinking; nosy beggars—damned children, politically speaking. Always asking impertinent questions; always expecting people to like them. He'd met an American on a train once, and they'd got to talking, as one does, and he'd told the fellow about a spot of trouble he was in with his wife and the fellow had had the cheek to ask him where he went for his clothes. He hadn't told him, of course; what business was it of his? Add a Jew to that—and this fellow's one, or I'm a blue-behinded ape—and you've got a fine merry-o on your hands.

"The only way you could possibly make it," he said, "would be through the Arab countries. I'd advise you to try the Egyptian Consulate. I'm sorry. That's the best I can do for you."

He rose to shake hands; it was, Joseph thought, like shaking hands with Crécy and Agincourt. "It is a curious fact," he said to O'Connor many weeks later, "that the English, more than any other people in the world today, trail their history around with them wherever they go. The ancient Romans must have been like that." "They must indeed," O'Connor agreed, "the proud, traveling creatures."

Joseph took the train to Naples and went to see the Egyptian Consul. The Consul was a tall, fat man who looked, Joseph thought, a good deal like King Farouk. He wore rimless glasses, and he peered suspiciously at Joseph over the tops.

"Who are you?" he wanted to know.

Joseph told him his name, his occupation, and the fact that he was an American. "I know that," said the Consul, fiddling with Joseph's passport on his desk in front of him. He gave him a sudden piercing glance over his eyeglasses. "But what is your nationality, sir?" he asked.

Joseph stared at him stupidly. He had just said that he was an American; the fellow had his passport open in front of him. What did he mean—his nationality?

"If you mean what I think you mean," said Joseph quietly, "what difference does it make?"

The Egyptian's black obsidian eyes snapped, and then veiled themselves. So, he thought, I was right; we have here another accursed Jew.

Still, it was not a good idea to slam doors shut in the face of Americans—and newspapermen besides. "Of course," he said smoothly, "what difference? I will give you a visa through Alexandria. Sometimes it is better to enter certain places through the back door."

Joseph left Naples the following day and returned to Rome. He was still puzzling over his visa "through the back door," when he happened to run into a couple of A.P. men in the bar of his hotel. "Alexandria?" said one of them. "Well, what do you know."

He made a clucking sound, followed by what Joseph recognized as a raspberry. "You go through Alexandria," he said, "and your life isn't worth *lire sixteen*. Any time they can knock off a Jew, particularly one who's going to cover a war, they'd be only too happy to oblige."

"Sure," said the other A.P. man, "what do you think the Arabs are? Boy Scouts? Brother, they play rough!"

"Not rough," said the first one, "mean."

"So what do I do?" asked Joseph mildly. "Get myself stabbed in the back or something?"

The first A.P. man chewed his thumb thoughtfully. "It's like anything else," he said; "you've got to know somebody."

"Do you know anybody?" asked Joseph.

"No," said the man.

"Thanks anyway," said Joseph.

He wanted to ask about Priscilla, but he was afraid to. For one thing, he wasn't sure that he could make it sound casual enough; and for another, he wasn't sure that he wanted to hear about her. Suppose they told him that she was in Milan? Or—for that matter—if they told him that she was back again, in Rome?

He had left the hotel and had taken an inexpensive

room in a small *pensione* in the old Jewish section near to where O'Connor lived. He kept himself as busy as he could; but it was hard. His mind wasn't on what he was doing; it was always behind him, looking back at the way it had been—or it was on ahead, wondering about Palestine. He thought about Priscilla a lot, more than he wanted to. It wasn't so bad during the day: he was running about Rome, in and out of trams and buses, and there were other newspaper people to talk to. But even so, there were plenty of moments when he remembered the figure lying in the gutter with its arms up around its head, and then all at once Priscilla's having left him would hit him like a blow, and he'd feel suddenly dizzy and frightened, and look around quickly, as though he were being chased. He didn't know what to do when it happened, or where to go; the only place he could think of was the nearest bar. But he could never afford more than one drink. The money from the sale of his camera was running out; there'd be more coming to him from Toronto, but not right away.

It was worse at night. In the white, bare light of his room, or in the dark as he lay in bed, the loss and the loneliness would be there like a lump in his chest. He found himself thinking about death again, the way he used to, and he was terrified, just as he used to be. He'd think about being buried: about how it would be to lie alone in the blackness and the nothingness forever and ever, moldering away out of sight and sound, never hearing anything, seeing anything, knowing anything; and he'd have to clench his jaws to keep from shaking.

Priscilla was keeping herself busy, too. She was in Rome again, and lonely, but in a different way: she felt that she had done the right thing, and that helped. Besides, she had friends, and they took her out at night, and sometimes went on interviews or errands with her during the day. Ariano was the only one she didn't see.

She thought that she and Joseph would surely meet somewhere, and imagined how it would be; she wanted it to happen, and she didn't want it, both at the same time. When her body cried out for him, as it did sometimes, she turned on it primly like a maiden aunt. What kind of a girl are you, anyway, Greene? she asked herself. Really!

She was with Kevin O'Connor when she saw him again. She and O'Connor were just rounding the Colosseum into the Via Fori Imperiali when Joseph got out of a green bus and started across the street. He and Priscilla saw each other at the same moment, and stopped, each with the same quick, sick feeling inside, as though the middle had suddenly fallen out of them. "Hello, Joe," she said.

They shook hands gravely, and she asked him how he was. "I'm fine," he said. "I'm all right. And you?"

"Fine."

They stood staring at each other, confused and sad and uneasy, not knowing how much it was going to hurt afterwards. It was O'Connor who asked Joseph what he was doing with himself.

Joseph told him that he was trying to get to Palestine. "I've got some kind of a visa through Alexandria," he said, "but they tell me it's murder."

"Did you try the English Consulate?" asked O'Connor.

"What do you think?" Joseph said.

"Ah, yes," said O'Connor. "That's what I thought. Well, then—the only thing is the underground."

"I know someone in Paris," said Priscilla.

Joseph smiled ruefully. "It seems I got drunk one night," he said, "and had my wallet stolen. I shouldn't have been carrying it around with me. I couldn't even buy a ticket to Milan."

He half turned and started away. "I've got to run along," he said. "It was nice seeing you. What's the thing they always say? *Ciao* . . . ?"

"Joe," said Priscilla helplessly, but he was already halfway across the street.

He felt light and empty inside; he had a sensation of moving swiftly and effortlessly, like a deer or an antelope. It lasted until he was well out of sight; then he went into the nearest bar and ordered a double brandy. He let himself down slowly into his seat, holding on to its wooden arms; he felt heavy as lead, exhausted.

That night there was a knock on his door. When he opened it, O'Connor was standing there in the hallway. "May I come in?" he asked.

"Of course."

"I'm not disturbing you?"

Joseph waved his hand at the room. "No," he said. "As you can see."

"It's a nice little room you have," said O'Connor, looking around. "Right in the heart of the city . . . or among its tripes, which is maybe the better way of putting it." And he added flatly without a pause:

"I have a note for you."

"Oh," said Joseph. He could feel the misery churning up inside again, and fought to keep it down. "Well," he said.

"It's from herself," said O'Connor. "And the hope that you'll listen to me, after."

Why should I listen to you? thought Joseph bitterly. Am I some sort of child, to be lectured at? Let her say what she has to say, face to face.

"All right," he said, holding out his hand for the letter. "Thanks."

"You could read it now," said O'Connor; "there might be some message for me to take back to her."

Joseph went off into a corner, as far from O'Connor as he could, and turned his back. He felt sad, and hopeless, and wished she hadn't written. The envelope smelled of her perfume; it was unfair.

Inside was a folded sheet of notepaper, and an American Express check for a hundred dollars. He immediately wanted to tear it up; his cheeks burned, and the muscles of his jaw stood out. "Take it easy," said O'Connor. "Read the letter."

Joseph stood still, looking at the writing, breathing the fragrance that he knew so well. It was as if Priscilla herself were talking to him. "Joe, my dear," she had written, "there's no use saying I'm sorry; you probably wouldn't believe me if I did. But there are some things you have to believe, and one of them is that what we had was very true and very beautiful. I think that it was that way for you too; I want so much to remember it like that, always.

"The check enclosed is a loan—or a gift to Israel— whatever you choose to call it. *Please, please,* don't refuse it! It will help get you to Paris. I wish I could make it bigger. The name of the man I know there is Davidow, 41 rue Jacob. He'll put you in touch with the people you want to see.

"Bless you, Joe dear.

"Pat."

He faced O'Connor, trying to sound scornful, but

uncertain and unhappy. "Does she really expect me to take this money?" he asked.

"Now, now," said O'Connor sharply, "get down off it! The girl is wretched enough, without you throwing her own last little gesture back into her face. You owe her that much, for the joy you had in Rome in this season of the year . . . maybe you remember the remark. How many people have joy in their lives at all—that would be gratified for the least bit of it?

"As for what she expected, I couldn't say, except maybe a bit of kindness from you."

"Kindness? What kindness did I get from her?"

O'Connor gazed at him reflectively. "I'd say you got as much as she had to give," he said, "and that's the most you'll ever get from anyone, man or woman, either.

"And that," he added, "is all she got from you, though it was enough for her; but don't take the grace of it away now with an ill-considered bit of temper you'll be sorry for in the morning."

Joseph stood there like a child, feeling ashamed, feeling the anger drain out of him, and in its place feeling a pity and a sorrow for them both—for himself and Priscilla, for the girl who wanted so much to believe that it had been good and beautiful between them, and who had tried to help him at the end in the only way she could.

"All right," he said at last, "tell her thanks. For the loan."

He hesitated a moment. "Tell her," he said, "that it was the way she said it was. For me too."

"I'll tell her that," said O'Connor.

"I'll be in Paris the day after tomorrow," said Joseph. "Tell her that."

He held out his hand. "You've been a good friend," he said. "Thank you."

The Rome-Paris express left in the late afternoon. Priscilla bought a platform ticket for it, but stayed off to one side, so that Joseph wouldn't see her. He came quickly through the gate, with his cameras slung over his shoulder, and went into a second-class compartment. After a while the whistles blew, and the train began to roll out of the station. Priscilla watched it until a curve in the track took it out of sight. Then she turned and went back through the depot and out into the street again.

Afterwards she drove down the Via Cavour, past the Hotel Mediterraneo. She wanted to see the place where she had been happy. As she went by, she lifted her hand in a salutation, and a farewell. *"Ciao,"* she said. It had been a season of her life; her spirit was making ready for summer.

Joseph, too, as the train wound its way north across the olive-dusty plains, was saying good-by . . . good-by to whatever it was he'd been. He was never again going to be able to say: I don't think about being a Jew. Priscilla had told him that it made him more of a person; and yet, in the end, wasn't his being a Jew the very thing that spoiled it for them both?

The shadow behind him. She had seen it, too.

Paris was in bloom, the flower stands at the kiosks were piled high with blossoms, and the marroniers were in delicate, full leaf. The sky was a soft blue, the air gentle and soft, and the boulevards curiously quiet after the noise of Rome. There were still a lot of American uniforms in the streets.

He found M. Davidow at the address Priscilla had given him in the rue Jacob. He was a small, round man,

who looked like a commercial traveler and reminded
Joseph of Signor Mancini. He listened to what Joseph had
to say, studying him meanwhile through half-closed eyes.
"Hm," he said. "Hm."

He played for a moment with a pencil on his desk.
"Of course," he said, "I do not do these things myself. I
am not an emissary, a *schliach*, you understand. But I am
not without friends."

"I know there is another way to get to Palestine,"
said Joseph. "Some kind of underground. If you could tell
me . . . if you could send me to someone . . ."

"It is a risky business," said M. Davidow.

"So?"

M. Davidow nodded. He spoke in Yiddish; it made
Joseph homesick to hear it. It was like being back in Cleveland again.

"You understand the situation?" he questioned. "It
is like the ancient times, with the hosts of the Egyptians
and the Syrians arrayed against us. The Mufti is back in
Gaza, and Glubb Pasha does exercises in Jordan with his
Arab Legion. Soon England will withdraw from her Mandate—if she is to be believed; then the Arabs will proclaim a Jihad, a Holy War, against us."

He smiled, and placed his finger against his nose in a
knowing way. "But who believes her?" he asked. "Who is
frightened? The Arab threats do not disturb us; they im-
press only each other and the United Nations. Also, the
British, who do not like the Arabs, but who like the Jews
even less. Is the Mufti England's friend? Is Egypt? Who
could imagine it? Egypt is very loud, but not brave. I think
that no one in the world is brave any more, except our
own people, for whom there is nothing else to be."

"I know," said Joseph.

"Britain was never kind," said M. Davidow, "but she was a lion in the world. What are we to think of her now, this lion who gave us a homeland and then withdrew it, who since 1939 waves a White Paper like a flag of surrender to the Arabs, who do not believe her anyway? Seven hundred and fifty Jews a month we are allowed into Palestine: a handful. And to Abdullah in Trans-Jordan what is allowed? An army.

"So in the end she will crawl away, this lion, having done her best to please a few Arab sheiks whose oil wells feed her pipelines.

"What is left of our people? A miserable remnant, with nothing but the will to live and the courage to endure. For them, there is nothing but Israel; nowhere else in the world to live in peace. For this peace they will do what their ancestors did in the days of Moses; they will cross the deserts and the Red Sea if necessary. They will endure anything, to be at home in their own land."

He was silent for a moment, gazing somberly out the window at the narrow rue Jacob with its old, gray buildings. "We do what we can," he said at last; "we take them from the filthy camps, from those countries where they are still hated, where they are treated like animals, and by secret ways we ship them to Eretz. Sometimes we are lucky, sometimes not; sometimes our ships are hunted down by the British Navy, fired upon and rammed, like the *Exodus*, the passengers sent back to Cyprus or to the German prison camps. You will notice, I said prison camps; they are prisons, and not a holiday for displaced persons.

"So. Do you still wish to go as a passenger to Israel? You will not have an easy time of it, my friend, even

though you are an American. You will have to take your
chances, like the others."

"When do I go?" asked Joseph.

"I will give you the address of a *schliach*," said M.
Davidow. "He is a young *sabra*, born in Israel. His wife
and child are in Tel Aviv. He will give you your instructions."

Joseph came out of M. Davidow's little flat, and
walked through the streets of Paris. He was thoughtful
and troubled; the couples strolling along the *quais* made
him think, for a moment, of the couples enlaced along
the parapets above the Tiber, and he waited, suddenly for
the old sick feeling to come over him again: the sense of
loss, the pain of never-again. But nothing happened; the
image, the golden memory which had ridden with him
all the way from Italy, had already begun to fade, to lose
its sharp edges—the anguish overlaid by new concerns,
and in a different air. He was lonely, but it wasn't a bitter
loneliness; he felt no desire to look for anyone, no need of
a woman, or any companion; he was content to be alone.
He had his memories: they were both sweet and sad; and
he had the future: it lay ahead of him, disturbing and
dangerous, leading in new directions.

The *schliach* to whom M. Davidow sent him turned
out to be a young man in his early twenties. As Davidow
had said, he was a *sabra*, which is the word for a certain
kind of cactus; that is to say, he was a tough specimen,
a Jew born in Zion, and not to be easily uprooted. His
name was Dov—the only name by which Joseph ever
heard him addressed. He spoke Hebrew to Joseph at first,
a purer Hebrew than that of Joseph's old teacher, the
"Hitchkock" of his days in shul, and Joseph had difficulty

in understanding him. Later, aware of Joseph's difficulty, he switched to English, which he spoke with a strange accent, now and then emphasizing the wrong syllables. He told Joseph that both he and his wife were officers in the Haganah, which was the Army of Israel, made up of both men and women, and was, so far at least, only for defense—a militia, a police force. He had been sent secretly with many others to Europe to help rescue the survivors of the Terror wherever possible, to help get them across the closed and guarded borders, always westward and southward toward the sea. Now he was in Paris, working with a certain Goldberg, who was the agent in charge of the illegal ships which sailed secretly at night, from the waiting ports.

M. Goldberg—after the first anxious moment—was very glad to see Joseph. "Perhaps someday you will write about all this," he said. "Perhaps you will be able to tell people how it was for us."

"I don't know," said Joseph honestly. "That's what I want to find out. I've got to see it for myself."

The next day Joseph took a taxi to the Gare de Lyon and caught the train for Marseilles. He traveled third-class, and he carried a forged identity card in his pocket.

He was now Menasha Goldblum, a paperhanger from Freiburg. The real Goldblum was dead; he had perished long ago in the terrible gas chambers of Auschwitz.

His name, at least, would reach Zion.

CHAPTER

((+((+((+((+((+((+((+((+((+((+((+((+((+((+((

9

THE WATERFRONT of Marseilles smelled of garlic and wine, of tar and the sea. Joseph took a taxi, following instructions, to the Café Royal, and presented his identity card to M. Sylvan, the *patron*. He was at once hustled into a back room, where he found a small boy seated with a worn-looking older couple, among the ragged cardboard boxes and suitcases held together with bits of rope, which constituted their belongings. "*Shalom*," he said, self-consciously, and the elders replied, also self-consciously: "*Shalom*."

In a corner of the dingy room, several young men and two young women were engaged in a heated discussion in different languages. They paid no attention to him.

"*Restez ici*," said M. Sylvan. "*Ne bougez pas*." He went on to explain that the city was full of agents, both British and Arab, and that it was best to keep out of sight.

Joseph, who spoke only a few words of French, understood a little of it but not very much.

He went over and sat down near the older couple and their belongings. He felt eager and excited; he wanted to begin to make friends, to be a part of things.

"What did he say?" he asked in Yiddish.

The man replied in German; in a low, dry voice, he told Joseph what M. Sylvan had said. "Thank you," said Joseph, and added, also in German:

"My name is Goldblum."

"Mandelbaum," said the man indifferently. "*Geheimrat*, wife, and grandson." He pointed an arthritic finger at his dilapidated baggage. "A life," he said.

"Are you going to one of the kibbutzim?" asked Joseph, also in German, more to make conversation than anything else; he had only a vague idea of what the communes were actually like. Mr. Mandelbaum shrugged his shoulders. "I am no farmer," he said, "no pioneer. In Berlin I was a lawyer.

"Long ago," he said with a sigh. "Long ago. In Tel Aviv there will be too many lawyers."

The child sat huddled against his grandmother, staring vacantly at nothing. She was a small woman, white-faced and frail, still with a little elegance, or what was left of elegance, about her. "We are educated people," she said.

During the night more refugees drifted into the back room of the Royal. They came in silently, and let themselves down on the floor among their bundles, and fell asleep almost immediately. Sometime before dawn, M. Sylvan came in and quietly roused them. "*Ça y est*," he said.

Lorries waiting in the dark outside took them to the darkened warehouse and the dock where an old Greek cargo vessel, the S.S. *Teti*, lay, a looming shadow in the black. A few naked bulbs cast stark circles of light around the gangplank, up which other refugees were already hurrying silently, like ants, carrying their possessions on their shoulders and in their arms. Each refugee had a slip with the number of his bunk printed on it; as each group reached the shadowy deck, it disappeared into the black hold below.

There were *gendarmes* on the scene, but apparently they were not there to make trouble. They looked at the identity cards, shrugged their shoulders, and passed the refugees along; if someone was called Goldblum, it was his affair, not theirs. When one young woman faltered on the gangplank and would have fallen, the *gendarme* waved her on, not without sympathy. "*Allez,*" he said. "*En avant!*"

The Jewish Agency had paid the captain of the *Teti* one hundred and twenty dollars for each refugee, for which in turn he had agreed to supply adequate food, water, and sleeping accommodations. How well he carried out his part of the agreement, they were to learn later. The *Teti* ordinarily carried eighty to ninety people; now she was to accommodate seven hundred. Wooden bunks had been built in her hold, in tiers of four and even five.

The hold was already crowded, and there were still more refugees to be picked up at Genoa. After one look into that airless hole lit by a few unshaded bulbs, Joseph decided to make his bed on deck. Choosing a corner in the lee of a life raft, he fashioned a pillow out of his valise and with his raincoat over him fell asleep in the cold Mediterranean dawn.

. . .

It was the seventh of May 1948. As the sun rose, the S.S. *Teti* was steaming along the coast of France toward the Estérel, an oily plume of black smoke trailing from her single, rusty stack. Below decks, in the hold, the older refugees slumbered in their bunks while the young people talked in low voices in the narrow aisles. It was the dawn, it was the hour of peace; without air, without room, piled above one another like sardines, they slept and smiled and whispered, nearer home than ever before.

As the sun rose higher in the sky, the wind freshened, and the *Teti* began to pitch a little in the swells, rising and falling, and rolling in the sea. To many of the older people, the motion was too much: they woke only to be sick. The *shomrim*, young men and women of the Haganah, ministered to them as best they could, with mops and pails, wet compresses, and pieces of lemon; but there was little ventilation in the hold, and to the seasick it was like the worst years all over again, the final insult. But the younger ones woke to a new world, fresh, free, and sparkling, and climbed eagerly to the deck to sit in the sun, to talk, to seek one another.

A group of Polish youngsters huddled together in their cabin, which consisted of a blanket stretched between two lifeboats. To the accompaniment of a concertina, they sang, with joy, the bitter songs of exile, of the ghettos and the gas chambers.

Joseph walked about the deck, looking into the faces of his shipmates. He was surprised at their diversity; he saw dark hair and golden hair, round faces, craggy faces, oval, heart-shaped faces, the tall and the short, the plump and the slender. He saw young men who looked like football players, girls who might have come from American colleges, Hassidim with their spare beards and flowing ear-locks, bankers with pince-nez attached to a ribbon, or more often a piece of string. Gray eyes, brown eyes, blue eyes . . . He thought with emotion of all the many efforts that had gone into this single gathering up, this rescue, which after all was only one of many: the courage, the perseverance, the charity, the coming together of a people itself diverse and scattered, strangers in all but blood, with only one aim: to lift these few remnants into safety.

He sought out the Haganah leader, Raphael Zelinsky. He was a stockily built young man in his early twenties, with an expression at once indomitable and anxious. "I am not really Menasha Goldblum," said Joseph diffidently.

"So?" said Zelinsky.

"I'm an American newspaper correspondent," said Joseph.

Zelinsky studied him thoughtfully. "You are sure that you are an American?" he said.

Joseph looked at him in surprise. "What else should I be?" he asked.

"You could be a British agent," said Zelinsky candidly.

Joseph took out his passport and showed it to him. Zelinsky looked it over thoroughly before he gave it back to him. "You are Goldblum," he said simply. "But it may not help you anyway."

He pointed to a young man, scarcely more than a boy, with scars on the back of his neck and slightly crossed eyes. "That one," he said, "was on the *Exodus*. In Haifa harbor he jumped overboard, to swim to freedom;

the scars are where the British shot him. They picked him up and took him back to the *Exodus;* he was sent to Cyprus, and then to Germany.

"His brother has been fighting for more than a year now, in the Haganah. They are Poles; their name is Kolinsky. The young one will escape from wherever they put him, in order to fight in Palestine."

He gave Joseph one of his rare smiles. "A newspaperman is also useful," he said. "Be Goldblum. Afterwards, be whom you please."

Toward evening some of the elders appeared on deck, to walk for a while on unaccustomed legs as the ship slid up and down the slippery valleys of the sea. The *shomrim* circulated among them, cautioning them to distribute themselves evenly about the deck.

Supper consisted of a watery soup and an orange. The dining hall was in the main cabin; the tables were simply planks stretched across two barrels. Narrower planks across empty boxes made benches for those present. Seated among them Joseph was surprised to see a Catholic priest in a long maroon robe, his cross dangling at his side. His name, Joseph learned, was Father Duvernay, and he was on his way to a pulpit in Egypt. He had the broad, shrewd face and the bright, amused eyes of a French peasant; and he shared a cabin with the first officer.

The sun went down, the air turned cold. Joseph stood in the bow of the ship, watching the water parting on either side in smooth green waves and falling away into foam. Ahead of him, to the east, night was advancing like a cloud, and beyond the horizon, already enveloped in evening, lay Rome, the flush of sunset dying on her hills, her narrow streets, fountains, and piazzas already in shadow, the lights coming on in the buildings; and from the Pincio, the great Dome floating in the green and peaceful sky. He felt a sudden grief and a homesickness, a longing for those mornings already so far away, when he woke happy with the Roman sun in his eyes and heard the trams and buses going by outside his window. Pat, he thought, Pat! This was the hour when they always met somewhere in the city: at the Spanish Steps, at the Tortoise Fountain in the Piazza Mattei, in front of the Farnese, on the Campidoglio—catching sight of each other from far away, seeing the delight, hearing each other's voice, rushing together across a crowded square.

But then the strangeness of his own surroundings swept over him, and the memories faded; he saw the Mandelbaums at the Café Royal among their possessions tied with string. A life, he thought; a lifetime. He saw the *gendarme* helping the terrified young woman up the gangplank. . . .

Night had come on, the ship's lanterns were lit behind him, the green and red running lights rolling against the faintly glowing night-blue sky. A few stars appeared, large and golden in the west. Joseph shivered and went to find his bed near the lifeboat, the valise, and the raincoat. The Polish youths were quiet, stretched out beneath their blanket.

Down in the hold, the Mandelbaums prepared for bed in the single bunk allotted to them. While Hermann slept, the grandparents spoke together in whispers.

"Is this the food they give us to eat?" asked Mrs. Mandelbaum querulously. "Soup and an orange?" "Believe me," said Mr. Mandelbaum, "I will make a protest to the proper authorities." "The proper authorities?" said Mrs. Mandelbaum bitterly. "Who are they? Galicians, maybe; or from Lithuania." "So?" asked Mr. Mandelbaum. "So," she said. "How do you speak to Lithuanians?"

Beside them, an old, pious Jew prayed in his bunk. His curled sideburns fell softly on his bearded cheeks; in his *yarmilk* and black mohair vest, he praised the Eternal One of Israel. Near him two young men brooded over a game of chess.

The night wore on; far off across the black water, the coastal mountains lay like shadows, all but invisible against the blue-black sky; the lights of the Riviera towns clustered at their feet like tiny golden glowing dots. As the hours passed, Cannes fell astern, low on the horizon, then Nice, and the distant lights of Monaco. Joseph stirred uncomfortably on the hard deck, burrowing under his raincoat for warmth. His dreams were swift and restless, and followed one another in a flickering pattern; once he heard the orchestra again, but the music was unfamiliar.

On the Italian shore a convoy of trucks wound its way along the old Aurelian road, under the silent, looming mountains. Filled with refugees to be picked up by the *Teti*, the trucks were headed for a fishing village not far from Genoa, where there was a small harbor and a battered wharf.

Once arrived, the refugees formed silently on the shore. The black mountains rose behind their backs into the sky, the invisible water lapped and whispered among the pilings at their feet. They waited, as they had waited so often before, in bleak patience, in stony acceptance, in the cold night wind.

"What are we waiting for?" asked a little girl in Hungarian.

"We are waiting for a ship," said her mother.

"Why do we have to wait?"

"How can I tell you when I do not know?"

"Will they arrest us again?"

"Not if we are quiet."

"All right. I'll be quiet. Only I'm so cold."

"I am sorry, Mia; perhaps if you came closer to me . . . here, under my arm."

Just before dawn a triangle of white, red, and green lights appeared suddenly at the mouth of the little harbor, and the S.S. *Teti* came sliding in, her decks and portholes dark. She came in silently, like a ghost ship; the water churned as she reversed her engines; she drifted quietly against the wharf. Ghostlike figures made her hawsers fast and let down her gangplank, and once again that ant-like line climbed the steep slope and disappeared into the hold. It was a long climb up and out over the black water: from the top they could see the lights of fishing boats far out on the horizon. Somewhere out there, too, were the British destroyers.

"*Shalom*," whispered the *shomrim* over and over as they helped the refugees, many of them stiff with cold, up the dark and narrow gangplank, passing the heavier bundles of belongings from one to another, their flashlights making little circles of light on the ground, flickering up and down. "*Shalom*; peace." It was, perhaps, premature, but to the refugees, cold and weary, standing at the sea's edge with the long years of terror behind them, it was a lovely sound. "*Shalom*," most of them said in turn; and a few: "Blessed be He."

Joseph, roused from sleep by the ship's stillness and lack of motion, went over and stood at the rail and watched them come on board. It seemed to him that there were a great many, and he wondered how the ship could hold them all. The shadowy figures, the low voices, the yellow circles of light—the bleak, black mountains in the background, massive and silent, and the deep night-blue of the sky overhead with its quiet, before-morning stars . . . the whole scene, hushed and mysterious, had the quality of a dream.

But this was Italy; he could smell the land: it had the same sweet pine and cypress smell, the sand and grass smell of that night at Fregene so long ago. . . . Was it so long ago? It seemed so, indeed. It was strange to be so near Pat again—not really near, but in the same country, and that made a kind of nearness. Yet that, too, was only a dream—a sad dream, but not altogether sad: a gentle sorrowing.

A young woman came up the gangplank with her arm around a little girl; for a moment, as she stepped onto the deck in a circle of light, he caught a glimpse of her face, and in that single moment felt, as though it were his own, her tired loneliness, and saw the proud and frightened way she held her child close to her. "*Shalom*," he murmured from the shadows, and she lifted her eyes for a moment in his direction. Then she and the child passed out of the circle of light, and Joseph, still seeing in his mind the quiet, weary beauty of her face, turned and stared blindly down at the wharf and at the steady, slow movement of people below him, as they came out of the darkness like moths toward the faint lights of the ship.

There was a little light in the hold, from two lanterns hanging from iron beams. Among the tired bodies huddled on the floor was that of a woman from Eger; her name was Rosa Hatvany, and she had fallen asleep among the bundles and suitcases with a torn and dirty rag doll hugged

to her breast. Alex Hatvany, her husband, slept with his
head in her lap. The doll had belonged to their daughter,
the daughter whom they had sent, long ago, to Israel.

In his bed in the cabin which he shared with the
first officer, Father Duvernay slept soundly. He had not
wakened when the *Teti* stopped and did not wake when
her engines started up again. He spoke several languages,
but when he dreamed it was always in French. He had
brought with him his own provisions for the voyage: a
huge sausage, bread, cheese, and wine. He was frugal; it
would last for quite a while, and he could replenish his
hamper at Tel Aviv. And he had brought along with him
several periodicals in both French and English which he
intended to study during the voyage. After all, he was
going to Egypt, to take up his work there, and it was a
good idea to know what was going on.

The old Orthodox Jew in the hold had also brought
his own food: hard-boiled eggs, salt, and bread. Tea he
could get on board, and oranges—but in a soup? Who
could know what there might be?

Anna and Mia were given a mattress together, in
the second tier of bunks; and there, grateful for the
warmth, and—for the moment, at least—unmindful of
the close and fetid air, they fell asleep.

Far away, across the night-dark sea, Alon deployed
his two Palmach battalions before Safed; and on the
Jerusalem–Tel Aviv Road, the Harel Brigade moved slowly
toward the heights overlooking the Bab el-Wad.

CHAPTER

❖❖❖❖❖❖❖❖❖❖❖❖❖❖❖❖❖❖❖

10

THE WEATHER was bright and clear, the blue Mediterranean sparkled in the sun. The *Teti*, her deck crowded, rose and fell easily on the small swells, headed south. An air of gaiety invested the ship; in the sunlight, in the fresh wind off the sea, the refugees relaxed, and with the past behind them, grasped at the bright moment of happiness. Here there was no barbed wire, no guard with a bayonet or submachine gun; men and women lay about on the warm, bare wood, dozed and drowsed in the sun, or sat huddled together smiling and talking.

In a corner of the deck next to the canvas-covered latrines, Milton Gutzman had opened up his little barbershop and was waiting for customers. He had a sign which read: "Shaves, ten cents." He had brought it with him from a camp in the American zone. Before the war, Milton had been a barber in Munich; it was his boast that he had once shaved Goering, before the *Putsch*. "Imagine," he liked to say, "there I was with a razor in my hand. If I had known! With one *sqvaaaak* I could have changed the course of history."

But then he would have his doubts. "So what?" he would say. "Someone else would have done us in just the same."

He considered himself a philosopher; he delighted to be the center of everything and to receive and dispense news and gossip. It was he who pointed out to Joseph a tall, lean man smoking a pipe. "Dr. Dreyfoos," he said, "from South Africa. Actually a doctor, a medicine, trained in London. That's good, no? So what does he do? He gives up his profession, to work on a kibbutz in Israel. With his bare hands: a *chalutz*."

"Maybe it seems like a good life to him," said Joseph; "that's possible."

Milton shrugged his shoulders. "What is a good life?" he demanded. "A kibbutz is a commune, where nobody owns anything himself, not even his own barbershop. A *mensch* works there for the good of everybody: he does everything, from teaching the children to carrying out the garbage. Meanwhile, he is also a soldier and fights the Arabs, who would like to slit his throat and steal his dairy cows. It is something like your own cowboys and Indians, no? What sort of work is this for a doctor? And from South Africa, besides?"

"What has South Africa to do with it?" asked Joseph.

"It is only," said Milton, "that it sounds like a safe place to be."

"I wonder if any place is safe any more," said Joseph.

"For a Jew?"

"For anyone. Jew or Gentile."

Joseph took his camera and went about the ship taking pictures. It was interesting to see how people acted when they saw the camera, all according to their age, their disposition, and their religious background. The Orthodox turned away; but the young people smiled, or stared fiercely and proudly into the lens.

It was the children who interested him most. There were two groups—the very young, who seemed healthy and happy, and those older ones with vacant, listless faces, and veiled and lonely eyes; those were the ones who had seen too much and suffered too much.

Two children were playing together under an umbrella: a little flaxen-haired boy and a chubby girl with a solemn squint and the broad cheeks of the Slav. Each spoke a different language, but they understood each other: the umbrella was a roof, so they were playing house. After a while, for the little boy, the umbrella turned into a parachute, and he imagined himself floating gracefully to earth, equipped with the paraphernalia of a space-traveler. There were many such travelers in the much-tattered paperback book of comics given him by an American soldier in the camp at Zeilsheim. It was his only library, and his greatest treasure; he pored over it, without understanding a word. The little girl, meanwhile, went on with her imaginary household chores; they were few and simple, because she had never seen a house; but cooking, sweeping, and rearranging things, one did even in a tent. There was no need for them to play the same game, just as long as they were playing together.

They paid no attention to Joseph's camera; neither did another little girl whom he found embroidering lengths of brightly colored yarn onto a piece of burlap. She wore a ribbon in her hair, and her face was set in a frown of concentration. Here, at last, was a world small enough for her.

With the tip of her tongue caught between her teeth, she bent above her embroidery, erasing from her mind the larger world that she could never understand.

With his camera, Joseph made friends. People are glad to have their pictures taken when they feel that they are engaged in something heroic or unusual; and Joseph had a professional air about him. This wasn't somebody taking private snapshots for an album; the fear that he might be a British agent, bent—in some way—on making trouble, vanished when they saw that Raphael Zelinsky himself allowed Joseph to take his picture. "He is a photographer for the United Nations," the barber explained to everyone. "Imagine that; they wish a report. An American, no less, from Freiburg, by the name Goldblum."

"So be so good as to tell me," said Mr. Mandelbaum, sitting upright on the wooden stool which the barber used for a chair, "how can he be an American from Freiburg? Is Freiburg in America, then?" "Maybe it is in the American Zone," said Milton. "Who knows?"

"And you, sir: you are named Mandelbaum? You know, of course, in Jerusalem the Mandelbaum Gates. A relative, perhaps? A connection?"

"*Gewiss,*" said Mr. Mandelbaum shortly. For all he knew, he was connected; a man like himself, who had enjoyed the title of *Geheimrat,* could naturally have been a member of that wealthy family. Maybe distantly.

Mrs. Mandelbaum, however, refused to sit for her picture, and insisted that her husband also refuse for himself and for their grandson. "Who would recognize us," she demanded, "looking like this?" To which Mr. Mandelbaum replied that there was no one left, as far as he knew, who would recognize them at all, no matter how they looked. "No difference," said Mrs. Mandelbaum positively; "a pic-

ture is for eternity. How would our Hermann feel if someday when he is a respected lawyer in Tel Aviv his friends
were to see him looking like this?"

"How would he feel?" demanded her husband. "How
do I know how he would feel?" "No matter," said Mrs.
Mandelbaum. "I want these days to be forgotten."

At noon, when the sun was overhead, Joseph aimed
his camera at the hold, and took a picture of the dark well
and the two iron ladders, and a few of the bunks in which
one or two people still lay, lonely and uncomfortable, but
too ill or too weary to climb to the deck. Faces looked up
at him, without interest or expression; it was like looking
down into a dungeon, he thought, a prison; and yet it was
the first freedom that most of them had known in more
than eight years.

In the afternoon sun he caught Father Duvernay and
Dr. Dreyfoos, the South African, engaged in conversation.
Dr. Dreyfoos was perhaps thirty years old, with the thin,
sensitive face and gentle inquiring glance of a good Jewish
physician. He would have been at home in New York or
Hollywood, but he was headed for the kibbutz of Givat
Brenner. "We also," he said quietly to the priest, "are a
dedicated people. *Nous aussi sommes les dediées.*"

"Ah yes," said Father Duvernay in his own tongue,
"one should never forget that the blessed Apostles were
people like yourselves. As the Holy Father has said: 'We
are all of us Semites, in a spiritual sense.' "

"I do not think that the Anglican Church agrees with
him," said Dr. Dreyfoos drily. "Nor the Greek, either."

The priest lifted his hands in a typical Gallic gesture.
"Let them pull their own artichokes," he said. "Our Lord
gave the keys of the kingdom to Peter, not to Paul.

"As for the Anglicans—isn't it a shocking thing, that

a King would become head of his own Church for the sake
of a woman?"

"Father," said Joseph when the priest's remark had
been translated to him, "you sound like an Irishman."

"Why not?" said Father Duvernay. "I'm a Breton—
which is to say a good Celt myself."

Joseph moved on around the deck, hoping to catch
sight of the young woman of the night before, but failed
to find her. All the time she was seated behind a life raft
toward the stern of the ship, her face turned to the north,
her somber eyes seeking out that land already lost over the
horizon—that vague, terrible land-mass of Europe, where
all her memories were, and where—except for Mia—everything she had ever known and loved was buried, in dirt
and ashes. A family, a home, a son, a father, a mother, a
husband—all, all gone, lost and gone forever. What lay
ahead? An empty sea, and an unknown land. Someone had
said "peace" to her when she came on board the night before. . . . Well, peace then. A bee, an insect dying all alone
of the cold has such peace.

The sun went slowly down the sky; a bell rang, it was
time for supper. At the tables she found herself with her
daughter near the one they said was an American, the one
who had been taking pictures all day . . . to what purpose?

He had wanted so much to find her; and there, quite
simply and suddenly, she was. The little girl with the hair
ribbon, who had been doing the embroidery, was with her
on the side nearer Joseph; that must have been the child
she had her arm around when they came on board. There
was a resemblance . . . they both seemed to have drawn
a circle about them to make a smaller, stiller place in
which to live. Her voice when she spoke to the child was

almost a whisper; the mother's arm, thought Joseph, is still around the child.

He addressed the little girl in German, offering her bread, and then in Yiddish. But she only raised startled eyes to him and drew back against her mother. The woman bent down in a swift, protective gesture, and spoke to her rapidly and softly. "She speaks only Hungarian," she said in German, looking at Joseph defensively. "She has fear."

"Of me?" asked Joseph in surprise, lasping without thinking into English.

Anna's eyes clouded; she appeared to draw back into herself. "She is only little," she said in English. "You must forgive."

Her voice surprised him, it was so musical; he thought he had never heard a more beautiful voice. It was not like any one instrument, but like many, all playing together. It was a voice like an orchestra, like something by Mahler, gay and grieving, but far away. Like long ago when there was joy in the world, and grieving for it.

And Anna, looking at Joseph, thought: This is not somebody like us, who has lost everything.

Strangely enough, it was a comfort to her. "Say thank you to the gentleman," she said to Mia in her soft whisper. "Take the bread."

The child looked questioningly at her mother and then at Joseph. Reassured, she held out her hand and murmured: "*Köszönöm.*"

"I took a picture of your daughter," Joseph said. "When we get to Tel Aviv I'll have a copy made for you."

He smiled at her a little awkwardly. "I wanted to take one of you, too," he confessed.

She looked at him, her head drawn back and a little to one side, wary and waiting; and their eyes met for the first time. Hers were blue, he saw—deep blue, with dark lashes around them—or were they blue at all? or violet, like the sky along the horizon on a summer day? Her dark hair hung down in a gentle wave to her shoulders. She had the high cheekbones of the Magyar; her mouth was full and generous, her nose small and straight, with delicate nostrils.

It was a long look between them, full of half questions and half answers and sudden reticences. "You are the one," she said at last, uncertainly, "who said to me last night: *Shalom?*"

"Yes," said Joseph. "I was the one."

"*Wahrscheinlich,*" she said. "I know now the voice."

But then again, the withdrawal, as though she had gone too far, had ventured too far into too wide a world, and might not find her way back again to her own. Nor was there any way for Joseph to follow her. She and her daughter ate the rest of their meal in silence and soon left the table.

As she rose to go, she gave Joseph a last shy glance, guarded and noncommittal. Mia bobbed him a little curtsy; it was so out of place that Joseph almost laughed aloud.

Where on earth did she learn that? he wondered. "*Köszönöm,*" she said.

Later, before he went to his corner of the deck to sleep, he sought out Milton the barber. "Tell me," he said, "you who know everything: who is the woman with the dark hair to her shoulders, and the child with the hair ribbon who embroiders?"

Milton pushed the barber's stool toward him. "Seat yourself," he said. "Sit, my friend. You are speaking of the beloved of King Solomon: 'Who is this that cometh out of the wilderness like pillars of smoke?' You are perhaps surprised to hear me quote from the Book? As a child I had training in the synagogue in Maisach, which is outside Munich. For my *barmitzvah*, I made a speech from the Song; my cousin Sara thought it was for her. 'Her eyes are like doves, and her teeth like flocks of sheep.' Later that night she pushed me into a closet under the stairs, and herself also."

He sighed. "It goes by," he said. "Life goes by."

For a moment he looked at Joseph as though he didn't see him. Then he recollected himself. "But you are asking me about something else," he said.

"Wait here. I will go ask my *melamed*. In ten minutes I will have found out about this one with the dark hair and the child who embroiders."

"Thank you," said Joseph.

"Ten minutes," said the barber. "Ten cents. The same as a shave."

"Did I charge to take your picture?" asked Joseph indignantly.

"Did I ask you?" said Milton. "Besides—I haven't got the picture yet."

Joseph sat and waited, and in ten minutes, as he had promised, Milton came back with the information. "The lady's name is Anna Muhlmann," he said, "born Czeffy, from a wealthy family from Buda Pesth. Of all her people, only the child Mia is left. The others"—he made an expressive gesture across his throat—"at Maidenek. But first over the head, with clubs, like in a slaughterhouse. This, I am told, she was forced to watch. Her husband was an architect from Vienna; the child was born after his death."

He gazed somberly over the ship's side into the foam-hissing darkness. "Death," he said at last; "that is too dignified a word to be used. A man must die sooner or later, in bed or on the battlefield; but there must be some other word for the final abomination which happened to these people.

"Keep the ten cents; I don't want it any more."

For the third time Joseph slept stretched out on the wooden deck, his head on the valise, while the *Teti* slipped through the ocean night, past Fregene and Ostia, where far to the east and out of sight the Tiber emptied its waters into the sea. Not even a faint glow in the sky marked the spot where Priscilla Greene and Count Antonio Ariano were dancing at the Rugantino in the Piazza Sonnino in Trastevere—and discussing the possibilities of linen for export instead of leather. It was in any case, at last, a matter of indifference to Joseph; he slept in good spirit and in a freshness of heart; there was no longer anything to grieve over.

Except the world, and man. But to a Jew that came naturally; there was nothing personal about it.

In the close air of the hold, in the wavering light as the lanterns swung to and fro, Rosa Hatvany was arguing with her husband. Alex wanted to live in a kibbutz, to work with his hands in the green earth. But Rosa had lived all her life in Buda Pesth; what would she do on a farm? And besides—their daughter, Toni: a young girl like that ought to have the opportunities of a big city.

Leaning over the side of her bunk, Anna murmured: "Excuse me; I could not help overhearing. You are from Buda Pesth?"

"Yes. No! From Eger. And you . . . ?"

Anna looked around at the dim hold with its iron bulkheads, its tiers of bunks from which stockinged feet protruded here and there, and sometimes a head. Am I from Buda? she wondered. Where am I from? I do not know. From Maideneck, from the frontiers, from the cold and the snow, always running, running, even before they caught us, Carl and me, even before that terrible thing which I mustn't think about . . . and afterwards. No, she thought, how could she tell anyone? She mustn't answer, she mustn't remember, she mustn't open herself to the world again, to people.

It was Mia who bent down to Mrs. Hatvany, and pointed to the ragged doll among the bundles on the floor. "Is that your doll?" she asked shyly.

Rosa gazed up at the little face peering down at her. "It belongs to my daughter," she said.

"It's very pretty," said Mia. "Is your daughter a little girl, like me?"

"Yes . . . in a way. . . ."

"Is she here with you?"

"No, she is in Israel."

"We're going to Israel, too."

"I know. We are all going together."

"How old is your little girl?"

"She is seven."

"For God's sake, Rosa," murmured her husband; "she was seven when she left us.

"Long ago," he said, appealing to Anna. "It was long ago."

"I'll be six," said Mia. "Someday."

"Ah," said Rosa.

Mia's face was like a little pool of shadow, out of which only her eyes shone in the dim light as the lanterns swung slowly this way and that. "I never had a doll," she said, "to go to bed with."

"Mia!" said Anna in consternation.

Rosa hesitated a moment. Then, picking up the little

bundle of rags, she placed it in Mia's arms. "Here," she
said. "Only for tonight."

Mia said nothing; she made a little crooning sound
and hugged the matted object to her breast. "I am so
sorry," said Anna; "she ought not to . . . you should not
have . . ."

"Please," said Rosa. "It is only for tonight."

"But it is so kind of you—"

"Believe me: a trifle."

Little by little the voices in the hold died away; after
a while nothing was to be heard but the creaking of the
ship, the sound of water rushing by against the hull, the
steady pulse of the engines, and the restless movements
and heavy breathing of the sleepers. But Rosa lay awake,
staring at the lanterns which swung overhead, to and fro,
to and fro. . . . Sometime during the night she rose and
reached into the bunk where Mia and her mother lay, and
took the doll gently from the sleeping child. It was her only
link between the past and the future; with it in her arms
again, she could sleep.

The east turned gray, and then faint green; then yellow. The yellow spread out through the air; a band of red
appeared in the east, low on the horizon, and above it
the green slowly turned blue and began to glow. The sun
came up, and suddenly there were long shadows everywhere. Those who were sleeping on the deck turned their
faces away from the bright, kindling light, aching in all
their joints and muscles from the hard wood on which they
had lain curled up like worms through the cold night.
From their holes and corners, from the bowels of the ship,
the Orthodox came out on deck to pray; with shawls and
phylacteries, they bowed toward the East.

Mr. Mandelbaum and Hermann stood in line, waiting

their turn to use the canvas-covered latrine and washrooms, which were located amidships next to the barbershop. On the afterdeck, Mottl, from Pinsk, the self-appointed guardian of the orphans on board, leaned over the rail and drew water from the sea in a bucket, to toss over his naked charges as they shivered and squealed and danced about in the early sunshine.

"Today," said Mr. Mandelbaum to his grandson, "we will find some nice young people for you to play with."

Hermann was not impressed by this remark. Play, he had learned, was usually fighting, either real or make-believe, or else running around and hiding, or trying to catch people. . . . He liked to sit quietly and not be noticed. "I'm hungry," he said.

"Never mind," said Mr. Mandelbaum. "In a little while you will have an orange."

But there were no oranges for breakfast that day, only a sort of porridge. To the murmurs of the refugees, Zelinsky, the Haganah leader, had only one reply: "We are seven hundred. Are we bringing Jews or oranges to Israel?"

To Joseph, in private, he expressed a different concern. "This captain," he said, "this Greek—I don't know. I'm not sure if he is honest."

He smiled thinly and shrugged his shoulders. "At least," he said, "he cannot sell us into slavery to the Turks —like so many did in 1492 when we had to leave Spain, also in a hurry."

As the morning wore on, people began to appear in every conceivable costume. Some men wore knickers; others, overalls. Most of the women had scarves tied around their heads, to ward off the sun, and to keep their hair from blowing about and getting tangled in the wind. The Orthodox alone dressed as usual, in their long coats.

A Polish girl with russet hair and freckles played her harmonica on top of a life raft. The Polish boys surrounded her; soon the harmonica was joined by the accordion.

It was the third day.

CHAPTER

I I

THERE WERE plenty of bitter tongues on board the S.S. *Teti*, and one of them belonged to Sophie Opisch. This elderly widow, originally from Riga, who had lived for the last three years in peasant huts and damp cellars, had created a life of esteem for herself out of dreams and fancies, and never failed to mention her nephew in America, although she had never seen him and never heard from him. It was her way of demanding deference from the people around her. She had no other defense against poverty, misery, and a lonely old age.

When they asked her why she had chosen to make the difficult journey to Israel instead of going to her wealthy nephew in the United States, she closed her eyes, bit her lip, and threw her hands up to heaven. "So what is," she demanded, "to be in America? For me, it is unnatural, like a fish out of water. My nephew belongs to the Country Club, U.S.A."

136

Like almost everything else, she had made up her nephew's life out of imagination. Who knows how much of it she believed? But in her opinion it explained everything. "*Goyim nachus!*" she exclaimed. "So all right, for Gentiles. But for a Jew? In Israel, a Jew lives natural, like a human being."

Joseph wanted to take a picture of her. But first she insisted on rearranging her hair. "I want you should send a copy to my nephew in Birmingham, Alabama," she said. "He will see how I am traveling first-class, like advertised!"

Near by, a discussion of another sort was taking place among a number of the passengers, including the pipe-smoking Dr. Dreyfoos, Father Duvernay, Mr. Mandelbaum, and Milton Gutzman, the barber. The British Mandate would be ended soon—if the news was to be believed—and after that, what was going to happen? Would the British actually leave? What did President Truman say? Would there be a Jewish state? Or would the Arabs rule? Or both, perhaps? No one knew.

Father Duvernay had just remarked that not all Jews were Zionists, a declaration which was generally denied by the others. "Very well, then," said Father Duvernay, "how does it happen that, in America, Mr. Lessing Rosenwald and the Council for Judaism have denounced the proposed Jewish state as a menace to peace?"

An uncomfortable silence followed these words, broken at last by the barber. "It is nothing off the nose of Mr. Rosenwald," he remarked, "whether we are a state. No doubt he is a rich man: comfortable—not like us who have no other country but Eretz."

The old Orthodox Jew from the hold, who had been walking past, heard him and stopped. "Let me tell you a story," he said in German with a heavy accent. "It is a story told by the Breslauer rabbi."

He cleared his throat, and took a step backward. "It seems," he declared, "that there lived on one side of a high mountain a hermit, whose entire belongings consisted of one old cooking pot. He was without family or friends; for company he enjoyed the visits of a rooster, a mouse, and a small bird like a sparrow. Came the moment, in God's good time, when these animals died, of whatever causes is not known. When this was related to the famous rabbi of Kotzenau, Avram ben Yehudi, he is said to have sent a message to the hermit: 'Do not be surprised that your friends died, for misfortune always awaits the wealthy.' "

So saying, the old man in his hat and his *yarmilk* moved on. But in a moment he returned. "Nevertheless," he declared, "I say unto you: 'Even the remnant of Jacob shall return.' "

With that he walked firmly away. The priest gazed after him thoughtfully. "A formidable character," he observed, "*formidable et mystérieux.*"

He roused himself abruptly. "Still," he remarked, "after all, one must not allow oneself to overlook the practical aspects."

"What are they?" asked Joseph defensively. "What are the practical aspects?"

"The practical aspects," said Milton Gutzman, "are that we are there. That is to say," he added quickly, "I am not there yet, personally, so I am only speaking in general."

"The Arabs are also there," said Father Duvernay. "And there are many more Arabs than Jews. If it came to fighting, it would be the Jews who would suffer the most.

These colonies which you call kibbutzim—do I have the just word?—are many of them in exposed positions. They would be under fire from the hills of Syria, Trans-Jordan, and the Lebanon."

"So?" replied Milton. "We have been under fire before—only, we hadn't as much as a toothpick to fire back. This time, you will see something."

Dr. Dreyfoos took his pipe out of his mouth, and nodded in agreement. "Give a duiker the horns of a buffalo," he said, "and he will stand his ground.

"Particularly," he added drily, "if he has nowhere else to go."

"With the horns of a buffalo," said Mr. Mandelbaum, who in happier days had often visited the Tiergarten, and had subscribed to zoological magazines, "the duiker would tumble right over onto his nose."

"It is as good a way as any of staying put," replied Dr. Dreyfoos, "and digging in."

"Allow me to disagree," said Mr. Mandelbaum. "For myself, I will say without equivocation that I am not in favor of wholesale immigration."

"No?" exclaimed the barber. "Then what is to happen to those left behind? Are they to stay there and rot? Or is it to be a quota system, like in Cyprus: so many today, none tomorrow?"

"They must take their chances," said Mr. Mandelbaum firmly. "I believe in everything orderly and in due course. Your little antelope with his horns in the ground is not in a good position."

"So you agree with the Gentile," said a young Rumanian; "or did I perhaps misunderstand him? Tell me, Reverend Sir," he said, addressing himself to the priest, "where do you stand in all this?" He spoke in French, and

Father Duvernay responded in the same language. *"Tout simplement,"* he said, "I am opposed to violence."

"Naturally," Dr. Dreyfoos agreed, "that must be the Catholic position. It was not always so—as, for example, during the Crusades."

"Ah," exclaimed the priest, "but they were for the liberation of Jerusalem!"

Dr. Dreyfoos's pipe had gone out, and he stopped to light it. "That is our aim also," he said calmly. "For us, too, it is a Holy City."

Other discussions were going on, meanwhile, in other parts of the ship. They were in many languages, but mainly in German, Yiddish, English, and Russian. Most Europeans as a rule speak more than one language; and in the camps—the concentration camps, the prison camps, the work camps, the displaced-persons camps—those who had survived had picked up a smattering of tongues. "Truly," said Mottl, the guardian of the orphans, "this ship is like that tower of Babel which the children of Noah built in the plain of Shinar."

Like his friends in the ghetto in Pinsk, he had studied, as a child, the history of God. However, a young Talmudic scholar corrected him. "The tower," he declared, "was not in the first place an edifice; according to Cordovero of Safed, the teacher of the sublime Loria, the tower must be considered to be a symbol of man's arrogance, to which the Holy One, Blessed be He, very sensibly put a stop, by creating suddenly a number of alphabets into which he poured the different tribes like soup."

To which a Rumanian Communist who had fought with the partisans in Yugoslavia replied:

"*Rahet.*

"The fact is," he insisted, "that men for the first time

140

were working together in harmony; they were probably building a large apartment house. So God is frightened that he is not going to have His own way any more, and he makes quarrels between them. Suddenly they don't understand one another; in short, there is no communication."

"So?" demanded the Talmudist.

"So," exclaimed the partisan, "divide and conquer! God is a capitalist. Do you deny it?"

"I deny nothing," replied the scholar, "because I deny everything. Is God interested in politics and co-operative apartment houses? 'Render unto Caesar that which is Caesar's, and unto God that which is God's'—which was spoken by the prophet Jesus bar Joseph of Nazareth, who was a monk of the Essenes, and a contemporary of the great Hillel. If the Lord, Blessed be He, created alphabets, do you imagine that he did so for the sole benefit of the Rothschilds?"

"It was the money of the Rothschilds," remarked a young accountant from the Camargue, "that built the first colonies in Palestine."

"Maybe so," said the partisan, "and I will not even bother to ask you where it came from. But it was the strength of the kibbutzniks that kept them there. Do you deny it?"

Like the Talmudist, the young accountant denied nothing. He himself was headed for a kibbutz near Galilee.

Neither the Talmudist nor the partisan nor the priest knew that the battles for Haifa, for Safed, for Galilee, for Jerusalem, were already being fought, so far away. No news of this had reached the ship, or of the confused and indecisive British withdrawal. But even Mr. Bevin himself, in London, was in ignorance of much that was taking place, and failed to understand it.

Seated on a life raft in the sun, Joseph was talking with Raphael Zelinsky, who meanwhile kept an eye on all the activity going on around him. "I was never an optimist," Joseph said; "even in America, no little Jewish boy is ever told to grow up to be President."

He was silent, trying to remember something, and then remembering it, and feeling suddenly depressed, with just a touch of something like homesickness. But it went away again in the bright ocean air and the bustle all about him. "But this," he said, "the things I have heard on this ship. . . . Why should the world hate us so much? Why should human beings do such things to other human beings? What have we done to merit all this hate?"

"Who knows?" said Zelinsky. "Maybe we killed Christ."

"If we hadn't," Joseph argued, "somebody else would have had to. Without the Crucifixion, how could there have been an Easter?"

Zelinsky shrugged his shoulders. "Look," he said, "I'm no scholar. A Jew is a stranger everywhere: a prickly character, a thorn. Who wants a thorn?"

"Just the same," said Joseph, "Jews have become Englishmen, Frenchmen, Germans. . . ."

"And remained always Jews," said Zelinsky. "A Jew is an actor, a good actor or a bad actor. He is well paid, but he is not invited to sit down at the family supper table."

"All right," said Joseph, "but is that a reason to hate him?"

Zelinsky gazed somberly off to the horizon, which rose and fell, appeared and disappeared, as the ship rolled.

"No one is born to hate," he said slowly, "he is taught; he takes it in with his mother's milk. Also, it makes for marching and speeches. When two people hate something, it makes a bond between them.

"Always, people hate the small things, the defenseless things. Who knows why? Hit the mouse with the broom, crush the May fly . . . but walk carefully around the lion and the hippopotamus. When Israel has an army, nobody will hate the Jews any more."

"Nobody?"

Zelinsky lifted his hands, palms up, in an expressive gesture. "Even the Mufti will not hate six divisions, fifteen brigades, with tanks and paratroops. Not for long."

"Six divisions?" said Joseph, looking around the crowded deck. "Out of this material?"

"For how many hundreds of years did our grandfathers dream of Zion?" demanded Zelinsky. "Let us enjoy this small dream of fifteen brigades."

The children also had their arguments; already Hermann Mandelbaum had been punched in the nose by a little Latvian. Mia found him crying behind a bench, and stood looking at him with sober curiosity. She couldn't imagine why anyone should cry, on such a splendid ship, and on the way to Israel—unless, perhaps, he was hungry; and breaking off a piece of a biscuit which had been given to her by Rosa, the lady with the doll, she held it out to him.

Hermann looked at the biscuit greedily, but with suspicion. "Go away," he said in German; but at the same time he felt that he must immediately reach out and seize the biscuit before it was withdrawn. In any case, he would prefer to eat it alone; he had learned that nothing is really yours until you have swallowed it.

Suddenly his grimy little paw shot out, seized the morsel, and stuffed it into his mouth. Then he turned his back on her.

Not in the least put out by this behavior, Mia rocked up and down for a while on her heels, while she nibbled like a little rabbit on the remaining half of the biscuit. "I saw you with your papa," she said presently in Hungarian. "You were going to peepee."

He didn't understand a word of it, but it didn't matter. A child is never really eager to listen, only to talk; the lonelier the child, the greater the need to find somebody to talk to. "In Berlin," he said in German, not looking at her, "we had a big house, and my father smoked cigars." He himself had never seen the house, but he believed in it. A word here, a word there, conjured up a picture of the past for him. There had been a world somewhere, a fine rich world, to which his father and mother had belonged.

Mia didn't understand him, either. It made no difference to her: she was having a conversation. Another human being, small like herself, and not at all alarming, was sharing the sun and the bright sky and part of her biscuit with her—someone who wept, it was true, but whose tears were understandable and not frightening the way her mother's were on those rare occasions when she cried and the whole world went suddenly to pieces.

She fished a small piece of chalk out of the pocket of her dress and, bending over, drew some wavery chalk lines on the deck. They formed a few small squares—small and few because there was so little room between the other people. Solemnly, with intense concentration, she began to hop about inside them; and presently Hermann joined her, and hopped too. His cheeks grew pink, his nose ran, he was happy; he couldn't have explained why.

All over the ship children were playing together, shyly or boldly, joyfully or spitefully, gathering other children into their group, and leaving still others to sit by themselves with dull eyes and hearts full of loneliness, to which they were accustomed. Mainly, the thing was not to show it, not to admit it.

The little boy and girl with the umbrella were together as before; this time the little girl appeared to be a strange creature on a distant planet, mysterious and powerful, but she was unaware of it. As far as she was concerned, she was still the important person who swept the floor. No one had ever told her the story of Cinderella, so she had no great expectations. Merely to have a floor of her own to sweep was happiness enough.

"Come, Dorschka," said Mottl, "it's time for the evening soup."

The little girl got up silently and left the umbrella and her friend. He had parents, and she didn't; it was as simple as that, though she didn't understand it very well. It seemed to her that she remembered something from long ago, but she wasn't sure. She was five years old; her father had died in the last year of the war, in a sealed cattle car somewhere in Poland; her mother coughed her life out two years later in a displaced-persons camp in Austria. She had never seen her father, and scarcely remembered her mother, except as somebody who used to bend over her bed and kiss her good night. Sometimes, in the dark, she wished that someone would do that again—bend over her and kiss her good night.

To hop from square to square on a slanting, rolling deck is not the easiest thing in the world, and it was not surprising that Mia landed, sooner or later, on Mrs. Opisch's foot. Mrs. Opisch, after the first agonized gasp, said nothing; she merely looked indignant, and very much pained. "I'm sorry," said Mia in her own language; to which Mrs. Opisch replied: "Little fool!" in hers. And turning to Joseph, who happened to be standing near by, she expressed the wish that she might live long enough to see the Promised Land, and to have somewhere to put her feet. "One thing for America," she declared—"there is room for the feet."

Hermann, recognizing in Joseph a familiar face, had gone to hide behind Joseph's back. But Mia stood her ground, and looked anxiously around for her mother. "What is wrong?" Anna asked, picking her way across the crowded deck; all she could see was that her child and a red-faced old woman were glaring at each other like a turkey and a dove. "I said I was sorry," Mia explained, "but I think she doesn't understand me."

"My daughter is sorry," said Anna to Mrs. Opisch, "for whatever she did. She speaks only Hungarian." She spoke quickly, in three languages, two of which Mrs. Opisch understood.

"It wasn't her fault," said Joseph. "I was watching; it was the roll of the ship that did it. It was nothing."

"Nothing?" retorted Mrs. Opisch. "You should get such a knife-thrust in the ankle! She is jumping like in a public park; she is leaping in the air like a balloon.

"Anyway—who asked you should make with the advice? A *chutspa!*"

Joseph began to laugh; he couldn't help it. Suddenly he was back in the little butcher shop in Cleveland, listening to his father and a customer—old Mrs. Cohen, from down the block. "What is this? Meat? From a cow, maybe?"

"I swear to you, this is best-grade Kansas City."

"Kansas-schmansas. An impudence!"

"Why are you laughing?" asked Anna, tight-lipped. "Because this lady called my daughter a balloon? I assure you," she said, turning energetically to Mrs. Opisch, "my daughter is no balloon."

Mrs. Opisch made a vague gesture of appeasement. "So all right," she said, "who is talking? A child jumps; in the air an angel directs her so she comes down on somebody's ankle. Excuse me for being there with the foot."

Joseph walked toward the bow of the ship with Anna; he could see that she was upset, and he wanted to comfort her. "It takes all kinds," he said.

"Pardon?" she asked helplessly. "What takes?"

"I mean," said Joseph, "that people . . ."

But it scarcely seemed worth explaining. After all, if someone landed on your foot with all his weight . . . her weight, that is . . .

Life wasn't all rosy, even for Mrs. Opisch.

"I had an aunt like that," he said, "my grandfather's sister. A great-aunt, really. She'd bite your head off; everybody was afraid of her. But when there was trouble in the family, or sickness, she was always there with the chicken broth."

He sighed. "I would gladly be sick now," he said, "to get some of my Aunt Clara's chicken broth with matzoth balls."

Anna made a little gesture of distress. "Oh, please," she whispered, "do not talk about things to eat."

She couldn't have said anything more effective—more simply and suddenly revealing. It brought Joseph up short: only a few days ago—how long? a week? two weeks?—he'd been dining in the restaurants of Rome. But she—how long had she been hungry? and homeless?

And face to face at last with the thing he had been trying for so long not to face, he put his hand on her arm. "Mrs. Muhlmann," he said earnestly, "believe me, if I could do anything . . ."

She shrank back, staring at him out of wide, frightened eyes. "You know my name?" she said in a shocked voice. "How can that be?"

"I asked someone," he said simply, surprised.

He could almost feel how she retreated, drawing back from him, shutting him out, shutting out everything around her. It was like a snail, he thought, going back into its shell; but there was something wrong with the image—it was softer than that, it was more like a moth. . . . Did a moth go into a cocoon? He was afraid it was the other way round.

"Is it so bad to ask a person's name?" he asked, but she only stared at him as though somehow by staring she could solve something, some question that puzzled her. "Is it?" he asked.

"It is a name I do not use any more," she said at last. "From a life I have forgotten."

And as she turned to go, she said with a note of infinite loneliness: "I am only Anna."

He watched her cross the deck and enter the main cabin, and noticed how lightly she walked, with dignity and with a gentle grace, but also in a sort of solitude.

When he couldn't see her any longer, he went up forward and leaned against the rail, looking down at the smooth blue-green water, listening to the hiss, the fall and follow of the foam as the ship's bows lifted and stayed suspended for a moment, shuddering a little, and then coasted down the waves. He felt the fresh, keen air on his face, and heard, in the rush of wind and water, the sound of violins and trumpets . . . the silver singing of the strings, cascades of woodwinds . . . snatches and measures, the shout of brass from the Don Juan, the mysterious snowy opening of the Beethoven Ninth . . . the oboe singing alone in the Brahms. . . .

The Brahms again.

And then suddenly, it was gone, and he heard instead the long slow ending of Mahler's great "Song of the Earth": "*Ewig, Ewig . . .*"

There was this sound of music within him and around him, washing over him, filling his mind and heart with peace and with delight; symphonies, concertos, all tumbling over one another like driven leaves, like tumbling fountains. . . .

Fountains. He could see them again in the pure Roman light—the Trevi, the Triton, the Tortoise. He walked around them, he watched them happily, without sadness; he waved good-by to them.

"*Ciao,*" he said.

But Anna, sitting soberly upright in her bunk in the hold, felt a vague regret, and a real disappointment—regret for something missed, something which seemed to have gone past without her quite knowing—and a disappointment in herself. Why had she drawn back? Was she afraid—but of what?—of this man who looked at her with warm brown eyes, with sympathy? What was it he had said? "Believe me, if I could do anything . . ."

As a matter of fact, there was no reason to be afraid of anybody any more. Or was there?

It did no good to talk about it: she always drew back. It had been going on for a long while now. Perhaps it always would, for the rest of her life.

What was the matter with her? She had been so good-natured once upon a time, so gay and friendly, so happy.

He had called her by name: Mrs. Muhlmann, and it had struck fear into her, as it always did; there was such a horror in that name, a feeling of panic which she couldn't control. It made her want to run . . . to run. . . . Once upon a time there had been joy and beauty in it. But after that came the terror. Not Muhlmann: not that poor slaughtered man, dragged from her side, hit over the head like an ox.

Her name was, simply, Anna.

Next time she would try to smile, to say something agreeable. Anything would do: a nice day, perhaps, or even, simply, thank you. She would try very hard; perhaps he wouldn't touch her, put his hand on her arm like that. Or, if he did, perhaps—perhaps she wouldn't mind so much.

She wiped a tear off her cheek. In heaven's name, what was she crying about? Maybe from hunger. From thinking about chicken broth with matzoth balls. . . .

CHAPTER

12

TO FEED seven hundred people for eight days is no simple matter, even for an ocean liner, and on a freighter like the *Teti*, it would have been all but impossible even under the most favorable conditions. By the fourth day, with Sicily behind them, the food had practically given out, and even the water in the tanks was at an uncomfortable level. To the excited protests of the passengers, the Greek captain replied curtly that he had his profits to consider; the provisions he had put in at Marseilles and Genoa had been sufficient, but had obviously been swallowed down in too much of a hurry. "Probably," Martin Gutzman suggested, "we should not have gorged ourselves the first two days." "On what?" asked Mr. Mandelbaum contemptuously. "On soup and oranges?" "For years already," said Martin, "my stomach has been growing smaller. What would seem like a snack to most people, is a whole dinner to me."

Outraged, the older people went in a buzzing mass to Raphael Zelinsky, but the younger people, the boys and the girls, treated the crisis with a certain grim humor. They were not surprised to find themselves once again the victims of indifference and falsehood—scarcely having had any other experience in their short lives.

"How long were our people in the Wilderness?" asked the young Talmudic scholar. "Forty years; yet they sustained themselves."

"They had at least locusts," said his friend, the Communist from Yugoslavia.

"Locusts we cannot get," said the Polish boy who played the accordion, "and roaches are too bitter."

It was pointed out that beetles were permissible, according to the Third Book of Moses; but it was agreed that roaches—even if they might be considered beetles—were disagreeable. "In the desert," said the scholar, "the Holy One, Blessed be He, sent down a rain of manna to the starving tribes. This was in the Wilderness of Sin, beyond the Red Sea."

"We should have somebody like Moses to part the waters for us," said the girl with the freckles and the harmonica; to which the student replied: " 'From Moses unto Moses there arose none like Moses.' Which was said of the great Maimonides by his contemporaries."

"One can learn to eat almost anything," said young Avram Kolinsky, "if only to throw it up again."

The Haganah leader addressed a meeting of the older refugees in the main cabin. "This is very bad," he told them; "I do not say it isn't very bad. But think—you who have lived through so much worse: if you could endure Belsen, Auschwitz, Maidenek, Buchenwald; if you could live all these last years behind barbed wire in Hamburg, on Cyprus, God knows where—surely for four more days you can live hungry to get to Israel!"

Angry cries greeted this exhortation, mingled with groans of acquiescence. "It is monstrous," exclaimed Mrs. Mandelbaum; "*Grauslich!* The Agency paid for my passage, did it not? So let me have what they paid for! Anything else is unheard of."

"The Agency," said Zelinsky patiently, "is powerless; it must take what it can get. We are not here on an excursion; we are running a blockade. For this we must pay large sums, and say thank you."

"Running is what we are doing?" Mrs. Opisch inquired. "First-class, no doubt; with all the delights."

"So where were you in the old days?" a Slovak woman asked. "In what first-class establishment?"

"My father was a landowner," said Mrs. Opisch bravely. "Everything was done in the best manner."

A sigh swept through the cabin. "So excuse the question," said the Slovak woman bitterly. "A *ganzer Macher* is on board; a queen!"

Mrs. Opisch left the cabin and went out on deck. Her eyes felt moist; no doubt it was the sea air made them so. But the sea air was no reason for the heaviness of heart. To feel oneself alone and not admired was one thing—but to be alone and disliked in the middle of the ocean? And with only one bowl of watery soup, besides, and a few dried peas, and a hard biscuit.

God was the Holy One of Israel; He was the Eye that looked at her from behind the red lamp in Temple; He was the mysterious Presence absent in the Ark; and He was like her own father, beard and all—a stern, implacable, just Being who loved her like a daughter, but not personally. In this she may have been unfair to her

temporal father, who was not a landowner but a small
factor, who had never learned to express himself except
in business matters, philosophy, and generalities. But who
knows? Perhaps the Jews are still waiting for their heavenly
Father to express a more tender emotion.

"Ah," said Father Duvernay, "but He did; and you re-
jected Him."

This was in answer to Dr. Dreyfoos, who had brought
up the subject.

They were seated in the cabin which Father Duvernay
shared with the first officer, dividing a small piece of
sausage between them. "I suppose I should feel guilty,"
said Dr. Dreyfoos, "to be eating when others are hungry,
but I don't. What I feel guilty about is not having made
the world a better place."

"That is what comes of being a Jew instead of a
Catholic," said Father Duvernay calmly. "A Catholic
would put himself in God's hands and leave the miracles
to the saints, but a Jew must always take it on himself."

Dr. Dreyfoos looked at him with a smile. He wanted
to say: A Jew once did; but refrained, and chewed on his
bit of sausage instead. He had to admit that in general
the Father was right; but like most generalities, there were
holes in it.

"We're a curious people," he said reflectively, "stiff-
necked, as the Book says, and hard to get along with. As a
matter of fact, we never got along with ourselves, in the
days of our own history. Nothing but quarrels within the
family, and bitter civil wars. We were first dispersed some
twenty-five hundred years ago, and then thoroughly scattered some six hundred years later. Now we are coming
back together again from the farthest corners of the earth,

and I have no doubt we'll quarrel with each other just as badly as before."

"How can you be a cynic," asked Father Duvernay, "for I am convinced that is what you are—and yet at the same time give up a respected and useful career in order to work as a laborer in the earth?"

"That is also peculiarly Jewish," said Dr. Dreyfoos, "to make the desert bloom. 'A land that floweth with milk and honey'; you won't find that expression in any other histories. It is purely Hebrew."

"Strange," mused the priest, "I had always thought of the Jews as a sedentary people."

"We had no other choice," said Dr. Dreyfoos, "but we are not sedentary by nature."

He smiled grimly. "We are to have Partition," he said, "but if I am not mistaken, we will have to fight for it. Six hundred thousand against thirty million.

"Then you will see how sedentary we are."

"Well," said the priest, "that is as may be. In the meanwhile, if you are running out of tobacco for your pipe, I know where there is some more; it is French, but it is perhaps better than nothing."

Dr. Dreyfoos smiled. "Will the first officer not miss it?" he inquired gently.

The sun was hot now during the day, and people sprawled on the deck sought whatever shade they could find. As the sun went down, a certain obstinate liveliness made itself felt; from the tent which the young Poles had constructed out of a blanket and two lifeboats, the accordion was heard again, joined this time by the metallic tones of the harmonica. Young people began to sing, which was better than feeling hungry in silence. The songs of exile, plaintive, wry, and indomitable, floated through the

155

ship, which smelled of soup, grease, coal-smoke and un-
washed human bodies.

"Me'eretz hatamar ad yark'tey k' forim
Anachnu po-b' mahovot v'isurim . . ."

"Never say that you have reached your journey's end . . .
Upon us yet will dawn the longed-for day . . ."

And the *B'Arvot Hanegev:* "A boy has fallen in the
desolate Negev. . . ."

In a corner of the deck, Joseph, Anna, and Mia sat
huddled over a small pot of stew which Joseph had managed to coax from the cook in exchange for his last
thousand-lire note. Anna had, besides, a hard-boiled egg
given her by Rosa Hatvany, which was one of two given
to the Hatvanys, after some hesitation, by the old man
with the sideburns. Joseph was embarrassed to be offered
a bite of the egg; he knew that he ought to refuse it, to
return his share to Mia, but he was too hungry. After all,
he thought, I am sharing my stew; and he accepted his
bite of the egg.

He was also a little embarrassed about the stew,
which he knew to be sheep's testicles broiled and gar-
nished with onions in the Greek manner. He thought it
best not to mention it to the ladies, who believed that
they were eating some sort of sweetbreads.

"You are kind to do this," said Anna.

"Mrs. Hatvany is good," said Mia. "Won't Hermann
be jealous," she added comfortably.

She wasn't able to talk to Joseph, except by looks and
smiles, but she had accepted him into her world, along
with the Hatvanys, and children like Hermann, who were
even more worried than she was.

Anna, too, communicated less by words than by a glance or by the play of feelings which came and went on her expressive face. She spoke several languages in addition to her own, but she said little; sometimes there seemed to be a wide distance between her thoughts and her remarks, unless it was a matter involving Mia, when she would deal with things simply and directly and without any hesitations. It was as if she lived an active life only in her daughter, waking from a kind of drowsiness, or sleep, and going back into it again when Mia was away.

It baffled Joseph. She was like a stream which has been dammed up; only a trickle makes its way over the dam, while behind and above it the great mass of water lies motionless, dark, and forbidding. If the dam ever broke, what a fearful force would loose itself on the valley below!

"Tell me," said Joseph, "when we get to Tel Aviv, what will you do?"

"I go to a reception center," she said indifferently, "and then to a kibbutz."

"Where?"

She was vague; she didn't seem to know, but Joseph had a feeling that she preferred not to say. It was part of the secrecy that always seemed to surround her. "If there's trouble with the Arabs," he said, "the farms will be in the front line of attack."

"One is used to that also," she replied calmly. And then, as though to change the subject, she inquired:

"And you? Were you always a—how do you say?— cameraman?"

"Not always," said Joseph. "I was a musician."

Her eyes widened at that, and she looked at him for

the first time as though she really saw him. How lovely her eyes were, in the shadow of her dark lashes . . . like the blue of meadow flowers shading into violet.

"A musician!" she breathed. "But I had no idea . . ."

"You didn't?" He gave a forced laugh. "Why not?

She seemed to be poised, in balance, waiting, not quite ready to draw back, but uncertain. "I too," she said at last.

"You too?" exclaimed Joseph, in surprise. "But I thought . . ."

Anna lowered her eyes; a little frown appeared between her eyebrows. "I studied at the Conservatory," she said, almost unwillingly. "Piano. I was not professional." Stretching her fingers out in front of her, she let them play on imaginary keys, studying them as though they belonged to somebody else. "It was nothing," she said, and shrugged her shoulders wearily. "A long time ago."

Mia, who had been watching her, turned to her curiously. "Are you playing music, Mama?" she asked in Hungarian.

"Once I did," said Anna gently. "But I prefer to forget it."

"I know what you mean," said Joseph, answering her gesture. "It's better not to think about it."

Again she gave him that swift glance of recognition. "Yes," she said, "it is better to forget."

"You can't ever be the same," said Joseph. "You can't ever be the thing you were. It's gone. There's no use being sorry about it."

"One cannot avoid to be sorry," said Anna quietly. "But you are right, it does not help.

"And you? Are you sorry for what you no longer are?"

"It was never my idea," he said. "It was my family's."

"They expected of you, what?"

"Everything," said Joseph somberly. "The works. I was to have been another Heifetz."

"Ah, yes; a violinist."

"One has to decide," said Joseph. "One has to make up one's mind, to commit oneself from the beginning. I couldn't face it."

"You played no more?" she asked in surprise. "Never again? That is extraordinary, I think."

"I played with orchestras," said Joseph. "But not solo."

She turned it over in her mind, obviously trying to understand. "Probably you were sensible," she said. "I have no way to know.

"So now you forget the whole thing? This is possible?"

"Yes," he said. "More or less."

"Ah! More or less. And with the camera you do solo?"

Joseph smiled; it seemed a curious way of putting it, but he was forced to agree: with the camera he performed solo. "It's better not to drag the past around with you," he said.

It was well meant, but it had an unhappy effect. Her face clouded over, and she made a little gesture of withdrawal, involuntary and almost childish, hunching one shoulder up, and tucking her chin down against her chest. The past! she thought; the lost, golden, gleaming fields of her home . . .

"When I was a little girl," she said, "we had a garden with grass and walks under the trees. In the morning there would be on the grass and walks the silver paths of snails.

"The past is like that," she said: "slime."

Joseph was silent, pitying her, trying to imagine, trying to see in his mind the young woman in the big house with the garden and the trees. Young, and happy, and beautiful; she must have been happy; she was still beautiful. But all he could think of was his own childhood, and the gloomy little room back of the butcher shop where he used to do his practicing day after day. "No," he said at last, "the past isn't slime." He wanted to say that it was like a shell, out of which one must burst one's way; but he wondered if that was really true. Only for some, perhaps.

She didn't answer him; she was embarrassed by what she had said, and ashamed. Why does he talk to me like this? she thought angrily. Why doesn't he leave me alone? But then she realized that she had been the one who had been asking the questions, not he. This is unfair, she told herself, but whether it was unfair to him or to her, she didn't say.

The elders were taking their evening promenade, with shawls and coats or sweaters as the air turned chilly. They were still arguing bitterly with each other over the food situation, some wanting to confront the captain face to face, others counseling patience. The Mandelbaums came by, stepping in a dignified way around the forms sitting or lying on the wooden boards, and seeing them so near, Joseph waved to them. He thought that Mrs. Mandelbaum looked even thinner and more worn than before. This is their bad time, he said to himself, though not their worst; that is behind them. After so many years of being of no more importance than an ant or a beetle, here on this ship they are still nothing. For them, that is very hard to bear. But they will be all right when they get to Israel: they will make demands and they will get respect from other people who are just like them. One could say that such a future is a sufficient defense against the past. But Anna . . . how will she get along with no defense, with only her sadness?

As the Mandelbaums went by, Mia arose suddenly, and running up to Hermann, took hold of him and breathed noisily into his face. Hermann started back in alarm. "Mama!" he cried. "Papa! She has been eating onions!"

Mr. Mandelbaum leaned down and sniffed. "It is true," he declared in a legal way; "someone has onions."

"But that is infamous!" exclaimed his wife. "While we are starving!"

Mr. Mandelbaum looked severely at Mia, and at her mother. "What else would you expect from Hungarians?" he asked. So saying, he drew himself up and brought his heels together. "Come, Mama," he said; and offering Mrs. Mandelbaum his arm, led his little family away in silence.

"And to you, too," said Anna in Hungarian, "a long and disagreeable life."

No one there understood her except Mia, who looked at her mother with her mouth open and burst into laughter. Anna gazed at her helplessly—and then, all at once, she too was laughing. Joseph had never heard a laugh like hers, so merry and so helpless, and asking to be forgiven at the same time.

"Excuse me," she said, "but I have been quite awful!"

"I couldn't be happier," he assured her. "Go right ahead."

She gathered herself together, and sat quietly, but after a while she rose to go. "Why do you leave?" asked Joseph. "It isn't dark yet."

"I think we have been here long enough," she said. "Thank you, Mr. Goldblum."

"Please," he said, "my name isn't Goldblum. That is only for the authorities. My name is Joseph Victor."

She looked at him gravely. "If that is what you wish," she said. "Good night then, Josef Victor."

"Say good night, Mia. And say thank you to Victor Úr."

"*Köszönöm*, Victor Úr," said Mia, and dropped the little curtsy.

Left to himself, Joseph stretched out in his own place on the deck, and lay with his hands clasped behind his head, staring up at the sky. He felt content, and even in a way happy, and at peace. Twilight was coming on, the ship's lights were newly lit and shone pale and starlike in the dusk. The stars themselves were coming out one by one as the colors ebbed away in the west and the night darkened above him.

He lay there thinking back over the past, trying to remember as much of it as he could. Strangely enough, the clearest memories were those he had once wanted to forget—his childhood, his mother and father, the aunt who had bought him the violin. When he got to the part about Rome, it was hard to see it as it was, or even to remember it very clearly; it was confused: so many things, ruins and fountains and comings and goings.

He tried to think about Priscilla, to recall how it had all happened, but already it seemed unreal.

Only this was real: the sea and the ship, the lonely night, and Anna—"only Anna." It flowered out of his childhood, out of his own life, out of a still more distant past. He thought of a poem he had read once, in a book:

> Men nobler than myself
> Have set me like a tree;
> My roots are in their dust.

In the middle of the ocean, in the darkness, under the golden, slowly drifting stars, he felt at home.

Little by little the voices faded out, and the ship grew quiet. There is nothing quieter than night on the sea, and a ship where everyone is asleep: everything is hushed, all is silent, one hears only wind and water. In the hold, Mia was sleeping, hugging to herself her triumph over Hermann Mandelbaum. Rosa Hatvany lay on her husband's breast, the rag doll in her arms; and only Anna lay awake, thinking and wondering. He asks me so many questions, she told herself; where can I hide?

But I do not want to hide, she cried out in silence, and it is I, not he, who asks.

Above, on the dew-drenched deck, Joseph also lay awake. But although his eyes were open, his thoughts were far away. He was thinking of his family in Cleveland; he could hear his mother's voice saying: "Yonnie, where are you going?"

He wasn't sure that he knew.

CHAPTER

13

JOSEPH was awakened by people running past him on the deck; and almost at once he received a request from Zelinsky to join him as soon as possible on the bridge. When he got there, he found the captain, the first officer, and the Haganah leader all peering through binoculars at a spot on the horizon over which he could discern a smudge of dark smoke. "A British destroyer," said Zelinsky, and handed him the glasses.

He could see her clearly against the horizon in the early light, a low, dark hull, long and knifelife, and dangerous. Perhaps she was one of the two which had rammed the *Exodus* the year before, and had fired tear gas and firecrackers at the passengers, and had killed the sixteen-year-old Hirsch Yakubovitch and Bill Bernstein of San Francisco.

"Trouble?" he asked. "Do you think they're after us?"

"We don't know," said Zelinsky. "They may be, or not. She hasn't sent us any orders yet."

"Perhaps she doesn't know we're here," said Joseph.

"Are you crazy?" asked Zelinsky.

The captain of the *Teti* looked worried. "Hide the people," he ordered. He spoke in French, but with an accent. "Put them off the deck, anywhere, in the hold, somewhere."

He didn't care what happened to them; they could all be sent to Cyprus as far as he was concerned—once he was paid, that is—but he didn't want any trouble with the British Navy. It was illegal to transfer refugees to Palestine.

"But surely," said Joseph to Zelinsky, as the two of them made their way down the ladder to the deck, "they know that we come from Marseilles. They must know all about us."

"Perhaps not all," said Zelinsky. "They know that we sailed, but where are we bound? The manifest was for Alexandria. A few passengers are allowed. And there is also another reason—"

They had reached the deck by this time, and calling one of the *shomrim* to him, he sent the boy off with orders to get everyone under cover at once. "Except the priest," he added, with the brief flicker of a smile; "if he wants to walk around the deck, all the better."

"So where were we?" he said to Joseph when the young messenger had sped away.

"You said there was another reason."

"Yes—perhaps. It is this: the Mandate is almost at an end."

"Why should that affect us here?"

"Who knows what is going on in the rest of the world? Perhaps they do not wish to displease the Americans."

Joseph made a wry face. Don't count too much on the Americans, he thought. But all he said was:

165

"Then why worry?"

"There is always somebody who hates the Jews," said Zelinsky. "So who knows who is the captain of that destroyer? His name might be Nebuchadnezzar."

It was hot in the hold with the sun beating down on them and only a trickle of air coming in through the openings in the tarpaulin covering the hatch. The refugees huddled together, staring fearfully upward at the dim light which was all they could see of the outside world. They sat on the edge of the bunks, they stood packed together like sticks of wood, and exchanged worried questions and comments. They were frightened, but there was still the bitter, Jewish well of humor which had never run dry in all the two thousand years of the Diaspora. One report had the entire British Mediterranean fleet outside, with its guns trained on the *Teti*. "They will blow us up," cried a Galician; "they will sink us to the bottom of the ocean." "Never mind," replied another. "Afterwards they will wave a White Paper over us."

The pious prayed; they recited the Shema, and the Psalm of Moses: "The Lord is my strength and my song, and is become my salvation." They waited with beating hearts for whatever was going to happen.

"This is all foolishness!" exclaimed Mr. Mandelbaum angrily. "We are outside territorial waters. Under international law, who has the right to interfere with a ship on the high seas? No matter what it is carrying. Why am I shut up in here? When we are approaching Palestine, then is the time to take care—not here!"

But few heard him, and of those, even fewer paid any attention. In a corner, a young Hassid was invoking the power of the Lord. "May they not see us," he intoned. "May we be covered by the glory of the Most High, as by a cloud." "Let Him show them His behind," said a young Communist bitterly, "like He did Moses."

"How can they do this?" Mrs. Opisch demanded indignantly. "My nephew is an American citizen, U.S.A."

"If he is such a *Macher*," said the Slovak woman, "let him send us Eisenhower."

Anna sat on the side of her bunk with her arm around Mia. She was not particularly frightened; the terror which she felt all around her only served to draw her back from the outside world into the quiet of her own. "Will they do something to us, Mama?" asked Mia fearfully.

"Everything that they could do," said Anna, "they have done. So everything is over."

"Then we can go upstairs and play?"

"Soon. Somebody will tell us when."

"Why are we hiding, Mama?"

"It is a game we play. We make believe they do not know we are here."

Anna found herself looking for Joseph. She hadn't realized how much she wanted to see him, and was a little surprised at herself; his warm, sorrowing, eager face . . . it was a comfort to her, it was a place to go, the only place she'd found. It wasn't because she was afraid, because she wasn't afraid; rather it was a desire—strange to her—to be with someone else. But why Joseph, then? She didn't know; all she knew was that in the hold, all but suffocated in that wedged-in mass of humanity, she was suddenly lonely because he wasn't there.

Fortunately, the ordeal of the destroyer didn't last very long; it was less than an hour after the alarm had been given when the all-clear sounded over the loudspeaker, and the refugees, old and young, poured up onto the deck, to breathe the fresh air and feel the sun on their bodies.

And they needed the sun, and the buckets of salt water which Mottl brought up from over the rail and carried to the lavatories or set down on the deck for them to wet their hands and their faces and their feet.

The problem of keeping clean, never an easy one, was made even more difficult by the lack of fresh water. Such soap as they had was all but useless in brine; and soap was not one of the things the captain had agreed to provide. Not that people used to life in the prison camps expected things to be made comfortable for them; but to have no fresh water to wash in—for the women not to be able to wash their hair—had a curiously depressing effect on the spirit. In the camps they had at least been allowed sometimes to wash their hair.

"How can I shave a face with salt water?" asked Milton the barber bleakly. "I cannot get a lather." "So who cares?" declared the young Pole with the accordion. "We will arrive like so many Samsons, and tear down the gates of Gaza."

"Do you object that I have a small beard?" he asked the freckled girl, who for answer blew a joyful note on the harmonica.

The feeling among the younger people was generally joyful, now that the British Navy had disappeared from sight. Toward evening a space was cleared in the main cabin, the tables were pushed out of the way, and to the music of the accordion and the harmonica, and to the rhythmic clapping of hands, the girls and boys danced the *hora*, linked together in a circle, advancing, retreating, bowing, and whirling in the dusty light.

Father Duvernay watched them with pleasure, reminded of his own Breton reels and jigs; and even Anna's face took on a faint animation, reflected from the smiling and solemn faces which, shining with perspiration, turned and circled in front of her.

She was still watching the dancing when Joseph caught sight of her through the porthole and, making his way inside the crowded cabin, came up behind her. "Shall we join the dance?" he asked, smiling.

"Ach!" she cried, surprised, her reserve lost for a moment. "There you are!"

She seemed so happy to see him. "I wondered where you were," she said.

A warm feeling spread slowly through him, starting from somewhere under his ribs. It was such a simple, small statement, but it went on sounding and resounding in his heart. *"I wondered where you were."*

That is the way a person sometimes says, quite simply: "I missed you," or even—"I love you."

The sun went down; dancing was over, the tables were put back again. Joseph and Anna together watched the sunset fade away in the west into the night. The silver sickle of the new May moon hung in the sky above their heads, over the evening star which swung below it like a locket on a chain. "What are you thinking?" she asked.

He was staring out across the water into the darkness. Beneath them and behind them, the wake of the *Teti* made a pale, foaming shimmer in the night, broken with little lozenges of star-shine and moon-shine. "I'm thinking of the rest of the world," he said, "out there, far away, across the sea. And how they don't know about this."

"I am glad, I think," she said. She felt the night enfold her; she drew it around her like a cloak. "I wish that no one knew about it," she said, "but ourselves."

She realized almost at once that he hadn't understood

her. "I mean not always," she said, "but now, for this one time, when it is night; I do not wish people to know about me."

"What is it about night, Anna?" he asked gently.

"Only that you can hide in it . . . as I have so often had to hide. It is safe. For small animals."

She spoke so simply that Joseph felt a wrench of pity for her, although she appeared to feel none for herself. For hunted people, he thought; the night is safe for hunted people. . . .

"The day is safe, too," he said. "Back there, across the sea. It's day there, now."

"Far away," she said. "In your country. Perhaps; I do not know, I was never there. But where I have lived, it will never be safe again."

"That's far away now, too."

"I know. I thank God."

"Anna," he said, "can't you look ahead?"

"To what?" she whispered. "To what?"

He was silent; what could he say? He tried to imagine her in a kibbutz: the daily tasks, the hard back-breaking work, the ever-present danger. There was no use pretending that life was going to be easy for her. And he was not committed yet, himself—not to Zion. Not to a dream; not to a new way of life in the world.

Only to Anna. And that not wholly. Not yet.

But the night has its own dangers, even for the wary, for those who move carefully and listen anxiously. There is a slowness in the night, a tide, gentle but inexorable, urging the heart; the still, hushed circle of the sky draws it upward with longing. Shadows take over soundlessly in the quiet light of the stars; everything is mysterious and beautiful. The spirit leaves the body, and

soars; it is unconfined, it travels to the moon on wings of
longing. . . . Let the world always be so beautiful! It is
peaceful, it is the abode of love. Past and future dissolve in
the arrowy darkness, in the faint and glimmering shadows;
there is no future, no past, only the present, the heart
beating a little faster, the breath tight in the chest . . .
and the longing, like a hurt, to be a part of the peace and
the beauty, to be whole like the night, to feel love without end and boundless like the night. . . .

Under the canvas cover of a lifeboat, Avram Kolinsky,
the boy from the *Exodus* and a dozen countries, lay in the
arms of the freckled girl. She was a year older than he, but
it made no difference—they were both of the same age in
the world's pain. And for the first time this young girl, who
in the crowded hold kept herself to herself, untouched and
immaculate, comforted a lover with tears, and with kisses
and sighs. In the darkness, he was her son, her brother,
and her friend; she poured out her pity as though it were a
libation to the thirsty sands of the Negev.

The mild night air touched their faces, for a moment
peaceful and soft with dreams. What had they to dream
about? The past was sad, and the future uncertain. In
Israel they would fight, with Avram's brother, side by side
in the Palmach, the striking force of the Haganah. But
they dreamed of happiness and freedom, of a good world,
of kind people and a good life. It could only be a dream;
they had never lived in such a world.

Anna let Joseph take her hand; it was icy cold. "There
is a song," she told him, "from the opera; about a land
where the citrons bloom. That is where the singer wishes
to live. In the opera she returns, I think, to this land."

She stopped suddenly. "There is not anywhere to
return," she said.

171

She stood motionless, with lifted head, listening, watching the night. "It is all darkness," she said. "Gone; vanished. The golden fields, the morning sun. As though it never was—all the light, the singing, the joy. Only darkness is there. Like Babylon, lost also in the night behind us. Who remembers Babylon?"

He could see that she was shivering. "Here," he said, "let me put my coat around you."

She let him wrap her in his coat; the chill wind off the sea struck through his thin shirt, but he scarcely felt it. He felt only the physical presence of this woman whose shoulders were firm and cold under his hands; the living, strong body—proud, secretive, imbued with its own purpose, alien to him, and yet in some strange way familiar. "Anna," he said.

But she wasn't listening. She was rapt in some faraway sorrow. "Only the moon," she said, "remembers Babylon, the lights, and the singing."

"Anna," he said, "stop it."

She turned a blind face toward him. "They were happy, too," she said, "before the Assyrians came down. Or was it the Assyrians?" She shook her head wearily. "I don't know," she said. "It was so long ago, in history class. Perhaps the Medes and the Persians."

"It was long ago," he said, "and it doesn't matter."

"Oh, but it does," she whispered; "this is what matters, it all goes by, it passes into the night, into oblivion. And I cannot bear it."

Suddenly she was weeping, and his arms were around her. Slowly, hesitantly, she lifted her face, pale and cold in the darkness, and slowly, as if without volition, her lips met his: they too were cold and wet, salty with tears.

172

His arms tightened around her; his throat ached with the words he wanted to say; he could feel his heart beating.

He said nothing; and she thrust herself out of his arms and turned away, her hands to her face. "Dear God!" she whispered. "Why do you do this to me?

"Why?" she demanded, rounding on him. "Why? Why?"

"Because I love you," said Joseph.

The moment he said it, he knew that it was true; but whether he'd known it before, he wasn't sure. Anyway, it made no difference. "I love you," he said.

She backed away from him as though frightened. "Such a thing is impossible," she cried. "Do not say it! Do not bring me again unhappiness!"

"Unhappiness" he exclaimed, shocked. "How could I?"

It was his turn to cry out: Why? But there was no answer; only, over and over, the single word: No.

"Why is it impossible? Why? Why?"

"Josef—no! Believe me—I cannot. Already I have such anguish. Please—it is not to be like this.

"I cannot love," said Anna. She was sorry, too—sorrier, she thought, than she could ever tell; sorry for herself, sorry for both of them. She was shivering again. "It is not able for me," she said.

"Without joy, one cannot love, one can only endure together."

Why was it, he thought, that the simple act, the good and natural conclusion, always failed him? Was he to be forever the boy at the Conservatory, sitting dumb and yearningful in the woods, unable to say a word, to move, to seize what might so easily have been his? Hearing only music in his ears instead of whispers and avowals . . . ?

"Anna," he said unsteadily, knowing it was useless, "love is for sharing, whether joy or grief."

She made a move to go past him toward the hatchway, from which a pale shaft of light rose like a mist into the night and was diffused and lost in the darkness. From the hold came a babble of voices in many languages. There, among people who scarcely knew her, who left her alone, she knew that she would be safe—safe behind the walls she had herself erected, safe from the hopelessness of trying to live again in the world.

"I have had both joy and grief," she said. "Joy is for sharing; grief one suffers only alone. One puts oneself, rather, to sleep.

"It is a kindness to those who sleep, not to waken them. Let me go, please."

He stepped aside; she passed him with averted face.

Late that night, on the floor of the hold, Rosa Hatvany propped herself up on one elbow and gazed tenderly down at her husband. "We are so very fortunate," she said, "for we still have what was in our hearts to begin with; this we did not lose, like the poor woman above us who weeps herself to sleep."

"It is her own fault," said Alex Hatvany drowsily. "The American would be kind to her and to her child, if she would let him."

"Imbecile!" exclaimed Rosa in a low voice. "Idiot! When the heart is in mourning, is that the moment to dress for a wedding?"

All through the night, as he lay sleepless on his hard bed, Joseph heard the whispers of the lovers in the lifeboat above him.

CHAPTER

14

IT WAS the fourteenth of May, the evening of the Sabbath. In the main cabin, the candles were lighted, and the women of the Orthodox congregation blessed them with the traditional prayers. Then, after the supper, such as it was, the foredeck was cleared for the Sabbath services. There was no rabbi on board; the young Talmudist acting as Reader, or *Tzadik*, read from the Siddur, and the people responded according to what they remembered.

The *Teti* was headed due east, and the last flushed colors of the day touched with a loving and mysterious light the gray, blue, and gold of the prayer shawls as the Orthodox prayed and chanted, bowing again and again to the east: to Zion, the Promised Land. "And to Jerusalem Thy city shalt Thou return in mercy, as Thou hast promised." The women stood back, as was proper.

It was their last service at sea. They prayed, not knowing what was happening elsewhere—what had already

175

happened; still with their burden of grief and dread, lifting their appeals in all innocence toward the Lord of Hosts, the God of their fathers.

Two hours earlier the state of Israel had been proclaimed in Tel Aviv. A short, stocky man, dressed in a light-blue suit, and with a crown of white, bushy hair, had announced:

"We, the members of the National Council, representatives of the Jewish people of Palestine and the Zionist movement of the world, being met together in solemn ceremony today, the day of termination of the British Mandate over Palestine, by virtue of the natural, historic right of the Jewish people and of the Resolution of the General Assembly of the United Nations, hereby proclaim the establishment of a Jewish state in Palestine to be called Israel."

For two hours in the streets of Tel Aviv, people had danced and sung, and with cheers or weeping had waved Godspeed to the truckloads of young soldiers bound for the frontiers, for Jordan, the Negev, and Galilee. The sun went down, and it was the Sabbath; and the people of Israel had gone into their synagogues to pray.

At midnight, as the cruiser carrying the last British High Commissioner slipped into the Mediterranean beyond the three-mile limit, a solitary flare rose from the Royal Navy Headquarters on Mount Carmel, arched slowly through the sky, and fell flaming among the dark cypresses on the mountain slope. The British Mandate had ended.

On such ships as the *Teti*, riding the night-darkened sea, the news broke like a roaring wave, incredible, heart-shattering, terrible with joy.

A woman's voice, speaking over radio Kol-Israel, made

the announcement; they came running from all over the ship to hear it. They cheered, they cried, they danced, they prayed: with faces shining, lifted to the stars, they sang the Zionist anthem, the "Hatikvah," the ancient longing to be fulfilled, to return to the land of their fathers: "As long as a Jewish heart beats, and as long as Jewish eyes look eastward, our hope . . . is not dead." With tears running down their cheeks, they embraced one another; soon, now, they too would see Israel; those who still had friends in the world would see them again. "Our Toni!" wept Rosa Hatvany. "Our little Toni!"

Down in the hold, Mrs. Opisch had taken off her blue petticoat, and had cut out two strips and a six-pointed star, the Star of David, which she was sewing on an old tablecloth. It was to make a flag, the flag of the new nation. "Tomorrow," she told the Slovak woman, "I will take it to the captain, to hang on the mast. We will go into Israel under the flag of our people."

Weeping, the Slovak woman embraced her. "For my sins, forgive me," she begged. And turning to those near by, she exclaimed:

"What a noble soul. A heroine!"

Mrs. Opisch also wept, from a mixture of emotions. "I ask God's pardon for everything," she said humbly.

Near by, three young girls with kerchiefs on their heads prayed silently, their hands over their eyes, before the lighted Sabbath candles.

Milton Gutzman, the barber, ran everywhere around the ship, embracing everyone. Wherever he went, people would suddenly start dancing, if only for a moment. The truth was that nobody knew what to do; the emotion was too great, the release of long-pent-up fear, the surprise, the joy, the sense of a great triumph, needed room in which to express itself, needed great parades, brass bands, and rockets. Only Zelinsky, the leader, had a revolver, which he would have liked to shoot into the air, but refrained out of respect for the Sabbath, and fear of frightening the older people. Coming across Joseph, he gave him a bearlike hug instead. "Fifteen brigades!" he shouted. "Beginning the day after tomorrow!"

Father Duvernay in his cabin listened to the celebration, to the dancing and the singing, and poured himself a little wine. But before he lifted it to his lips, he crossed himself. "Father," he murmured, "Thy will be done. But be merciful with Thine oldest children, who, having closed their ears to Thy voice, may yet in Thine own time be reclaimed to Thy Grace. Do not let them be consumed, neither by the Moslem in his pride, nor by the soldiers of the Anglican heresy in their ignorance; for the sake of Jesus Christ Thy Son, born of Mary in Bethlehem, Who went to dwell in Nazareth, in Galilee."

And holding up his glass, he murmured to the starlit, joyous world outside:

"*Shalom.*"

Joseph found himself in a strange state of mind. He was greatly moved; the wave of joy carried him along with it like a chip on its crest. He felt a lump in his throat; he too wanted to sing and dance. Yet all the time, somewhere inside him, someone stood and watched and asked: Why?

It was himself, the outsider, the foreigner, the man with an American passport, who no longer had to be Menasha Goldblum. He had no friends in Israel; he had no home there. The Sabbath was only a childhood memory to him; the responses of the prayers came from long ago and far away.

And at the same time, he understood at this moment what these people had suffered, what they had been through—with what courage and strength, with what obstinacy and cunning, and in what anguish they had survived; and he felt an exultation for their sake and for his own, a feeling of triumph which he was able to share, of heaven and earth opening out for him also.

But it was something new to him, and after a while he didn't know what to do. He would have liked to join the celebration, but his enthusiasm began to flag. He stood undecided, not knowing what he wanted, looking for familiar faces, and finding them transfigured and unrecognizable. It was their celebration, not his; they had come thousands of miles, through fire and death for this. And what had he come for? To take pictures.

Well—that reminded him; he had better take some pictures, then.

He wondered where Anna was; he wanted to be able to say: Now you know where you're going. He wanted to enjoy this mass outburst of joy with her; he needed her, if he was really to be a part of it.

He wanted to say: This is my great happiness because it is yours. He wanted to hear her laugh again, so sweet and unexpected and merry; he wanted her to cry, but with her head on his shoulder. He wanted to share with Anna whatever she would let him share—whatever it was that this great happening might mean to her. Whatever it was, that is what it would mean to him. Only that, and nothing more. And nothing less.

That was what he really wanted.

And catching sight of Mia among a group of excited children, he made his way up to her, and asked her where her mother was.

Mia had no idea what he wanted. Happily, followed

by Hermann, and by the space-traveler and the little housekeeper-orphan, she danced around and around, chanting "Úr Victor," and singing a little song in Hungarian:

> *"Eszterlánci cérna*
> *Cérna volna selyem volna . . ."*

The children understood her no more than Joseph did, but for them the occasion was a joyful one for reasons equally unknown. In a child, terror lies at a deeper level than joy, which is near the surface; and the two are very often at work at the same time, some gleam or glint bringing amusement and jollity, while underneath the fear persists like a toad in a well. It would be a long time before those children would forget the fear, but in the meanwhile there were such times as this, when the grown-ups were happy, when there was general rejoicing, and children could shout and hop up and down and sing and be part of it.

And this, too, was part of the grown-ups' happiness, that the children were able to do this, and that they would have a home to grow up in where they could be proud and secure, where they could play and dance, where no one would have to wear the yellow star or walk in the gutter or have numbers tattooed on his arm, or be strung up on meat-hooks.

It didn't seem like too much to want for the children. And there it was, across two hundred miles of ocean, in the menacing, joyful, fearful, quiet Sabbath night.

Already Mrs. Mandelbaum walked with a new step and a new purpose; one could see that she had once been rich and accustomed to having her own way. "My husband," she said to her acquaintances left and right, "the *Geheimrat,* told me that such a thing as this could happen, but he did not expect it at such an early date. Imagine—while we were still at sea!"

But then her expression changed, and looking down at her shabby dress, in which for so long she had both slept and waked, her face fell. "To make an entrance," she murmured, "into the new land, in this . . . !"

All at once people were beginning to talk about what life would be like in the new state. "For one thing, we will be clean again," said Mr. Mandelbaum vigorously. "This is a matter of some importance to a person."

"Just the same," said a Russian woman doubtfully to her friend, "for the Sabbath, where will we look for a *shiksa?* Who is going to lay the fires, draw the water, bake the bread?" "In Israel," said the other joyously, "we will not need *shiksas;* on the Sabbath everything will be done for us by God's angels."

"Why not?" the first one agreed. "They owe us at least that much."

Dr. Dreyfoos went smiling among the passengers, the young and the old. Here itself, he thought, is a state, a small nation; people of every kind, which is what are needed: the fighters, the pious ones, the scholars, the trouble-makers, the lowly and the proud. And the children, who must grow up to be Solomon and David, Deborah, Einstein, Freud, Heine, Spinoza, Mendelssohn. . . .

He realized that he had included no bankers among those names. Never mind, he told himself, we have done enough banking to last us for the next two thousand years. It will not be by the bank, but by the kibbutz that this phase of our history will be remembered; by our *chalutzim,* and Zelinsky's fifteen brigades.

But being a fair-minded man, he had to admit that it was the bankers who made it all possible.

The people on the *Teti* didn't know that Abdullah's Arab Legion was already on the march into Palestine, that Kfar Etzion had fallen with all its defenders, men and women—save three; they knew only elation: Israel was free! And it was this general sense of joy and wonder, beating on Anna like a sea, which dazed and confused her as she wandered blindly through the throngs in search of her daughter.

Everywhere she saw smiles and tears, an opening of hearts to life again, to hope, to the future; people unfolding like flowers. And wherever she looked, she saw some form of love: the thanksgiving of parents, the shy merriment of husband and wife, the exaltation of lovers. She watched Avram Kolinsky and his girl locked in each other's arms; she watched them as they kissed, their young taut faces alight with wonder. She greeted the Hatvanys with an absent smile, her own eyes blurred by the sight of joy. Little by little, she could feel herself coming alive again, like a foot or an arm that has gone to sleep—the prickle and pain creeping through the numbness, the heart aching with returning memories. . . . She fought it; it was against her will. . . . And then, suddenly helpless, unable to struggle any longer, giving in . . . feeling the sweep of it, the longing to lose herself, too, in the happiness, to exult, to be a part of it . . . all the walls falling, tumbling, the great dam breaking, the terrible reservoir of longing, of need, of loneliness overflowing at last, crashing down, lifting her up, sweeping her away in a blind breathless panicky rush. . . .

She stumbled into Joseph's arms, not even knowing that they were around her—only knowing that she was holding him, nestling his head against hers, crushing herself against him. "Anna," he cried, "this wonderful news!"

But it was hers, her news, her freedom, not Israel's, that caught her and shook her.

It had all happened so suddenly, too suddenly for her to be any longer in control; there had been too many emotions in too short a space piled one upon another. They stood folded in each other's arms, eyes closed, scarcely moving, barely breathing, feeling the warmth of their bodies pass from one to the other, feeling a long-drawn-out ebbing away of tension, an almost tearful peace. "It has been so long," she whispered in her own language.

They drew apart, staring at each other, smiling a little uncertainly, doubtful, self-conscious. Then she was in his arms again, her face this time pressed tight against his chest. "I am so shaking inside," she said.

He felt wonderfully strong and protective, tall, calm, and at peace. He kissed the top of her head; her hair was soft and cold from the night air, and dark as the sea; he buried his face in it.

After a while she disengaged herself, and uttered a deep sigh. "I do not know if this is good," she said. "Perhaps I have only imagined something that was not true."

She glanced at him shyly, and then looked away again. "Is it that I remember truly what you said?" she asked.

He waited without answering; he was a little wary, a little fearful, not knowing what she meant, what he had said, what she had remembered. What had he told her? —about himself, perhaps—

"That you loved me?" she whispered.

He was flooded with relief and delight. "I do," he cried. "It is true. You remembered truly."

She seemed to take it in, to fold over it, to draw it into her heart. "I am so glad," she said simply.

They stood there hand in hand, gazing into each other's eyes. There was nothing else to do, there was nowhere to go. "I did not believe how that could be," she said. "I did not know even that I wanted it to be. But yet I think I did. I did not sleep at all that night."

"I didn't sleep either," said Joseph.

It was different from anything he had ever felt; there was such a sense of home-coming in it. But to a more distant home than Cleveland—and yet closer to his heart.

They didn't know what to say; they had come together from separate ends of the earth, they were one, they yearned toward each other, and they were still strangers. They were like children, awkward and self-conscious. "I love you, Anna," he said again.

She pressed his hand; and the way it felt, the knowledge it gave him that this hand was now his to hold and to love, filled him with a fierce, incredulous pride. Was this soft brave strong sad beautiful woman really his? Did she accept him, take him for her own? He longed to say: Are you mine? but dared not; it was too soon, it would seem too urgent of him.

She said it for him. "I also, Josef," she said. "Why should I deny it? *Szeretlek*; I love you. So is it."

He found himself trembling, he thought perhaps from cold. But rather it was from a sense of awe at the incredible richness of life, of destiny, the unprepared surprises . . . each one inevitable, sorrowful or beautiful, fated. . . .

The life of the boat swirled around them. It was Anna who roused herself first. "I must go to find Mia," she said. "I have not seen her."

"She's all right," Joseph reassured her. "I saw her

playing with the other children, and Mottl was watching them."

"Oh, then, good," said Anna contentedly. "I do not have to go."

The Polish boys went by with their accordion and a pride of young followers, and suddenly the night around them was full of singing and clapping, dancing forms weaving in and out of the light. And, at that moment, Joseph felt a sudden terrible impatience at the rejoicing crowds; he wanted desperately to be alone with Anna, to be able to say the things he had to say, to hear the things he had to hear. . . . Where could they go? He thought of the hold, in which there was no privacy at all, of his own little bare corner of the deck with people all around him, inches away. . . .

For the first time, he realized what it was like to be homeless—really homeless, without anywhere to go. As it had been for Anna, for so long. "Is there nowhere?" he asked mutely, with his eyes, and she shook her head helplessly.

"We have no place to go," she said.

The sea rolled beneath their feet, the night stood over them; but there was not a single place for them to be alone, to be quiet, to lie side by side, to talk, to open their hearts to each other. No private place at all.

CHAPTER

15

DAWN STAINED the air above the Moabite hills, and the sun rose for the first time over the state of Israel. It was the Sabbath day. All night the lights had burned behind the blackout screens in the house by the shore where the Haganah commanders, Israel Galilee and Yigal Yadin, had been deliberating with the Prime Minister, David Ben-Gurion.

They were waiting anxiously for two things: the arrival of desperately needed supplies from the transports taking off secretly from the airfields of Europe, and for the first act of open warfare from the other side. It was essential to Israel's stand in the United Nations that this act should come not from the Jews but from the Arabs.

It came. In the clear morning light, three Spitfires with the markings of the Royal Egyptian Air Force swept in from the sea and dropped their bombs on the Tel Aviv airfield, a little way inland from the shore. The solitary machine gun mounted on top of the power station knocked one Spitfire out of the sky. But one plane dropped a small bomb within a few hundred feet of the S.S. *Teti*, then entering the harbor with Mrs. Opisch's flag flying from the mast.

It was a cloudless day; the water was of a deeper blue than any Joseph had ever seen. He and Anna, with Mia between them, were standing on deck, staring at the city which rose from the low shore, with its crowded docks and sheds, its hotels and balconied apartment houses shining white in the sun, beyond the beaches to the south.

It was then, as the *Teti*'s engines were reversed, and she slid more and more slowly through the water, that the bomb exploded harmlessly off her starboard quarter.

There was a second or two of stunned silence, followed by shouts and cries; many ducked, or fell on their faces, and tried to make themselves small. But after a while, when nothing more happened, they picked themselves up again. From then on, however, they watched the sky apprehensively, over their shoulders.

"Well," said Zelinsky bitterly, "there you are. If we had even one fighter plane . . .

"But give us time. You will see."

"Who gives us time?" asked the barber.

Time, thought Joseph; but for what? To be with Anna —but where? He held her hand tightly, with a kind of desperation, and she returned the pressure tranquilly. She has more faith than I have, he thought; even though she has had to learn not to expect anything.

"It's going to be all right," he said.

The flood of Anna's emotions had ebbed a little, drawn back again from the high tide of the night before. For the first time, now, she was able to think seriously about the future, and she realized that it was not going to be easy or simple. Still, that was better than no future at all, which was the way it had looked to her before.

Joseph was wrong in thinking that she had faith: what she had was acceptance. She had accepted loneliness and hopelessness for so long, and the world's darkness; now there was a little light. She accepted that, too, humbly and gratefully; she didn't ask it to be anything more than it was.

"Where will you stay?" she asked. "Where will we see each other?"

"I don't know where I'm to stay," Joseph confided. "But we'll see each other."

"If we did not," she said steadily, "I would say to myself that I must always remember to give thanks because of you."

"Don't worry," said Joseph. "I'll find a place."

She smiled at him, a little sadly. "I will have to go where I am told," she said. She seemed to hesitate for a moment. "I go to the Kibbutz Degania, in Galilee," she declared.

"They won't send you right away," he assured her. "We'll have time."

"No," she said, pressing his hand, "not right away." But to herself she thought: So it is someday instead of right away: a mixed blessing. God gives, and He takes away; I will try to be grateful for what is given.

"Perhaps," she said, "someday you will come to visit us there. Mia would be glad of that."

"And you?"

"Oh—me! If you did not come . . . I would be very sad."

She spoke lightly—or, at least, she tried to. But Joseph

heard the entreaty under the lightness, the appeal, the longing to be comforted, if only with a promise; something to take with her into the days ahead. "I'll come," he said.

The immigration officers of the new state were now on board, going over the passengers' papers in the main cabin. "*Shalom,*" they said warmly and in a friendly way to everyone; "peace." It was time to say good-by to one's shipmates, to make farewells.

Instructions began to issue from the loudspeaker. The passengers stood anxiously among their worldly possessions: tin cups, pots from a yesterday, bundles of clothing tied together with string, cardboard boxes, old suitcases with rope around them; one gnarled old woman carried all her belongings in a faded burlap bag marked "National Sugar Refinery, N.Y., N.Y." The young Pole had his accordion strapped to his back, among his smiling companions.

Dr. Dreyfoos went to the priest's cabin to say good-by to his friend. "My sedentary days are over, Father," he said; "I will soon be growing vegetables, with a rifle in one hand."

"Then I shall ask St. Michael to look after you," said Father Duvernay with a smile, "who is the patron saint of swordsmen, as well as St. Eloi, who looks after farmers and farm-workers."

"Thank you," said Dr. Dreyfoos, "but I would rather you asked Paris for some seventy-fives."

"Fill your pipe once more before you go," said Father Duvernay. "You will miss the French tobacco, I think."

"I confess," said Dr. Dreyfoos, "I have developed quite a taste for it."

Avram Kolinsky and the girl with the freckles stood

close together, holding each other's hand. They intended to be married, and they were both going into the Army. In less than ten days they would be thrown into the battle of Latrun, with the Seventh Brigade, made up of recent immigrants. If they had had a choice, that is what they would have chosen.

Mrs. Opisch said good-by to the Slovak woman. "Come see me sometime," she said. "Believe me, I will be glad of a friendly face."

"I have a sister in Haifa," said the Slovak woman; "maybe you should settle there, instead of somewhere else."

"What did I tell you?" said Mrs. Opisch. "In Israel, a Jew is a human being."

The Mandelbaums were among the first to leave the ship. Before leaving, Mr. Mandelbaum shook hands with the Greek captain. He had forgotten the deprivations, the unsanitary conditions, the lack of food and water; he was about to step upon the land of Israel, where the name of Mandelbaum meant something, and he felt that he would like to shake hands with authority, for the pleasure it would give him. At the same time, he expected to make a few remarks to show that he, also, was a person of authority.

"I would like you to testify," said the captain, "to the good treatment the passengers have received on this trip."

Suddenly, to Mr. Mandelbaum, the captain looked like one of Hitler's men, an S.S. officer; and despite himself, something inside him turned to water. "Why not?" he said. "Certainly; with pleasure."

He was frightened, and ashamed. But later, when he thought it over, he realized that he had, after all, done the right thing. "Who knows?" he said to his wife, "but we will need this brute of a captain again someday, to make other trips for us, bringing arms and supplies? One cannot afford to make enemies at this stage of the game, when the ones we already have drop bombs on us the very first moment!"

It took a long time to get the *Teti's* passengers disembarked, for the harbor had no facilities for the handling of large craft. Small barges ferried them from the ship to the shore, a few at a time; they stared around them in a daze, laughed, joked, knelt to kiss the ground, and rose again with tears in their eyes. They were home! . . . at last, after two thousand years.

And from all sides warmth flowed out to them: "*Shalom, shalom,*" everyone said over and over: "Peace, peace."

Everywhere women of the Hadassah handed out oranges, sandwiches, and soft drinks; with smiles they welcomed the newcomers to the young nation which was already at war on the first day of its life.

Joseph, Anna, Mia, and the Hatvanys were standing together in the customs shed, looking at the crowds, listening to the excited voices as long-lost friends and relatives greeted one another. Suddenly there was a cry, and a young woman with a revolver strapped to her waist came rushing up to them and threw her arms first around Rosa Hatvany, and then around her husband. Mrs. Hatvany gave a gasp, turned pale, and staggered. She was unable to utter a word; speechlessly, with one hand pressed to her heart, she held out the rag doll to her daughter, who was taller than she, brown with the sun, and had already seen service with the Harel Brigade in the Jerusalem hills.

It was time for the kibbutzniks to leave. They were

going in several large buses to centers where they would rest for a few days, be fed and clothed, before being sent on to their destinations.

For a long moment Joseph and Anna gazed into each other's eyes. It is all right, those glances said; be patient, everything will be arranged. Joseph bent and kissed the top of Mia's head. Then, almost shyly, he turned to kiss Anna good-by.

She clung to him for a moment with the same sudden abandon as the night before. But then she dropped her arms, and stepped back in confusion. "Forgive me," she said timidly, and grasping Mia's hand, turned and hurried toward the buses.

There were no taxis, but he found a car to take him to the Press Club, and as he drove through the city he looked about him with interest. What sort of a city was it, he wondered, this white, seaside metropolis which less than forty years before had been nothing but empty sand dunes? He could see that it wasn't going to be anything like Rome.

He had never seen a city at war before. At every intersection he noticed barbed wire and bomb-shelter signs in Hebrew, English, and French. Once or twice he passed a gun emplacement and caught a glimpse of soldiers, young men and women—girls, actually—in sandals and faded khaki trousers, with rifles in their hands. Yet all the time the sun glinted peacefully on the stone and concrete buildings with their wide, shaded balconies, and on the young trees which lined the streets, the small squares and patios with their flowering bushes; and all around him he heard the bustling, peaceful city-sounds: the cries of street vendors, the rumble of buses, strains of music from open windows, bells, voices, footsteps; and smelled the city-smell, of wine and restaurants, the sharp odor of coffee, fumes of oil, earth-fragrance, flower-fragrance in the sun, the sudden cold smell of buildings in shadow, of doorways opening into shadowy halls.

At the Press Club, Joseph showed his credentials and was assigned to the Hotel Yarkon, down the street. There he was directed to a room with three beds, on one of which a young man was sprawled, half dressed and tight asleep. The sound of a bomb exploding somewhere in the city failed to waken him.

After the hard deck of the *Teti*, the bed on which Joseph threw himself seemed unbelievably soft. It was dusk when he awoke, and the young man was no longer there. He washed, shaved, and went down into the city in search of something to eat.

A block or so south of the larger hotels he found a cheap restaurant and went in and ordered a big meal of soup, sweet corn from a simmering pot, and *falaphel* stuffed with cabbage, fish balls, and chopped peppers. His stomach, after the starvation diet of the last eight days, stretched itself like a balloon; it was not very comfortable, and he let his belt out a notch or two.

As he sat there, resting, trying to breathe, and with his stomach aching a little, he saw the young man from the hotel enter the restaurant and hesitate in the doorway. It was obvious that he had recognized him, too, and after a moment he came over to Joseph's table.

"Mind if I sit here?" he asked.

"Not at all," said Joseph.

The young man sat down, smiling shyly. "My name is Greenfield," he said, "Hyman Greenfield. I know who you are; they told me at the hotel."

And holding out his hand, he added:

"We got the same room together."

"I know," said Joseph. "I saw you there. How many are we altogether?"

"Seven," said Greenfield, "counting you. That is, there's five others, besides me; but they come and go. Sort of in relays. They're mostly with Avidan's Brigade in the south, or with Carmel in the north. There's never more than one or two here at the same time."

"What about you?" asked Joseph.

"I work at night," said Greenfield.

He was a flier in Israel's tiny air force. A pilot from Brooklyn in World War II, he flew a Piper Cub over Arab territory every night, locating his targets by the light of flares; then he and his bombadier, who was a girl, threw or kicked their homemade bombs out of the open door of the plane. "We don't do too much damage," he said, "but it keeps them watching the sky.

"We got to make them think we got an air force," he said.

He told Joseph that he was married to an Israeli girl whom he had met at the University of Jerusalem. "I was there on the G.I. Bill," he explained, "but this girl, my wife, she lived there." And she was still there, he explained, in the Old City, beseiged by the Arab Legion. There was very little water or food; it was impossible to get convoys through to the defenders. "I don't hear from her," he said. And he added simply:

"It kind of worries me sometimes."

"I should think it would," said Joseph.

There was so much for him to learn; he realized that he knew almost nothing about this war, which had been going on for a long while. Yet, as he walked back through the darkened city, it seemed to him that everything was serene: there was no feeling of dismay or fright. The air was calm and still, the city-voices muted, but unhurried. A young man and a young woman of the Haganah went by on patrol, talking in low voices, carrying a Sten gun. From an open window hung with a blackout curtain he heard the strains of David Rose's "Holiday for Strings," which he himself had helped record a year before; it gave him a strange feeling to hear it there, in the cool, jasmine-scented Palestine night.

At the Press Club he sent his first cabled dispatch to Toronto:

CANADIAN PACIFIC TELEGRAPHS
RA GZ 366 COLLECT PRESS VIA MARCONI 1/53
TELAVIV MAY 15 2130
PRESS WORLD NEWS SERVICES
45 AVENUE ROAD   TORONTO CANADA
DISEMBARKED SS TETI SATURDAY FIFTEENTH HISTORIC OC-CASION OUR SHIP FIRST ENTERING FREE TELAVIV WATERS NEWLY PROCLAIMED JEWISH STATE PALESTINE FLYING MOGEN DOVID EVERYONE YOUNG OLD MOBILIZED TO EXPEDITE UN-LOADING MATERIAL FROM SHIPS AMID SINGING SHOUTS SHALOM TAKEN THROUGH CUSTOMS EFFICIENTLY PROUD MO-MENT WOMEN MEMBERS HOMEGUARD ATTENDING NEEDS OF THESE TIRED HAPPY PEOPLE SHALL NEVER FORGET SIGHT FIVE MINUTES AFTER DISEMBARKING TELAVIV AGAIN ATTACKED FROM AIR EGYPTIAN PLANES ALREADY BEEN BOMBED TWICE BY TRANSJORDAN BRITISH SPITFIRES FOUR PEOPLE KILLED MA-CHINE GUN FIRE SEVEN WOUNDED DAMAGE NOT ASCER-TAINABLE AMAZED FANATICAL RESOLUTION FAITH HAGANAH WITHSTAND ANY ONSLAUGHT FOR THEM PROBLEM SIMPLE NO ISSUES NO DOUBTS NO DISCUSSIONS CLEAR HAVE NO OTHER

WAY PROBLEM MATERIALS SUPPLY WIRE RESTOGRAM TEL-
AVIV FURTHER INSTRUCTIONS MILITARY CENSORSHIP WILL
SEND PICTURES BY AIR WHEN POSSIBLE TRY TO GET NEWS WEST
COAST PAPERS LOCAL BOY ETC WIRE MONEY BARCLAY BANK
TELAVIV

He was still leaning over the cable desk when he felt
a hand clapped on his shoulder, and a familiar voice remarked:

"Haven't I been expecting you these whole two days?"

Startled, Joseph turned to find himself gazing into the
face of Kevin O'Connor. The bearded Irishman looked
him over carefully. "You're a touch thinner," he said
judiciously, "but not as bad as I expected."

"I didn't expect to find you here at all," said Joseph.

It was strange; there was no grief attached to seeing
him again, no sudden wakening of an old anguish. He
remembered the last time, when O'Connor had come to
his room with Priscilla's letter—Pat's letter. It was like
someone else's sorrow, like a scene on the stage: poignant,
but at a distance, small, and not his own.

They sat at the bar, each with a double scotch in
front of him, and O'Connor told him how he'd flown in
two days before from Athens in a plane bringing arms and
ammunition from Czechoslovakia. "It took a bit of doing," he said, "though the how and the why of it isn't
worth the telling. But you, now, on the *Teti*—there's a
story for you!"

"I've got pictures of it," said Joseph.

"There's a *Time-Life* man here maybe should see
them," said O'Connor. "For there's no other story to be
had at all, beyond the proclamation of the new state. They

196

keep us bottled up, for fear the news might leak out to the other side."

"What news? If there isn't any?"

"The news of how they do it, then. I do know this much—that there's cruel few of them, and little to fight with; it's hit and run, and hit again some other place, and away."

"Jerusalem's besieged," said Joseph.

"It is," agreed O'Connor; "it is indeed. There's eight hundred men and women and children in the Old Quarter, cut off from the rest."

He looked soberly into his glass. "The poor devils," he said. "It's been going on now, these last four months. But they've the obstinacy of the I.R.A. itself.

"What's more," he added, "there are generals and captains here no more soldiers by rights than myself, or less so. Like Ireland in the Troubles—farmers by nature, and scholars besides. Like Alon, or Yigal Yadin, the archaeologist. And the little fiery man himself, Ben-Gurion, who wouldn't know a platoon from a regiment. A labor leader, no less; another David, with a slingshot."

"We've never had more than a slingshot," said Joseph, "and a Book. And a Pillar of Fire by night."

O'Connor glanced at him curiously: so it was "we" now, was it? There was certainly a change in him, there was no mistake about it. For one thing, he looked browner, though that might have been the effect of the long sea voyage; but more important, there was a different look in his eye. In Rome he'd been like a child at a party; here he looked as though he'd grown up a little.

"I've a message for you," said O'Connor, "from Pat."

"Oh," said Joseph. He couldn't help feeling a little

shortening of breath—the way something that once struck the heart like a great wave can still move it a little if only in memory.

"She says: 'There's a time for everything,' " O'Connor declared. " 'A time to keep, and a time to cast away.' "

"She's a smart girl," said Joseph. "Tell me: is she going to marry whatshisname—the Count? Ariano?"

"I don't think she has marriage in mind," said O'Connor. "No more than she had with you."

He sighed, and raised his glass slowly to his lips behind the brown beard. "There's a thing about women," he said, "that makes them dangerous to the world, being the weaker vessels, but the more desirable. And bold in the attack, and swift to maneuver. Many a man has been brought low in his pride and his strength by a brief, darting beauty with no more scruples than a pirate. Then there's the other type, that molds a man to her fancy, body and soul, and has him on his knees in wonder before her, the poor deluded sod."

"You've never been married?" Joseph inquired.

"I have not," said O'Connor. "I am convinced that man is woman's natural victim.

"Willing enough, God knows," he added ruefully, "myself included."

"There's one you haven't mentioned," said Joseph. "A girl with a Sten gun in her hand."

"I do confess," O'Connor admitted, "that the military female is something new to me. Young girls, mostly, that should by rights be setting out the tea, or calling home the cows. . . . We never thought to put our own Bridgets and Noras in uniform during the Troubles. Not that an Irish lass isn't the equal, pound for pound, of any fighting woman in the world; but the sentiment of it! It would break a man's heart to think about it."

"But if it's to be broken anyway—" Joseph began.

"I'd rather it was done in an old-fashioned, decent way," said O'Connor. "Let the wounded hero return to his house, and find his wife making preparations for the wake —and not off with the family claymore, hacking away at Mrs. Moriarty down the block."

He drank for a while in silence, musing. "The fact is," he admitted, "we take our honor and pleasure in our dead. Whereas your heroes are those that survive."

Joseph considered this solemnly. "I guess you're right," he said; "we have a real hunger for life. If we didn't"—he shrugged eloquently—"we'd never have made it."

He was thinking of still another woman, but he didn't know how to describe her. Only that with her, a man felt that he was himself, and at peace. His best self, too. Whether it was the quiet, or the grief, or some great kindness or tenderness, he didn't know. Or a sense that if she gave her heart, it would be a complete gift, pure and whole . . . a place for him on earth, to live in, to move and breathe in, to work and rest in.

He didn't know. Maybe it was a dream.

A grace, a something in the bones, a sweetness of desire and beyond desire: a homeward dream.

CHAPTER

⟨⟨⟨⟨⟨⟨⟨⟨⟨⟨⟨⟨⟨⟨⟨⟨⟨⟨⟨⟨⟨⟨

16

IN THE MORNING, Joseph went around to a photographic studio on Allenby Road and had his *Teti* pictures developed. They came out very well. While he was there, bombs were dropped in the city by Syrian planes, operating thirty miles forward of the Syrian and Iraqi columns advancing on Samakh and Jenin.

At the Press Club, Joseph met O'Connor, who introduced him to a number of other journalists: Malvois, of the Paris *Combat*; Jacob Kastler, of *Ce Soir*, a big, rough, laughing, moody bear of a man; Izzy Stone, of New York's *P.M.*; Bonneau, of Metro Newsreel; and among others a man from Reuters. "What's an Englishman doing here?" asked Joseph indignantly, to which O'Connor replied in a matter-of-fact voice:

"Spying for the Arabs, no doubt."

"There'll always be an England," said Izzy Stone.

He was dean of the foreign correspondents in Tel

Aviv. Round, cherubic, he was a "hot" man, an ardent Zionist; his hearing-aid, which he kept turning on and off, helped him to silence a world which often seemed to him to resound too loudly with the wrong voices.

He examined Joseph's contact prints with deep interest. "You have been particularly good with children," he said. "Those two, playing under the umbrella. And the little girl with the embroidery. What did you say her name was?"

"Mia," said Joseph, experiencing a strange clutch at his heart. How was that? he thought—merely to speak the name of Anna's child! He was surprised, and he became thoughtful; he wondered at himself.

His first written dispatch gave Davies in Toronto little more information than he already had. It merely re-affirmed what he had already said in his cable: Israel's resolution, and her will to fight. He wrote about the bombings in terms which the rewrite desk thought best to omit.

In the Café Ginati, under the rounded balconies of Allenby Road, Joseph showed his *Teti* prints to Schershel, of *Time-Life*, who found them interesting. "I can't use them," he said, "but whenever you have anything else, let me see it. Any time; any time at all."

"I know who could use them," said Stone. "Agronsky, of the *Palestine Post*."

"As a matter of fact," said Schershel, "how would you like to do some work for *Life*? A kind of special as-signment—"

"I'd like it very much," said Joseph.

"Good," said Schershel. "Keep in touch."

In the Press Club there were plenty of stories going around. "I have it on good authority," said the man from Tass, "that the bombing of Ben Yehuda Street in Jeru-

salem on February twenty-second was done by a British
soldier in the pay of the Mufti, Haj Amin."

"That," said the Reuters man frostily, "is a cheap
canard."

"For five hundred pounds," said the Russian. "Besides, he was never paid."

"No British tommy would accept a bribe," said Reuters.

Bonneau shrugged his Gallic shoulders. "*Galéjade,*"
he muttered.

To such correspondents as Malvois, who was in Palestine for the first time, the appearance of the young men
and women whom he saw on the streets and at the tables
of the sidewalk cafés was a distinct surprise. "From what
one had observed of these people in Europe," he declared,
"one got the impression of their being ambitious, sensitive, obstinate, and out of place. One was reminded of Chal-
dea, Moab, Ammon, and so forth; of Babylon, and so
forth and so forth. But among these youngsters, so many
of whom have been born here, I receive the impression
that the gaze is proud, the features strong and even merry,
and the entire expression one usually associated with the
Aryan type. This presents me with an interesting question:
is it possible that the ancient Hebrew or Habiru were indeed not at all like their Chaldean neighbors, but of a different race entirely? Or is it possible that two generations
on a Galilean farm-settlement can affect the genes?"

"The theory is," said Izzy Stone, "that ultimately you
get to look like the people around you."

"That explains the Moroccan Jews," said Malvois,
'the Yemenites, the Africans; but who is around the *sabras?*
No, my friend; there is a spirituality at work, a refinement
which is the result of courage and hard labor, pride, orange

juice, and the knowledge that one is armed for the first
time in centuries!"

"You can be right," admitted O'Connor. "I have a
nephew in Dublin; the first time his Da gave him a pop-
gun for Christmas, he grew two inches overnight. It was a
pure spirituality; the very next day, for having hit his sister
in the eye with it, his Da took it away again, and he ended
up the same size as before."

No one—except Ben-Gurion and the Israeli General
Staff—knew the exact number of effectives in the Israeli
Army. There were only rumors, guesses, bits of information, official, non-official. . . . The communiqués from the
government were usually evasive, their purpose to conceal
rather than reveal. A Palmach battalion would move from
settlement to settlement, giving the impression of an army.
Izzy Stone had heard that Israel had only sixteen homemade Davidka mortars and four ancient 65-mm. guns; Malvois that the Egyptians under Naguib were moving on Tel
Aviv along the coast road from Gaza. In the north they
heard that Acre had fallen to Carmel's Brigade, but Alon
was in difficulties: the Syrians had come down against the
settlements of Afikim and Degania. Ben-Gurion had sent a
young Haganah officer, Moshe Dayan, northward with orders to hold the Jordan Valley settlements at all cost. With
Dayan had gone two of the old sixty-fives and a locally
made flame thrower.

Rumors, bits of gossip, guesses . . . but Degania?
That was where Anna was being sent. Anxious and worried, Joseph tried to find out what was happening, but
without success; it was all uncertain, veiled in doubt; the
situation seemed to change almost from hour to hour. Nobody knew anything for certain, no one was sure.

In Tel Aviv, a bomb fell on a bakery in the southern

part of town; two children were killed outside a school on Kerem Kayemeth Boulevard. Many windows were broken in the neighborhood.

That evening Anna took a bus from the reception center to Hayarkon Street in search of Joseph. Not knowing where he was staying, she had hoped to find him at the Press Club; at least, that was what the woman at the center had suggested to her. Loneliness was no longer enough for her; her heart, awakened against its will, longed to be comforted again and again. She was like a house which has been empty too long and, suddenly opened to light and air, cries out to be filled with voices. All the way in, she was smiling timidly—and a little foolishly—to herself.

But Joseph had left the Press Club when she got there, and with a feeling of panic she set out to search the streets and restaurants near by. Yet when she did find him, finally, seated with O'Connor in a small café near the little park by the sea, a feeling of shyness came over her, and she almost turned to leave. For a moment she stood helplessly in the doorway, unable to advance or retreat; fortunately, O'Connor saw her in time, and nudged his companion.

"There's a young lady," he said, "who looks like maybe she knows us, but it can't be me, for I've never seen her in my life, worse luck to it."

After one incredulous glance, Joseph was on his feet, and running. In the doorway, without a word, he folded Anna in his arms. Then, self-consciously, he brought her back to the table.

"This is Anna," he told O'Connor; and added, inconsequentially, "the mother of the little girl with the embroidery."

O'Connor nodded his head wisely. So that's it, he

thought as once before. Ah, the poor loon. But he had to admit that Anna was a beautiful woman; and—from the way she looked at Joseph with those deep, sea-blue eyes of hers, and her whole soul in them—a loving one, too. "Well, now," he said to Joseph. "You didn't tell me."

"I would have told you," said Joseph. "I was going to tell you."

"No matter," said O'Connor. But he thought to himself: I brought the right message. Pat was no fool.

Anna and Joseph gazed at each other across the table. They didn't know what to say or how to begin; but so much that was unspoken was in their eyes that O'Connor began to feel uncomfortable. "Look you, now," he said at last, "I've a cable to send off. I'll be leaving you, if you don't mind."

It was at that moment, as he left the table and went out of the café, that Kevin O'Connor felt, for the first— and last—time, an unmistakable twinge of envy for Joseph Victor.

Anna leaned forward and touched Joseph's hand. "I came at the first moment," she said. "I thought that you did not know where I was."

They were unable to look away from each other, staring into each other's eyes, their hands clasped across the table. "Have you had your supper?" he asked, and when she nodded her head, he drew in a long breath like a sigh. "Then let's get out of here," he said.

The moon, not yet at half, was overhead as they walked arm in arm toward the Esplanade. From the sidewalk cafés as they passed, from behind the blackout curtains, music floated out into the night: Viennese songs, American jazz; the young flowering trees made a sweet cold fragrance in the air which came in off the sea. In their dappled shadow, he stopped and took her in his arms. "Anna," he murmured. "Anna."

"I am so glad I found you," she said. "I thought: he does not know where I am. So . . ."

She hesitated a moment. "Would you not have looked for me," she asked in a small voice, "if I had not come?"

"I would have turned the whole city upside down," he said.

She gave a little sigh of content. "I cannot stay very long," she said; "there is a final bus which I must not miss."

Joseph felt an indescribable sweetness in the night. His ardors rose, held him taut, as he felt the warmth of her soft body against him. The night air made him shiver; the moon looked down, people were in the streets, there was no privacy. He had so much he wanted to say to her.

But the vocabulary of love is limited; it expresses itself more naturally in embraces, in ardent looks and sighs, in every action; merely to talk is only to repeat, after a while, over and over again, the same words—the same wonder, the same longing. The lover hesitates, he waits, there is something more to be said, to be done—some miracle, some revelation, some word from heaven. A silence grows, an awkwardness takes shape; perhaps something inconsequential, some little detail, gossip, news of his day may save him:

"I'm to be a special correspondent for *Life*," he said.

But she had never heard of *Life*, and he was obliged to explain. "That is very good—yes?" she asked; and he said: Yes, it was.

"Then it goes well with you," she said.

It broke the spell of silence and of mystery—only to create another in which each one longed to talk, to tell the

other everything there was to tell, to open his life like a
book, to explain, justify, point out. . . . Joseph went back
over his childhood for Anna. He told her about the butcher
shop, about his mother and his aunt, between whose pos-
sessive love he had been all but crushed like a grain of
wheat. "They had such jealousy over me," he said. "I was
like a no man's land between them, trying to be great."

She regarded him solemnly; he could see that she
sympathized with his family, even though she loved him.
"What they did," she said, "they did for you. Here in the
Negev the desert itself is made to bloom, by women's
hands."

"I am not the Negev," said Joseph.

"In Buda," she said slowly, "it would have been not
the same. There, one did not have to be very much great,
one only had to be a little great. Even without being Isaac
Stern, there would have been a good life for you; you
would have been honored and respected, maybe a professor.
In the old days. In the days that used to be."

He asked her about her work at the center, where the
chalutzim were being prepared for their ultimate destinations among the kibbutzim of Galilee. "It is very good,"
she said earnestly. "We are taught; there are classes.
When it is five o'clock we are free, just like in the kibbutz.
Mia is in good care; here people are very much concerned
for children. She is not at all sad or unhappy."

They were walking along the beach now, hand in
hand, listening to the lapping of the water which stretched
out into the dark beyond them. For a moment Joseph
thought of Fregene, and the picnic on the sands; but it
was all different. There were no lights along the shore, all
was darkness; and his own feelings were different, too: no

longer apologetic, but free and resolute. He had no desire to bury his head in Anna's lap, or to weep; he wanted to talk; he strode along, talking.

Anna had no Fregene; to her the sea which rolled in at their feet in little waves was the same dark, immense, hissing expanse above which she and Joseph had stood on the *Teti*'s deck along the rail, where they had spoken of happiness and unhappiness, where they had watched the moon go down; where she had opened her heart to him. . . .

"This good sea," she said. "This blessed sea."

She wanted to talk about the past, her own past. "It was like this," she said. "In Buda there were three classes —the great families, the rich people, and the artists. One did not have to belong to more than one; an artist could be not rich at all, and not from one of the great families, yet he would have respect. Unless, of course, he was very bad; but even then . . . in that case, he would spend all his time in the coffee houses and give himself the sad expression as one who has suffered a bad love affair."

Her sweet laugh rang out, a little muted in the quiet night. "There were no coffee houses in Cleveland," said Joseph. "Not when I was there."

"Everywhere," said Anna gently, "a man must have his little world in which to be somebody. A small island, a coffee house, maybe only with his wife—but this can be terrible, too, this need to be somebody; it is when it grows too big, too much uncontrolled, that other people suffer. Then it is a madness that takes no account of man or woman or child; it strides with terrible eyes across the land; it is a nightmare, a hideous thing, not to be believed, oh fearful, unbelievable—and innocent and good people are made to crawl like naked cattle on their hands and

knees to where the butcher is waiting to knock them over
the head, to slit their throats, to hang them up on meat-
hooks. . . ."

Her voice, which had started low, had risen, growing
more and more out of control as she admitted, for the first
time, what had been the fate of her husband, her father,
her brothers. Joseph halted, and put his arms around her;
she was shaking, her breath coming in little gasps. He held
the struggling, convulsive figure tight.

"Why?" she cried. "Why? Whom did they harm? My
own father, a good, kind man; Mia's father . . ."

"Hush," Joseph whispered, "hush, Anna. Hush, my
darling."

For a moment longer she trembled and shook in his
arms; and then she mastered herself with an effort. "Yes,"
she said, "yes. I must hush. I must not have these
thoughts."

She grew limp against him; he felt her full weight in
his arms. "I was so strong," she said; "I would not let myself think; I would not let myself remember."

"You were dying," said Joseph. "I want you to live."

"To live," she whispered. "But I am so very—how
shall I say it?—so *wehrlos*. So defenseless. How am I to
live?"

A feeling of infinite sadness and helplessness over-
whelmed him. They were two strangers blown together in
a whirlwind, two cockleshells on a wild sea. How could he
comfort her? how shield her from her memories? To be
with her, to stay with her . . . to be with her always.
. . . But their lives were so separate, so different! They
needed a place in which to be together, a land, a home;
they needed to know each other; they needed peace.

These thoughts scarcely even took shape in his mind;

they were no more than a flicker in his brain, which took form in the one word: wait. Someday, when there was peace, when all this was over, when one could think . . . Yet at that moment he wanted Anna more than ever, wanted her secret warm beauty, wanted her sorrow— wanted her sorrow for himself, wanted her salt tears to be for him, wanted to possess her utterly, to be possessed by her in turn. He could sense how her body responded to him, to his urgency, to the charge within him; she, too, felt a quickening, a longing—to be possessed, to belong again—at last—to someone, to be taken with gentleness and power, to give love and wonder and delight, to share kindness, to experience glory.

But where? Where? Not there, on the beach, on the cold sand—with people stumbling over them in the dark. Not with watching eyes, with voices and footsteps all around them!

"Oh, my dear!" she wept, pressing herself against him. "Oh, Josef!"

There was no place. When and where there would be, he didn't know. He clenched his jaws together, to still the trembling in his body. Someday. Wait.

It was time for her to catch the bus back to the center. "I will come tomorrow," she whispered.

"I'll wait at the Press Club."

"So . . . until then . . . ?"

"Until then."

"*Lilah tov*, my Josef."

"*Lilah tov*," he said. "Good night, my love."

CHAPTER

❊❊❊❊❊❊❊❊❊❊❊❊❊❊❊❊

17

JOSEPH was busy all the next day. He went to the office of the *Palestine Post*, where he sold his *Teti* pictures; he attended a press conference held by Moshe Shertock, then Foreign Minister; and with Jacob Kastler discussed the possibility of getting out of the city long enough to visit one of the nearby fronts. This was more difficult to accomplish than it seemed, since the government had put tight bounds on all correspondents, foreign or domestic. No journalist was allowed to leave the city. It was of the greatest importance that none of the Israeli Army dispositions be made known to the enemy—or, for that matter, to the Jews themselves, who might become discouraged and even frightened.

Kastler and the Frenchman Malvois thought that it might be possible to arrange something through the Irgun, which had not yet been brought into the regular defense forces, and which was conducting its own operations, though combining with the Palmach in defense of some of the settlements, but under its own officers.

In the meanwhile, Joseph had a chance to explore Tel Aviv. He discovered a city of outdoor cafés, of avenues of trees not yet fully grown, of boxlike hotels and apartment houses with rounded balconies shaded from the sun and wherever posssible facing the sea. People of all races passed up and down the busy streets—though for the most part, they had one thing in common: they were Jews. He saw dark-skinned Yemenites with their long, braided ear locks; bearded Karaites; Druses in their desert robes; Jews from India, South Africa, Abyssinia, from Tunis and Tangier, Jews in the curly sheep's-wool hats of Bokhara; and always the Europeans, with their coats and ties and brief-cases. In the beauty salons of Allenby Road, women sat under hair driers, as they did in Paris and New York.

Near the Zoo on Dizengoff Street he passed a bearded young man in the broad-brimmed fur hat, the long black coat, the wide trousers of one of the Orthodox Hassidic sects, pushing in front of him a chrome-trimmed perambulator from which a child's face peered out like a young bird from its nest. He stopped to take a picture, and almost missed Mr. Mandelbaum, who went by a moment later.

Mr. Mandelbaum carried a brief-case; he walked rapidly, with an air of having a great deal on his mind, and did not bother to return Joseph's greeting. He was on his way to the Museum, hoping to see some official of the government; he wanted, he hoped for, he needed to find a position of some sort which would enable him to establish himself in the new land in such a way . . . in circumstances that . . . well, after all, when one has been a Mandelbaum of Berlin, there are certain requirements. . . .

But for the most part, Joseph felt himself to be in a foreign city. The many languages he heard all around him, on the streets and in the cafés, made a blur of sound in his ears; and in addition, the sight of young girls dressed in the uniforms—or part of the uniforms—of soldiers, with revolvers strapped to their waists, or carrying guns, gave him a constant sense of strangeness and of belonging to a different world. On one occasion, he asked Anna what she thought about it. "I shall be learning to be a soldier, too," she said simply.

On that day the Haganah headquarters—which had just been moved—was bombed again. "There is a spy at work," said Bonneau, the newsreel man; "he will be one of three types: an Arab, an Israeli, or a foreign newspaper correspondent."

O'Connor stroked his beard reflectively. "Look out for Reuters," he said.

"But why, O'Connor?"

"Don't forget—the British want the Arabs to win. Else why do you think Cadogan is holding up the United Nations from putting a truce on us? He's waiting for Abdullah to take Jerusalem. After we've lost the middle valleys and the Negev—or what's left of it—then you'll see him plump for the Truce, for he'll have got what he's wanted all along, him and Bevin—a bloody nose for the Jews."

"We?" asked Joseph, straight-faced. "After *we've* lost . . . ?"

"Ah, well," said O'Connor, "in a manner of speaking.

"Not," he added, "but what there's something to be said for poor old England—all but bleeding to death in two great wars, and with the rug pulled out from under her with the end of Lend-Lease. That's the fault of *your* government," he said, pointing to Joseph; "for if ever there was a greater bit of bungling in foreign affairs than you'll find in Britain, you've only to look to America, and there it sits like a mushroom."

"Why a mushroom?" asked Joseph.

"*Enfin,*" said Malvois, "it was an Englishman, Milord Balfour, who made the declaration to return the Jews to their own country. This was two thousand four hundred and fifty-six years after Cyrus of Persia had returned them from Babylon. *Formidable!* Nevertheless, Milord Balfour was no Cyrus, and the declaration proved to be an *offre de Gascon.*"

Back in his room, Joseph found a communiqué from the Irgun slipped under his door.

Irgun Zvai Leumi
b'Eretz Israel

May 17, 1948

At 5:30 A.M. our combat-units stormed Samakh, which had been occupied by strong forces of the Syrian Army. The entire area has been cleared of the enemy, who suffered heavy losses.
Our casualties: six dead, and six wounded.

In the late afternoon, toward sunset, Joseph and Anna walked together along the Esplanade, where young and old took their evening promenade as though there were no enemies in the air. "When one lives always with danger," said Anna, "one grows accustomed to it as a part of life. It is probably in our blood since many generations; maybe for a while we forget, but then we remember again. So many of our festivals are for difficulties overcome: the Passover, Purim, Hanukkah. . . ."

She took his hand. "My own festival," she said shyly, "is when the announcement came to us on the ship, and I found you, among all the people."

They went to the terrace of the Park Hotel for dinner. There a small orchestra played the music of Strauss, of Offenbach, of the old Europe which was still deeply in the hearts of so many to whom Europe had been a grave and a calamity—who would never again see the Vienna Woods, the Danube or the Rhine, attend theater in Berlin or opera in Bayreuth, drink beer in Munich or coffee in Buda Pesth. "*Wien, Wien, nur Du allein* . . ."

Anna looked with an air almost of disbelief at the decorations, at the gleaming china and glassware, the silver, the waiters in their dinner jackets. It was so long since she had seen anything of the kind, she had forgotten what it was like. "All this," she said, "it is unreal to me, as though it did not exist. Although I was brought up so— It is just as well, since I do not think it will be like this at the kibbutz where I am going. I do not know when it will be, because of the fighting there."

"The Syrians have withdrawn from the settlements," said Joseph. "At least, that is what we've been told."

Anna sighed, and looked around her at the terrace and out across the beaches to the sea, shining golden in the last rays of the sun. She seemed to be trying to drink it all in for the last time: a memory of her life long ago and far away.

"Then I will be leaving soon," she declared.

"I do not mind," she said after a while; "in effect, I have learned to put my faith in whatever is ordering me from day to day, and not to make wishes. Mia will be happy in the settlement, with other children, and with studying and things to do. . . ."

She broke off, and her eyes, behind their dark lashes, grew misty and lilac-colored in the sunset light. "You see," she said, "for Mia's sake I still make wishes."

"Both of us," said Joseph. "We both do."

"Yes," she said, smiling at him gently. "Someday, perhaps, we will make a wish together. For both our sakes."

At first dark, two Blenheim bombers came in from the sea and swept over the city. The sirens wailed, too late; and Anna and Joseph, walking together along Allenby Road, slipped into a bomb shelter. It was almost empty, and very dimly lit. There they crouched against the wall, their arms around each other, while near them a member of the sect of the Agudath Yisrael, in his long, black coat, stood arguing an obscure point with a rabbi from Rumania. "The question," declared the sect member, "is this: what are the damages?"

"The Galizianer once remarked," said the rabbi, "that he who is desirous of being a saint, let him fulfill that part of the law which deals with damages. Thus, he avoids everything that might result in an injury to his fellow man."

"So who tells these persons in the sky where to find us?"

"As the Psalmist says," the rabbi decuared: " 'Therefore my heart is glad and my glory exults; my flesh also dwells in safety.' Please to pay attention to the word: safety. But in the matter of damages: by damage is also meant anything which might cause one's fellow man to feel nauseated."

Poomh! went a bomb in the distance, and the shelter shook a little. "He who hates an Israelite, hates also Abra-

ham, Isaac, and Jacob," said the rabbi. "He who hates
man, hates the Holy One, blessed be He, who created
man."

Poomh!

Crouched in the semi-darkness, their mouths one
upon the other, Joseph and Anna exchanged murmurs.
Their hands searched for each other ardently, and nerv-
ously; frustrated by the presence of others, and by their
own timidity, they drew apart, sighing noisily. The all-
clear sounded, the shelter emptied, and the rabbi and his
friend went out into the street, still talking. Joseph and
Anna followed them silently, their cheeks flushed, and a
look of distraction on their faces.

They walked gazing straight ahead, unable to look at
each other. When, a block or so farther, they found a cinema, they turned and went in as though of one mind, and
—still without saying anything—sank into seats in the
back row. There, in the flickering darkness, hidden from
their own embarrassment, from the world, and from each
other, they slowly grew calmer and found some comfort;
and once again their hands touched and their fingers
twined, gently and with pity, asking forgiveness and giving
it.

The theater was presenting a French comedy, with
subtitles in four languages. The sound track itself was
French, while English, German, Hebrew, and Arabic
translations of the dialogue—such as they were—flashed
on and off at either side of the screen, and above and below it. The result was complete confusion, for the translations were never quite on time, one usually running
ahead of another; laughter would break out in different
parts of the house, often at a solemn moment, as one part
of the audience found itself laughing at dialogue from the

scene before. But the confusion itself was comforting to Joseph and Anna, and helped to isolate them from the world around them; little by little they drew closer together again in a world of their own.

When they came out of the theater they were able to talk again and to smile at each other. There was still a little time left before the last bus for the Center, and they sat for a while at a sidewalk café. Joseph ordered an anisette for Anna, and a brandy for himself. "Tell me about Mia," he said; "is she happy? Does she have friends?"

"Yes; already a few."

"And you?"

"I?" She gazed at him blankly. "Friends?" she murmured, half to herself.

"No," she said. "I think I have forgotten how to have friends."

"When you're at Degania," he said, "you'll remember; it will come back to you."

She shook her head seriously. "To make friends," she explained, "is something which takes time. For a child, yes—it is very quick; even when I was grown up, a young woman, it was still a thing to arrive at very soon. But the old do not make friends so quickly; and when one is marked for death, it is the same as being old, and one is very much alone, and there is besides no time. Everyone then is the same, without time."

She looked out beyond him into space, at something far away. "There is no place in the mind," she said, "or in the heart, to look for friends. Kindness one finds, and moments of helping others. But in the middle of fear, one does not go outside oneself to strangers. And the friends one had—the old friends, the friends of childhood or later . . . they are either dead, or they are afraid to speak, even to give a greeting; they do not know you any more, which is even worse than dead. So one forgets how to make friends—just as one forgets how to love. Friends are not quickly to remember."

But at Joseph's downcast expression, her face grew soft, and she leaned across the table and lifted his fingers to her lips. "Love is more quickly to remember," she said.

Surprised and touched, he drew her hand to his face, and kissed her open palm. "I can't imagine ever not having been in love with you," he said.

"Do not say such a thing," she said. "It is to tempt God . . . Who, besides, does not like it when something is not true."

"I swear it!" said Joseph. "It's true. All my life . . ."

"You have known me only ten days," she said gravely.

"All my life," said Joseph stubbornly.

She made a little gesture of consent, charming and rueful. "So," she said, "all right—a lifetime. But you have lived other lifetimes, my love. Was there no one at home, in Cleveland, Ohio?"

"No one."

"And in Rome? No one?"

He hesitated for the fraction of a second. "No one," he said, much too firmly.

She was smiling at him now. "It makes no difference," she said gently; "it was, besides, another lifetime. Like the music, like the child practicing his violin, of whom you told me—who did not know that someday he would be sitting at a café in Tel Aviv, telling untruths to someone he loved. One lives many lifetimes, my Josef—if one lives at all."

He felt unhappy; he wished he hadn't lied about Pat. How could he have denied her like that? He was as bad as

St. Peter. And besides, he wished she wouldn't call him Josef; it sounded too much like his aunt.

"There was someone in Rome," he said slowly. "But it wasn't like this. I mean . . ."

She wasn't surprised, and she didn't let him finish. "I do not ask about anything else," she said simply; "only about this."

"I wish you wouldn't call me Josef," he said. "I wish you'd call me Joe."

"Please?"

"People do, sometimes," he said.

"If you like," she said, and tried it. "Joe," she said. The way she said it, it sounded more like "Joo"; and they laughed at each other across the table. It made him feel better; it brought her closer to him.

But on the way back to his hotel, after putting her on the bus, he thought of the clumsy, frightened love-making in the bomb shelter, and he groaned aloud. It was so different from the way he wanted things to be—simple and whole and clean and shining. . . .

Anna was all of that; and bruised and hurt besides. She deserved better of him. Joo, she had called him, in such a sweet way. . . . He smiled despite himself. He loved her desperately.

Hyman Greenfield was in the room when he got back, lying on his bed and staring at the ceiling. "I'm glad you got here," he said. "I've been having the willies."

"So have I," said Joseph.

"Lonely thoughts," said Greenfield. "I've been thinking about dying, and such."

"What's the good of that?" asked Joseph.

"None," said Greenfield. "It's no novelty; I've seen

it, plenty. What I mean is, being alone. Being by yourself
—that is, without anybody. Being alone with it."

He was thinking about his wife in Jerusalem. "I guess
I know what you mean," said Joseph.

"To die all alone," said Greenfield, "man, that's really
solitary! You can't even tell anybody what's happening
to you."

"Even if someone was there," said Joseph, "you
couldn't tell them."

"I know," said Greenfield soberly. "But at least,
you'd get a last look, and a word or two.

"I get the willies," he said, "when I think of Miriam
in Jerusalem all by herself."

"You don't believe in the hereafter?"

"You mean complete, with bones and a name?"

"No," said Joseph, "I mean the spirit."

"I want my own name," said Greenfield. "I want my
wife, too, and the bones included.

"Eternity doesn't worry me," said Greenfield; "what
worries me is being nothing, forever and ever. . . . That's
what keeps me awake nights. Buried away somewhere,
and being nothing. Know what I mean?"

"Yes," said Joseph. "I know what you mean. I used to
be the same way—"

He broke off in the sudden realization that what he
had said was the truth: that he used to have fearful
thoughts about dying, and that he didn't any more. When
was the last time he'd lain awake, filled with panic, terrified of the dark—not the good dark of earth's night, but a
deeper darkness, unknown and unknowable? He couldn't
remember. But he did know that what he thought about
now was life, not death; that Israel, alive, ardent, fierce,

argumentative, fighting for her life against all but hopeless odds—planning, hoping, working, making the desert bloom, building cities . . . that this small, intense, indomitable, beleaguered country had swept all thoughts of fear and hesitation out of his mind.

As for Greenfield—he was married, he missed his wife, he had too much time with nothing to do but lie on the bed and stare at the ceiling. Presently, Joseph knew, he'd get up and go out to the airstrip and take his little plane up into the night sky, headed for some Arab fortress or strongpoint; and then, with actual death all around him, he wouldn't think about it at all.

Before dawn, fourteen men of the Irgun, specially trained, set off in jeeps to raid an Iraqi ammunition dump back of Rasel 'Ain. Most of the Irgunists were North African Jews, who spoke only Arabic. Stealing through the orange grove which masked their target, the young Irgun leader spied the gleam of a rifle barrel; in a fluid, almost single motion, he seized it, pulled the Arab holding it into the open, and killed him with the knife he held in his other hand.

The fourteen men then proceeded to the dump, loaded their jeeps with the precious ammunition, blew up what they could, and came safely back to Tel Aviv before the sun was well up.

The young Irgunist who led the raid wore a heavy black beard. He was the eighteen-year-old Arieh Herzog; and Joseph was to see a great deal of him in the days which followed.

Next morning in Tel Aviv the Haganah headquarters was bombed again, as well as the bus station on the Jaffa Road, where several people were killed, and many wounded. In between the bombings, life went on as usual, except for a smell of burning throughout the city; toward evening, families paraded up and down the Esplanade, beside the sea.

In Jerusalem there was bitter fighting in the Old City, around the hospital and convent of Notre Dame and the Damascus Gate. At 3:35 A.M. the Hapotzim Battalion of the Palmach breached the Old City wall at the Zion Gate, and contact was made for a short while with the defenders of the Jewish Quarter. The dead were taken out, and the wounded evacuated.

Among them was Miriam Greenfield, who died on the way to the hospital.

CHAPTER

﹙◖◆﹚◖◆﹚◖◆﹚◖◆﹚◖◆﹚◖◆﹚◖◆﹚◖◆﹚◖◆﹚◖◆﹚◖◆﹚◖◆﹚◖◆﹚◖◆﹚◖

18

THAT EVENING, Joseph and Anna stopped for supper
(of a sort) at the Brooklyn Ice Cream Parlor before going
on to the Ohel-Shem Hall, to a concert of the Palestine
Philharmonic Orchestra. It seemed to Joseph that Anna
was quieter than usual, but he laid it to the bombings.

He tried to cheer her up, to take her mind off the
present. "Do you remember the first supper on board the
Teti?" he asked. "When I offered Mia the bread, and she
didn't want to take it?"

"She had fear of you," said Anna. "Gentlemen did not
so often offer her anything."

"I thought you had the sweetest voice I'd ever heard
in my life," said Joseph.

That made her smile. "Even when you are seeing me
for the first time," she asked, "and I am eating an orange?"

"Even then."

"It was the first orange I had eaten in many months,"

she said reminiscently. "In years. I did not know what it tasted like any more."

"And the watery soup?" asked Joseph, looking down at his own large dish of ice cream with hot-fudge sauce and whipped cream sprinkled with walnuts.

"It tasted good," said Anna simply, "like heaven. It was a freedom soup, or almost; and an orange from Eretz Israel. For two days this lasted; after that, the freedom went out from the soup, and there were no more oranges. And we ate, from a small pot on the deck, something shared to us by a kind friend."

She smiled at him warmly across the table, and sucked noisily at the straw embedded in her tall glass of chocolate ice cream soda. "Now freedom is back," she said, "for the moment; for now, at least."

The hall was crowded for the concert, to which Joseph had received complimentary tickets from Mr. Mahler-Kalkstein, the General Secretary. He wasn't sure why—whether it was his being a foreign correspondent or his having been himself at one time a member of the Los Angeles Philharmonic—but it didn't matter: he was there, with Anna, and Izler Solomon was conducting the Tchaikovsky Fourth and Mahler's "Lied von der Erde."

He was there with Anna. Hand in hand, fused into one spirit, one body, they listened, drinking in the music like water to the thirsty; hearing once again the sound of beauty, not only with their ears but with their hearts, with their bones . . . the great moments still greater and more deeply moving, the small moments even sweeter and more touching, because they were together.

Feelings of grief, and summer light, washed over them, tides of longing flooded them, currents of peace and of delight; they closed their eyes, hearing the rush of strings, the trumpets of the host, drums and cymbals, the brooklike runs of flute and woodwinds sweep over them like wings.

But it was no angelic host above them. Halfway through the Tchaikovsky, the air-raid sirens sounded. No one moved; the orchestra never stopped playing; people sat for a moment a little straighter in their seats—and that was all. Even the frightened ones took courage from those around them, and from the music. Death they could have at any time, but beauty seldom; and besides, they had paid for it.

Afterwards, walking through the moon-shadowed streets in the Palestine night, he still heard in memory the long, slow ending of the Mahler, and thought how once before, on the deck of the ship under the stars, he had heard it in his mind: "*Ewig, ewig* . . ." Forever. Beside him, Anna sang the closing measures to herself: "I am seeking rest for my lonely heart. I turn to my homeland; everywhere the lovely earth blossoms in spring, turns green, renews itself. . . .

"*Allüberall im ewig blauen Licht die Fernen.
Ewig . . . ewig . . .*"

"There is such sadness in Mahler's music," she said. "But it is a peaceful sadness: very Viennese."

Joseph agreed with her. "Compared to the Russian sadness," he said, "it is very innocent."

"There are occasions for different kinds of sadness," she declared. "For the heart which is so solemnly breaking, Tchaikovsky; but for the farewell of lovers, Mahler."

"The farewell of lovers?"

He felt a sudden alarm; he had a presentiment of what was coming. "Is it time?" he asked.

She nodded. "We go tomorrow," she said. "Mia and I."

Her voice trembled a little; she smiled at him, and took his arm, and her fingers clenched themselves in his. "I am glad we are having this night with the music," she said. "It will be something for me to remember."

She sighed. "I will also not forget the Brooklyn ice cream," she said valiantly.

Joseph tried to laugh, but he felt lost and miserable. He'd known that it was coming, that they had to part; he'd even known it would be soon. But now that it was here, he didn't know how to deal with it.

An old spiritual came into his mind, a song he'd heard years before . . . who had sung it? Marian Anderson? He didn't know. He sang a little of it as they walked along.

> "Sometimes I feel like a motherless child,
> A long way from home."

Anna gave a shaky laugh. "It is not as if I were going very far," she said. "Thirty miles, perhaps, only."

"I know," he said. "But it doesn't help. Not to see you every day. . . ."

"But you will see me!" she cried. "You will come to see me!"

"They say they won't let us out of Tel Aviv," he said. "But I'll find a way."

"I will write to you. I will tell you everything that I am doing."

"We've had so little," he said.

She made a little-girl face in the darkness, which he didn't see. "To you, little, perhaps," she said.

"And to you," he asked, faintly disturbed, "not? I mean—this is all you want?"

"It is all I have," she said simply.

"And it's enough?"

When she didn't answer, he declared almost roughly: "It isn't enough for me!"

"Whom the gods would destroy, they first make fall in love," she said mournfully.

"So?"

"Then they are not any longer grateful for what they have."

All of a sudden Joseph felt angry; he couldn't help it. Why should people always be so humble and grateful—for what?

"You sound like my mother," he exclaimed.

"Do I?" she answered gently. "Perhaps. She also loved you."

"What do you mean, 'loved'?" he demanded. "She still does."

"So do I," said Anna.

She laughed suddenly in the darkness, and hugged his arm. "Oh, Joo," she cried, "we have had our first quarrel!"

He laughed, too, vexed at himself, and feeling foolish, and just as suddenly happy again. "I'm hopeless," he told her. "I love you."

"I know," she said.

"Tell me," he whispered. "Say it in your own language."

"*Drágám. Te vagy a szerelmem.*"

"What does it mean?"

"Beloved. You are my beloved."

Then suddenly she was clinging to him with all her might. "Oh, Joo," she cried, "I do not want to leave you!"

Around them were the peaceful sounds of the city, the rumble of a bus on Allenby Road, the click of footsteps, a strain of melody from behind the blackout curtain of an apartment-house window, low voices bidding one another good night:

"*Shalom. Lilah tov. Shalom.*"

"I will come to Degania," he said.

Anna and Mia left the Center the next morning for the northern settlements, and that night Joseph got in touch with the Irgun. After the proper people had been reached, and certain arrangements made, he found himself being driven through the city along dark, winding streets to a house on the outskirts, where Arieh Herzog was waiting for him. "I am pleased that you have come," said the bearded young officer of the underground organization, whose terrorist activities had done so much to drive the British from Palestine and about which there was such a difference of opinion in Israel itself. "I wish that you will inform the whole world what we are doing. Let me tell you."

"I'd rather see it for myself," said Joseph.

Arieh regarded him somberly, and Joseph reflected that this young man, scarcely out of his teens, had already fought in many battles, and had killed many men. "You know that the military does not allow the correspondents to leave the city," Arieh said at last.

"Since when does the Irgun take orders from the Haganah?" asked Joseph boldly.

The black beard smiled a wintry smile; apparently it was the right thing to have said. "Where do you wish to go?" he asked. His voice was deep, and grated a little; he spoke English with a heavy accent.

Joseph wanted to visit eastern Galilee and the Jordan front, for the reason—as he put it—that many battles had been fought over that ground. There was still another reason, one which he forgot—or perhaps chose not—to mention. The settlement of Degania lay in that direction.

Arieh studied his hands, lying idle in his lap—the strong, sinewy hands which closed so easily over the haft of a knife. "There are still battles going on," he said. "Dan Laner, of Alon's command, is moving on Malkieh and Kadesh. There are Irgun units with the Yiftah Brigade."

He hesitated, and pulled at his beard. "But I will not do this for you alone," he said. "There must be more people."

"Why?" asked Joseph.

Arieh shrugged his shoulders. "The Irgun does not make a guide of itself," he said, "for one newspaperman."

"I see," said Joseph. "You want coverage. Is that it?"

"If that is the word for what we want," said Arieh carelessly, "then that is what we want."

Joseph counted off in his mind the names of the men he could trust: Kevin O'Connor, of course—Bonneau, Malvois, Kastler.

"There will be five of us in all," he said.

"Good," said the Irgunist. "I will arrange for a car and a driver."

He stood up and shook hands with Joseph. "The day after tomorrow," he said, "in the morning, at seven hours, a car will come for you. Be ready with your friends."

Tall and gaunt, he escorted Joseph to the door. He was like a dark angel, Joseph thought—an ancient figure out of the Judaean hills, bedded with the lion and the hawk. With black wings outspread, he might have soared upward against Jehovah—or with a sword and shield, struck terror into the Philistines. "There will be plenty of fighting at Malkieh," he said.

Joseph went back to the Press Club and put in a call for O'Connor, Kastler, Bonneau, and Malvois to meet him there as soon as possible. Then he sat down with a bottle of brandy, to wait.

O'Connor was the first to arrive, looking somewhat tousled from having been wakened from sleep, demanding to know what had happened to drag him out of bed at such an hour. When he learned what was being planned, he poured himself out a stiff drink of the brandy and raked his long brown beard with his fingers. "We'll be shot at," he said.

"So?" asked Joseph.

"You haven't been shot at," said O'Connor. "I have; and I can tell you it's damned unpleasant."

"Would you rather not go, then?"

"Ah, now," said O'Connor. "That's something else again."

The others, too, were glad to go along, to be included in the plans. "One cannot make history," said Malvois, "by refusing to act. If I am to stay during the whole affair here in Tel Aviv, I would do better to be in Paris, in my flat, where everything is comfortable."

It was agreed that they would meet in front of Joseph's hotel at seven in the morning of the following day. "Of course," said Joseph, "this will all have to be kept a secret. The Haganah . . ."

"*Foutre!*" said Bonneau. "What do you take us for?"

Joseph felt himself flushing. "I'm sorry," he said. "I didn't mean . . ."

231

"Of course not," Kastler grumbled. "Of course not. So if you will just pass the brandy bottle, we will forget whatever it was you didn't mean."

All the next day Joseph was busy, putting his cameras in order and getting his gear together; but underneath all his activity, he was restless and strangely lonely. The knowledge that Anna was gone, that she wasn't coming in to meet him any more, gave the hours a dreamlike quality, and made the city seem empty and on the edge of nowhere, full of staring strangers.

He tried to remember it as it had been; he went back to the *Teti* in his mind, to the time when he had first seen her standing in the circle of light, her arm around Mia. He thought of her face in the moonlight, turned to him, her eyes dark with love . . . or was it anguish? "This sea," she had said, "this blessed sea." He retraced their steps: he walked at sunset along the Esplanade, as they had walked; he went at night to the café where she had first found him; he even visited the Brooklyn Ice Cream Parlor, trying to make her come to him again, to warm her into life with his memories, to feel her near him. . . . It was no good. He was alone; the moonlight pouring down on Dizengoff Square, dappling the trees in the park, merely made him feel sad and filled him with longing. All Israel was only Anna for him now—nothing else existed; nothing else was real. That was how it was: the whole world started and ended for him in her face.

That night he sent his mother in Cleveland a picture postcard of Tel Aviv, and signed it, "Yonnie."

They started out in the early morning, in an old Ford station wagon, driven by its owner, Moshe Halevi. Bon-

neau and Joseph both had their cameras; O'Connor carried
the brandy, and Kastler brought along several bottles of
vodka. "It is a pure alcohol," he said; "good either outside,
or in."

They were bound for a group of three religious colonies of the Hapoel Hamizrachi, bordering the Syrian front.
By what maneuvers and evasions Arieh managed to get
them past the guards and the barbed-wire stations and out
of the city, Joseph never knew. But midway in the morning
they reached Ein Hanatziv, and there took on a guide, an
Orthodox young scholar by the name of Ezra Ben-Solis,
who knew the upper Galilee intimately, having done ar-
chaeological research around Tiberias.

They stopped at noon, to rest and eat their lunch
outside an abandoned Arab village whose inhabitants had
been ordered by Abdullah either to fight—which they had
no intention of doing—or to flee, which they did; all except one old man, the owner of a few goats, who came out
to sit with them, and to share a bit of their bread and
some cheese. "*Malesh Abdullah Chon f'i Kuzza Misheni*,"
he remarked philosophically, which Ben-Solis translated
somewhat freely as: "My goats are here; to the devil with
Abdullah."

To Joseph's surprise, the old man seemed to hold no
enmity toward the Jews. "But why are you surprised?"
asked Ben-Solis. "There is no need of hatred between the
Jews and the Arabs. It is the leaders, the *effendis*, who
have brought about the war, not this old man with his
goats. I tell you, it would be possible to live peacefully,
side by side, as they did at Mishmar Haemek, until Kaukji
of Lebanon . . ."

"That is your opinion," said Arieh, "and I spit on it."

Nevertheless, Arieh managed to elicit from the old

man the information that Tiberias was—as far as he knew
—in Arab hands. "In that case," said Malvois, "would it
be wise to proceed? I mean to say—we would be sticking
our heads into the noose, would we not?"

"Well, now," said O'Connor, "we didn't exactly come
out on a picnic, did we?"

"Perhaps we should take a vote," said Joseph, "seeing
that we are all in this together."

But Arieh shook his head. "Listen to me," he said. "If
we do not get to Tiberias, we are without direction. I do
not know where Alon is to be found, or what is developing
at Malkieh. To go blindly is not wise. Unless I can find
these things out in Tiberias, we may as well return where
we came from."

"There you are," said Bonneau. "*Le couteau sous la
gorge, le cul dans la merde: choissisez!*"

"Hell," said Joseph, "let's go."

They reached the city at sunset, having had to lie
low at one point to avoid an Arab column which appeared
to be moving east from the direction of Naharaim. As they
approached the outskirts from the west, they found Syrian
units already there, but managed, with Ben-Solis's help,
to slip through, and made their way into the town, where
they presented themselves at the Hotel Guberman on
Ahad Ha'am Street.

Arieh went off at once in search of information, and
returned at midnight with several bits of news: that the
Haganah High Command had ordered them apprehended
and returned forthwith to Tel Aviv, that the battle at
Malkieh was over, and that a considerable force of Iraqis
had crossed the Jordan south of Gesher to attack the
heights of Kaukab el Hawa as a preliminary to the attack
on the fortress of Gesher itself.

He had been told that the Palmach had a small company at Kaukab and that it was being reinforced by volunteers. "We should try to get there as soon as possible," he said.

"That is," he added, "if you wish to see fighting."

It seemed to Joseph that Arieh was looking at him with a certain constraint. He remembered the arms embargo declared against Israel, and it occurred to him for the first time that the young Israeli did not altogether forgive him for being an American.

At the same time . . . he had wanted so much, so very much, to stop at Degania. He realized with bitter disappointment that his reunion with Anna would have to be put off.

"Well," he said, "let's go. What are we waiting for?"

"We are waiting," said Ben-Solis, "for the Sabbath to be over."

They all stared at him in astonishment. "Are you serious?" asked Bonneau.

"It is the Sabbath night," said Ben-Solis calmly. "It is forbidden to travel on the Sabbath."

Arieh laughed harshly. "So," he said, "are we to hide here while the battle for the whole of Galilee takes place a few miles away?"

The battle for the whole of Galilee . . . Joseph thought again of Degania, so near to him now, and of Anna waiting for him. To be bottled up in Tiberias—to be shipped back to Tel Aviv . . .

"Look," he said, "we have absolutely got to get out of here."

Ben-Solis spread his hands apologetically. "I am sorry," he said. "I cannot leave; it is the Law. Not until the Sabbath is over."

"It will be too late," said Arieh grimly. "Already by tomorrow the roads will be blocked."

There was nothing to be done, Ben-Solis told him. To travel on the Sabbath was forbidden.

"Think, man," exclaimed O'Connor, "is there no one can give you absolution from this Sabbath of yours?"

"Only the chief rabbi of Tiberias," said Ben-Solis. "But he will not."

"*Merde, alors!*" said Bonneau.

To have come so far, Joseph thought, and to find himself boxed . . . what a thing to have happened! They could be killed, right there in Tiberias, for all this fellow cared . . . without even getting to Degania at all! Suddenly he was furiously angry. "Where is this chief rabbi of yours?" he demanded. "And how do I find him?"

"I do not know," said Ben-Solis simply.

"Well—will you go with me to find out?"

"I will go. But it will do no good."

It was almost two-thirty in the morning when Arieh, Joseph, and the young Talmudist arrived at the chief rabbi's house on the outskirts of Tiberias. They had been obliged to go slowly; part of the way the road was mined, the work of the Arabs when they had last been in possession of the city. They went carefully, keeping in the shadows of the buildings wherever possible; but no one noticed them. The Arab armies slept like the hosts of Midian.

Arieh knocked for a long time on the rabbi's door before it was opened and the chief rabbi of Tiberias himself appeared in front of them, dressed in a long white nightgown, and with a purple yarmilk on his head. His bristling gray beard reached to his chest; and his entire person, even in the nightgown, exhaled an odor of dignity and awe, of piety, and of severity. For a moment, transported back to his own childhood, Joseph quailed. The God of Israel is an angry God, he thought—dark, and inscrutable, and unforgiving. What does He care about the human heart? My grandfather never knew me.

The old rabbi was speaking, answering Ben-Solis; his voice sounded deep and musical in the still, cold night. He spoke in Hebrew, and Joseph had difficulty understanding him. "What are you?" he demanded of the young Talmudist. "Are you the Prophet Isaias? Are you so great in the sight of the Lord that for you He commands the sun to stand still, as He did for Joshua? Is it for you, perhaps, that the Holy One of Israel stops the war, from sundown to sundown, and the enemies of Israel also cease from fighting, out of respect for the Sabbath? It is written: 'The Philistine drew near morning and evening and presented himself forty days.' Is it also written that he took a holiday? But wait!—for you, for your sake, Goliath rests; he takes off his armor and drinks wine!"

The young Talmudist was shaken; he stood shivering in the cold night air, but he had not yet given up. "Then have I your permission to leave, Rabbi?" he asked.

The chief rabbi held up one finger in exhortation. "The war is a war," he declared. "Let it not be lost, between Friday and Saturday."

"Yet if it were Yom Kippur," Ben-Solis argued, "or let us imagine, the Passover . . ."

With a look of indignation, the old rabbi stepped back and shut the door firmly in his face. Ben-Solis turned uncertainly to Joseph. "Well," he said, "I suppose, in that case . . ."

"All right," said Joseph. "So now you know. Come along."

"Nevertheless," said Ben-Solis, "when the Tyrant Antiochus Epiphanes invaded Jerusalem on the Sabbath in the year 3834, his easy victory ended in defeat some three years later, giving rise to the festival of Hanukkah."

"That was three years later," said Joseph impatiently. "Come on! Step on it!"

In the last hours of the night, the station wagon crept out of Tiberias by a different route from the one by which it had come, and the little group of journalists, with Joseph in the front seat between Ben-Solis and the driver, headed south along the lake, past Degania, where the dawn bell was ringing to waken Mia in the children's house, and Anna in her room.

CHAPTER

19

DEGANIA, the oldest of the kibbutzim, lay on the gentle slopes above the Lake of Gennesaret; below the settlement, fishermen still cast their nets into the blue waters of the lake, as they had in the time of Simon Peter. In the settlement, men and women worked together; what a man could do, a woman could do. It was the rule of the kibbutzim that men and women shared equally in the common effort, and in the common rewards.

And these were the rewards to those who came to it as refugees from the fire-storms of the world. But even to others it offered peace to the heart, and manna to the spirit. It was like a monastery and a convent combined, whose members, having vowed themselves to one another, labored and prayed together, worked hard, loved, married, and brought up their children to be strong and healthy, to praise God, and to respect themselves and one another.

But it was also like a fort surrounded by enemies,

with watchers on the walls. It was only a little while since the Syrians had taken the nearby settlements of Massada and Sha'ar ha Golan, and had attacked Degania itself, only to be driven off by the defenders.

If no one in the community owned anything that he could call his own, the kibbutz itself had the best of everything to offer its members: the most modern equipment for farm and kitchen, a full library, a theater, music and the arts, several small factories, comfortable living quarters, good food, and work for everybody.

No one was idle at Degania. Some labored in the fields or in the dairies, some baked the bread or ran the laundries, some taught in the children's schoolrooms, some stood watch with rifles and machine guns. Anna worked in the orange groves, in the clear sunlight, within sight of the lake. The air smelled of oranges and bees and other blossoms.

The people around her were kind, and for the most part she was happy. She could see Mia during the play hour, teaching the other children her own little dance, walking in a circle, each child turning outward at the end of a verse, until they were all inside out:

> *"Lánc, lánc, eszterlánc,*
> *Eszterlánci cérna*
> *Cérna volna selyem volna . . ."*

The children lived together in their houses, studied together, worked, slept, played, ate together, all under the watchful eyes of their teachers. Every evening, after the children's supper, they came to visit their parents, bringing with them some sweet in a little basket, which was their dessert; and then for two hours the families were united, the problems and the joys of the day discussed, and the dessert eaten, after which the children went off to their dormitories, and their parents went to dinner in the great dining hall of the kibbutz.

After dinner there were occasional lectures, or concerts—a traveling theater troupe, or even motion pictures in the auditorium where the Philharmonic orchestra had been heard in happier times, where Menuhin and Isaac Stern had played and Marian Anderson had sung.

The orange and lemon groves and all fruit trees were in the charge of Menasha Feigen, and Anna was set to work as his helper during the period of her initiation into the life of the kibbutz. Menasha was one of the founders of Degania. Well into his seventies, burned by the sun, and tough as leather, he had a singularly gentle nature; with his long, white, flowing beard and his sparkling blue eyes, he might have been taken for Kris Kringle, or an early Christian martyr.

This old man had at once become Anna's friend. As they labored among the busy workers in the sunny groves below the settlement, he told her how the kibbutz had been founded, how he had come from Russia as a young man, and how he and others had bought the land from the British; how they had taken the rock and swamp and turned it into fertile earth, and built the houses; and how, even in those days, they had to fight off the Arab bands that came to plunder or destroy. He told her how the early settlements had armed themselves in defense, and how the Hashomer was organized, from which, in the nineteen-twenties, the idea of the citizens' army, the Haganah, was developed.

On her part, Anna would ask him such questions as what it had been like to live in Russia under the Czars, or to explain how it was possible to grow oranges without any pits—or whether he believed that widows should marry again.

"In the old days," Menasha told her, "in the Ukraine, a widow was considered class number One-A by the marriage brokers, because of her experience, her knowledge of cooking, and her deceased husband's household goods. Of course, if he left her nothing, that was a different matter. A woman of wealth owed it to her heart and to the community to give some worthy man a comfortable life sitting and studying the Torah."

"But if she had no wealth?" asked Anna.

Menasha's eyes danced. "A woman would have to be poor indeed," he declared, "not to give some comfort to a man. At least, for value received. But as for a young woman . . ."

He paused. "A beautiful young woman," he said. "A young Jewish woman . . ."

"With a child," Anna reminded him.

"This only multiplies the blessings," Menasha asserted stoutly. "Of course," he added, "I am not speaking now of the Ukraine. But in Israel—"

"It would not have multiplied the blessings in Buda Pesth," said Anna. "And I do not think Cleveland, Ohio, is so different."

Menasha gazed at her thoughtfully. "That is in America, perhaps?" he asked.

When she said yes, he nodded his head. "In America," he said, "everyone is wealthy. Even in the smallest houses they have running water, hot and cold, like in our own kibbutzim, and machines for washing clothes. I am sure that American men do not marry in order to sit and study the Torah. If they love, they marry.

"So, in America, where there is so much love going on, there are very few marriage brokers."

"Is that good, or bad?" she asked.

"I have not made up my mind," he replied. "There is still something to be said for the old ways."

He let his mattock rest for a moment, and scratched his head. "The tree that grows slowly," he said, "puts down the deepest roots."

The few, small days passed; and the week ended. Anna was tired; her bones ached. She tried not to think too much about things: it was peaceful at Degania, and she was grateful. It was already drawing toward the Sabbath; the evening was coming. Tomorrow they would rest, and she and Mia would be together all day. The blessed Sabbath, she thought; and thought: Josef is still in Tel Aviv.

But Joseph was on his way to Tiberias. She had no means of knowing, at that moment, how near he was to her.

As the day drew to its close, Anna and Menasha rested for a while in the shade of a carob tree, whose aromatic pods, dried in autumn to the color of old leather, are called St. John's bread by Christian children.

A plane rose suddenly above the hill behind them and passed overhead with a sound like a hornet, on its way to the airfields of Amman. For a moment, as it hung above them, solitary and dangerous in the clear blue of the heavens, Menasha gazed up at it soberly. "We are like mice on the ground," he said, "with a hawk in the sky."

Anna felt her skin prickle. "There is something terrible about a single plane," she said, "even more terrible than the great flights which used to pass over us at Maidenek. That was like a wave, like the sea, like thunder; but this single one in its loneliness is like a hunter, peering and seeking, spying out. . . .

"What have I done, Menasha, to be hunted?"

"You were born," said Menasha simply. "And so was I, and all of us since Abraham. Ask God what He wants of Israel, not me."

"But I do ask you," said Anna.

Menasha lifted his gnarled hands, palms upward. "To live," he said; "what else? To beautify the earth, as here in this soil which our hands have made to blossom. That is what God asks of Israel."

"I remember at home," she said, "from when I was a child, the fields glowing golden in the sun—the gleaming fields. I did not like to think of it for a long while, but now there is such happiness in that memory."

She smiled at him timidly. "I am only once more beginning to believe in life," she said. "For so long I believed only in death."

"Death is no enemy," said Menasha simply. "The true enemy is not he who destroys the body, but the spirit. To have made mankind distrust itself—that was the work of the enemy."

"You are not afraid to die, then?"

"Why should I be? Has it been so great, to be Menasha Feigen?"

"Perhaps it has," she said, looking around her at the green land glowing in the late afternoon light.

"Thank you," he said, smiling. "But simply to wake every day—that is not important. Even to taste life, to enjoy the sun and the fragrance, that is only for a little while. What is important is the spirit that lives on in what one loves. The truth is that God's love is like a lamp in the world; otherwise there would be only shapes of darkness and terror. To be a witness to this love, that is what God asks of Israel.

"To die without leaving love behind, without leaving behind anything one has loved, that is a death to be afraid of. Even God would be afraid of such a death. But to leave behind some light of the spirit, something one has loved: a child, a wife, a grove of orange trees . . .

"When the time comes, that is not a bad way."

Anna listened to him half dreamily, hearing also the coming and going of bees before the night, and an occasional cricket in the grass. She felt comfortable, but lonely; where was Joseph? Was he coming soon? Sometimes, she thought, when she was with Menasha, she felt like a child, a young girl with her father, waiting at home for a beau, a young lover, a visitor . . . someone. There was the same feeling of safety, of being protected . . . and of impatience. She realized that deep in her heart she had always expected her father to take care of her, to stand between her and calamity, to keep death away from her. And then he himself had been taken away, had left her all alone. She was pierced with a sudden grief, with a feeling of weakness and fright. I cannot protect anyone, she thought; I am not strong, I am only little.

The memories came back, and she shuddered, and clenched her fingers in the earth. "There is no good way to die, Menasha," she said. "I know, because I have seen it."

"I do not remember if I said there was a good way to die," remarked Menasha; "only that it was not a bad way. The moment of dying is in every case the same: a light is turned out. What is different is the state of mind; one would like to die not in an ugly manner, not in sorrow, and not in pain; better it should be over quickly when the time comes.

"But best of all, if one is with a beloved friend, in a happy moment, or else in the heat of battle: plock, a bullet, perhaps in the heart. In either case one is not thinking about it. Suddenly the light goes out, and that is all there is to it. One moment smiling or shouting a war-cry, and the next—where are you? Who knows? Wherever you are, there is no more rheumatism and growing old. No more little losses, little griefs; they are all canceled out by the big loss."

"You sound as though you looked forward to it," said Anna.

The old man gazed around him at the groves and fields which he loved. "I have been happy here," he said. "It has been a house full of joys to me, a home of delight. But man is given only a short lease, and must be prepared to leave at any time. Maybe afterwards to be with God; who can say?"

He smiled shyly. "I also whistle in the dark," he said. "It does not make the day come any sooner, but it makes a little sound."

At five o'clock Anna returned to her own clean, light, airy room, and a little later Mia arrived with her basket. It was the eve of the Sabbath. She had a lot to tell her mother; for one thing, there were three other Hungarian children in the school, one of them in her class. And the class had visited the dairy, and they had fed the chickens. Someday, when there was no danger any more, they would be allowed to go fishing on the lake. "It is the lake where the Rabbi walked on the water," she explained, "and fed everybody. Seven is a magic number, like the Menorah; did you know that?

"When is Victor Úr coming to see us?"

Anna fed her daughter a little cake from the basket. "Soon," she said. "He will come soon."

"Did you see the airplane?" Mia asked. "It went over us, and Bela said if it wished to, it could blow us all up."

"And who is Bela?" asked Anna.

"He's a boy in my class."

"Well, he shouldn't say such things then."

"I didn't care," said Mia stoutly. "I told him I'd seen lots of airplanes, and they didn't do anything. Anyway, you wouldn't let them hurt me."

Anna pressed the little head against her breast in sudden anguish. No, she thought. No! Don't say that! I cannot save you, my darling. Others, now, must keep you from harm.

After Mia left, she washed her face and her hands, and changed her dress. But she didn't go down to the dining hall, where the Sabbath candles were lit; instead, she stood by her window, looking out at the darkening light. Why didn't Josef come? She missed him so much. . . . Why had he roused her back to life again, only to leave her like this?

Presently she found herself pacing up and down in her room. It wasn't true, of course; he hadn't left her. She had left him; they had left each other. But why? Why? They had been together for such a short while. "Those whom the gods would destroy . . ." How unfair she had been! She could imagine the two of them, wandering through the orange groves, gazing down at the blue waters of the lake, stretched out in the shade of the carob tree, breast upon breast, mouth upon mouth. . . .

She pressed her hands to her flaming face. Why don't

you come? she cried out to him. Even for a day . . . for a few hours. We could picnic by the lake.

She sighed deeply. Was that why she was at Degania —to go on picnics? Such things belonged to the old world, the one that had ended in Maidenek, the one that she would never see again. Perhaps someday people would go on picnics in Cleveland, Ohio; perhaps lovers would lie together on the grass, lie sweetly together, appeasing each other's longing, assuaging each other's grief . . . together, quietly and gently, hungrily, tenderly, alone together, with no one to watch or listen or to come upon them suddenly where they lay. . . .

She didn't really believe it; she didn't believe that she would be one of them. ". . . *Then they are not grateful any more for what they have.*"

As the night darkened outside, her loneliness deepened. It was like something . . . it was like a feeling she had had long ago. . . . What was it? Something out of her childhood. She tried to think back, to remember; and then, suddenly, it came to her. It was the way she had felt that first year when she had been sent away to boarding school. She was homesick.

But where was her home? It was gone. She felt the long, empty, echoing corridors of that year of her childhood closing around her, the old forlorn clutch at her heart. Does one never grow up, then? she wondered. Does one stay only little forever?

She held her hands out in front of her and looked at her fingers, so worn now, cracked and grimed, and moved them up and down, lightly and tentatively, as though playing scales. There was a grand piano in the auditorium; she had seen it; it had stirred an old longing in her; perhaps they would let her play it someday—by herself, of course, when nobody was there. She must start to practice again, to take up the old things, to begin to remember something besides loneliness.

To help her forget the terrible years. And to help her forget Josef.

Yes . . . she must begin; at least, she must make a start; she must try to forget him, perhaps not altogether, but a little. Enough to make it possible for her to live, to wake up joyfully in the morning, to sleep peacefully at night, to spend the day at work in the orange groves—or wherever they might send her—to be happy with Mia in the evening, to rest on the Sabbath . . . to be without longing, without the never-ending ache.

Wearily she undressed, and went supperless to bed. On Sunday, the day after the Sabbath, there would be rifle practice. Everyone in Israel had to be a soldier—men, women, and children. She was frightened of guns, the terrible noise, the kick at the shoulder like the blow of a fist.

She must practice on the piano; she must start to play again. She and Josef would do sonatas together. They would teach Mia to play the cello . . . trios, quartets. . . .

But it was very wrong of the little boy—what was his name? Bela?—to tell Mia about airplanes and bombs. One shouldn't try to frighten people. There was enough trouble in the world.

The first movement of the Schumann Concerto went through her head: the rich, strong, masculine music, and yet so tender. She was back at the Conservatory again, in the big room with the little stage and the great Bechstein —and the notes rippling off her fingers. . . .

She slept, in darkness and in silence. She woke to hear the dawn bell ringing. Joseph heard it too, as the Ford swung west, crossing behind the settlement, above the lake. Kastler was sleeping; Ben-Solis was offering up the first prayers of the day.

Arieh was listening for the sound of gunfire in the south.

CHAPTER

[decorative rule]

20

KAUKAB ɛʟ HAWA stood high on a cliff overlooking the
Jordan Valley. It was an ancient fortress of worn stone and
crumbled mud-brick, reinforced here and there with tin
and corrugated iron and sandbags. Once, long ago, it had
been used as a signaling station to send messages by torch-
light from Jerusalem to Upper Galilee. Low, flat, and
earth-colored, it stood in a jumble of cavernlike rooms and
arched-over caves on the very brow of a precipice; it was
like a warren; in front of it the ground fell away in a sheer
drop to the floor of the valley many hundreds of feet below, while behind it the land, covered with rank grass and
with furze, sloped gradually downhill and rose again to a
saddle from which it made a sharp descent, with the road
winding and coiling like a snake.

It was this road they were on, starting from the base
of that ascent, some ten miles from Kaukab, and climbing steadily. It was already well into the morning, and the

Arabs—who fought when it suited them, never at night or during the hot hours of the day—were engaged in an assault on two lesser kibbutzim to the north and west. This was a small force of Syrian Irregulars, and not part of the attack on Kaukab el Hawa, which was facing the main Iraqi forces ten miles away.

Halfway up the hill, the station wagon ran into rifle fire, and Arab bullets began to plock the earth around them. Joseph looked at the little squirts of dust with surprise and with a curious sense of unreality. Someone was shooting at him; he felt very calm and cold inside, and amused in a superior sort of way. It seemed so unreasonable and impersonal, and that made it appear somehow ridiculous; he felt that he wanted to tell somebody about it.

But the station wagon was having trouble; the clutch was slipping, which caused the machine to go forward in sudden jerks, and finally to stall altogether. At that point the brakes also failed, and the car started to roll backward. It was too much for Moshe Halevi, the driver, who let go the wheel and dived for the floor under Joseph's feet.

Both Joseph and Arieh lunged for the wheel at the same moment, but Joseph, being nearer, reached it first, swung his legs up over the scrambling Halevi, and put the car into reverse, guiding it back down the slope to where the road leveled off enough for him to be able to bring it to a stop.

They sat for a while, considering. There was no other way to get to Kaukab el Hawa.

"I think we can make it," said Joseph, "if I give it the gun."

"Go ahead, then," said Kastler. He had already made a good breakfast of vodka and an orange from Tiberias.

"There is nothing worth seeing here," he said; "the view is from the top."

"Well," said Joseph, "hold on to your hats!" He realized that he was enjoying himself.

They roared back up the hill, the clutch slipping and Joseph playing it like a piano pedal, and gunning the engine for all it was worth. Once again they slid through rifle fire, the engine racing, wheels spinning, and the bullets missing them by inches. Everyone was shouting; in the general tumult Joseph thought he heard O'Connor's voice raised in the battle cry:

"*Abu! Abu! Eire Abu!*"

A mortar shell exploded a short distance away, and they drove through a shower of dirty smoke and flung earth, the wheels struggling in the dirt and the whole car moving for a moment crabwise, lurching and rocking. Then they were over the rise, and pointed downward again, and moving easily and fast, and Joseph found himself shaking. Now that the danger was over, for the time being at least, he felt a lurch of fear, and had to fight to keep himself from joining Halevi on the floor. "Well," he said bleakly, "wasn't that something?"

Bonneau leaned over the seat and gazed down at Halevi still sprawled at Joseph's feet. "*Cochon!*" he said. "*Espèce de chameau!*

"*Imbécile!*"

"He's the only one of us," said O'Connor mildly, "with any sense at all."

The road was rising again toward the fortress which hung on its cliff, facing the gray hills of Golan across the valley. They came up to it from the rear, past a pile of old Arab mattresses left out to rot, and two donkeys left behind by those same Arabs who had occupied the place at one time and, apparently unaware of its military importance or else afraid of being attacked by a superior force, had gone elsewhere, leaving the old stone ruins to be taken over by a company of the Palmach under the command of an eighteen-year-old sheepherder.

They found him at his command post, which was the only room in the rubble that still had a door. Lining the ridge, like sharpshooters, were about thirty young boys and girls: they looked to be little more than children. Another score or so were resting in the shade behind the walls, attending to a variety of things—talking, cleaning their rifles, writing letters, sewing, reading, and—in the case of two young women—washing their hair.

When Kastler asked the commander where his army was, the young sheepherder replied: "You are looking at it." And it was true: he commanded little more than a company. He had one Davidka mortar, some of whose parts were held together by string; a light machine gun, some rifles, and a few Sten guns. On the parapet he had mounted some dummies with broomsticks in a nest made out of sand bags, to give an appearance of watchfulness and strength.

At his order, a brown-haired, brown-eyed young woman showed them to the cavelike recess which was to be their headquarters. There they found straw mattresses already laid out on the hard earth under an overhanging arch, and were given blankets, and told where to find the latrines and the kitchen.

"You are welcome here," she said gravely in Hebrew, which had to be translated by Ben-Solis for the others. "It is good to think that from other lands someone is watching us."

She looked to be in her late teens; she could be,

Joseph thought, a co-ed in almost any American town, president of the student body, the popular halfback's date for the movies and a malted . . . except that she was carrying a Czech rifle. Her face looked as though it had dimples in it. She wore a copper bracelet on one arm, and a wrist watch on the other, socks and sandals, khaki trousers, a white blouse with the sleeves rolled up above her rounded elbows, a sweater tied around her hips, a yellow scarf around her neck . . . the high-school girl on a weekend hike in the country.

But on her head, like a warrior out of some antique battle frieze, she wore the great turtlelike helmet of the Royal British Navy.

Her name was Deborah, and Joseph felt his throat tighten as he looked at her. There was nothing tragic about her; she was a young girl, but she was Israel. There was something lovely about the proud and almost gentle way she looked out at the world. She should have been laughing and whispering with girls her own age, going to dances, dressing up, keeping a diary, dreaming, falling in love—eating ices on the terrace of the Park Hotel in Tel Aviv—or in front of a café on the Via Veneto in Rome. . . .

Or at a soda fountain in Cleveland, Ohio.

Joseph took many pictures of the fortress and its defenders that first day. He was excited and moved by what he saw: the Irgun fighters with their dark, eagle-fierce eyes under their woolen stocking-caps; the peach-fuzz cheeks of the girls, the clear, sad, gentle eyes of a young woman with a woolen scarf around her neck. He took pictures of men in discarded naval bailers and tipfors, old felt hats, helmets, and helmet-liners; the dreaming face of a poet, the open smile of an athlete, the contemplative gaze of a

scholar. Under a camouflage of nets between narrow, high
walls of brick and rubble, he took a picture of a girl with
earphones, talking into a radio transmitter and scribbling
on a pad, her helmet on her knees. Next to her, under the
nets, stood the company's armored truck. Rough ladders
made of cedar logs, like those in the pueblos of New
Mexico and Arizona, led from the lower levels to the
parapet: Joseph took a picture of a young woman on her
way up one such ladder, carrying her gun. On the parapet
itself, a light-machine-gun crew stood guard, watching and
waiting.

Smoke rose from the valley below, where the Iraqi
army camped; across the Jordan, in the distance, above the
grim, gray-brown and olive-colored hills, a bank of clouds
rode like a storm.

During the day, the Arabs kept up an intermittent
shelling of the ridge by two Sherman tanks, and during
the afternoon a Blenheim bomber came over twice and
dropped bombs. Whenever one of the 57-mm. cannons on
the tanks was fired, the watchers on the ridge could first
see the tank recoil, then a burst of gray smoke, and hear
almost at once a whir like a passage of grasshoppers, and
a thud as the shell hit—usually short, or to one side. The
tanks, the plane, were all part of the equipment left behind by the British for the use of the Arabs in their war
against the Jews.

"What I don't understand," said Joseph to the young
commander of the garrison, the sheepherder Dov Ben-
Abba, "is why the Haganah hasn't reinforced you."

Dov Ben-Abba, speaking through an interpreter,
took the time to explain that there were simply not enough
soldiers. In all of Galilee, the Haganah had only two brigades. It was the way of the Palmach to move in battalion

strength, to attack or to defend—and then to go elsewhere, wherever they were needed, leaving behind only a handful of the very young or the very old as a holding force. Reinforcements had been promised, because of the importance of Kaukab, but no one knew when they would arrive.

A few volunteers had come in from the nearby settlements. Ben-Abba's orders were simple: he was to hold the fortress with what he had.

As for the children—"Why not?" he asked. "They do not ask to be spared."

He gave a bitter smile. "We have no other choice," he said. "We are six hundred thousand people, men, women, and children, against thirty millions.

"And you Americans, with your easy riches—you do not help us very much."

Joseph didn't try to argue with him: what was the use? One Jew was never like another, and yet there was a bond; even between himself and this *sabra* to whom he could never explain what it was like to be born in the American Middle West, to live in New York and in Los Angeles, to work in Rome, to kneel in the Church of the Bambino. . . .

Arieh, too; to Arieh, Joseph was a Jew who had nothing to give but money. It made Joseph smile sadly: it was so much like his own bitter picture of his family, his rebellion against what had seemed to him, once, to be the thing above all things Jewish—the giving, and getting, of money.

The Chief Medical Officer, Dr. Morris Feinberg, once of Stuttgart and later of Buchenwald, came over and sat with him for a while. "Tell them," he said, "that we need medicines. Tell them that we are men, not rats. They are so used to thinking of us as rats."

The doctor had seen men naked, starving, racked to skin and bones, with great eyes staring hopelessly out of their skulls—animals set for slaughter. He had been one of them; and he had no illusions. "Men have only one improvement over animals," he said—"the thumb."

"Then why," asked Joseph, "are you here at the risk of your life: to save a few animals?"

"I am a doctor," said Feinberg simply. "What should I do? Take pictures?"

"Isn't it the soul," said Joseph, "that makes the difference? Rather than the thumb?"

"I don't know," said the doctor. "What is the soul? Did the Germans have a soul? A soul is perhaps something you fight for. Like the dignity of man: not to be a rat."

He glanced at the shoulder patch on Joseph's jacket which proclaimed him to be a foreign correspondent. "Maybe a neutral also has a soul," he said, and shrugged. "Who knows?"

Joseph went to his own cavelike shelter and lay down on his mattress. A neutral? he thought. Am I really a neutral? How can I be? My heart doesn't allow it; and the world calls me a Jew anyhow.

He tried to think about the Arabs, but he wasn't sure how he felt about them. For one thing, he didn't know any Arabs. These young Israelis, these *sabras*, had lived with them, had helped them with their crops and fields, had ministered to their health—and now they were fighting them. But it seemed to him that they felt less hatred for the Arabs than he did. Except for Arieh, of course. Arieh was what a Zealot must have been like, long ago, at the time of the destruction of the Temple. Men like Arieh, loaded with chains, marched in the Triumph, under the

Arch of Titus. But men like Ben-Solis and Dr. Feinberg marched there, too, and young girls like Deborah . . . and others, like himself and Anna. What a sad, strange, wild, tragic procession it must have been; he wondered if the faces would have looked familiar to him.

At sunset Jews and Arabs alike faced the east and bowed themselves in prayer; the blue dusk came down, and night rose over Amman like a sea. The Iraqi campfires twinkled in the valley below, while on the heights kettles of soup were heated, and small, round cakes of bread, made of flour and water and salt, and pounded thin, were baked on flat stones over fires, and sprinkled with sesame seeds. With the soup, made of vegetables, the bread, called *pita*, and a green pepper, Joseph made a satisfactory meal.

Afterwards he sat with O'Connor, Malvois, and Bonneau in the starry dark, with a bottle of brandy between them, and they talked about life at home in their respective countries. "I will tell you something which interests me very much," said Bonneau: "it is when I reflect upon Ireland, which has never won a war, but which nevertheless commands a respectful attitude from the great nations of the world."

"Ah, well," said O'Connor, "there's nothing like a quarrelsome poet or two to get respect for a country." "There it is," said Malvois ruefully; "we French are an industrial people, and so forth."

"You are also," said Joseph oratorically, "the refuge of the exiled and the oppressed." "Naturally," said Bonneau, "but within limits, *hein?* We do not let ourselves be carried away."

"Chopin," said Joseph. "Heine. Berlioz."

"They did not cost us a centime," said Bonneau.

Above them, on the parapet, Kastler was talking to the girl Deborah. The night, the wide and peaceful sky overhead, the clear shining stars, the high desert wind, cold and sweet, the deep moon-shadows on the cliff, all conspired along with the vodka he had consumed to fill him with a sense of boldness and romance, and he did not wish to waste it. They spoke in Hebrew and occasionally English, for Kastler knew several languages in addition to his native Russian. "Tell me," he said, for he was also very direct, "do you never want a man?"

The young Palmach girl looked at him in surprise; she had not expected such a question. "For what?" she asked.

"Well," he said, somewhat taken aback, "hm. That is to say . . . However . . ."

"If you mean, do I have a lover," she said simply, "then the answer is yes. He is with Yigal Yadin in the south."

"A lover?" exclaimed Kastler, in a shocked tone of voice. "At your age?"

It was Deborah's turn to be confused. "But," she protested, "you asked me, only a moment ago . . ."

"That was entirely different," said Kastler solemnly. "For a girl to have a man, or a man to have a girl—that is altogether natural, from the age of thirteen onwards. But to be in love! That is something serious; it takes experience. And in the middle of a war, besides!"

But he knew how to accept defeat, and to make a joke out of a rebuff. All at once he gave her a great clap of his big hand between her shoulder blades, which almost knocked her over. "God bless you," he said, laughing; "you are an honest girl; and I hope your lover comes safely back to you. Otherwise I would offer myself at this very moment."

"I'll remember that," she said, smiling. "After the war is over."

"Good," he said. "We will raise a large family, for Israel. Meanwhile, please give me a kiss, on credit."

Deborah put her face up, and kissed him dutifully, in a friendly way. "Hm," he grumbled, "I did not ask you to be sorry for me. I can see that your heart is somewhere else."

"I told you so," she replied calmly. "Besides, as you say—in the middle of a war, a girl is simply too busy."

Joseph lay on his mattress, looking up at that part of the sky which he could see from under the arch, and thinking about the fortress Kaukab el Hawa and its defenders. How young they were, for the most part! and how little they seemed to fear what might happen to them. Their duty was to kill. What was going to become of them? Was it possible for a young boy, a girl, to face death, to shoot down other human beings, and not have it affect them? Would they grow up without hearts, with only sadness where their hearts ought to be? But even as he questioned and wondered, he thought of the faces he had seen around him all day—the frank, high-spirited looks, the gentle expressions of the women, the lofty, devoted faces of the men; and he remembered that they had no hate for the enemy, only a love for their land, and for the company of mankind in which—in the world's despite—they proudly and obstinately counted themselves.

This little hilltop, this fortress dating back to Biblical times, this bare ridge of worn stones and packed earth, this warren of caves under the high desert sky—this was Israel.

Here, in such keeps and strongholds perched on the rim of valleys and in the Judaean hills, the Jews had faced their enemies from the days of Joshua, from the time of David.

But never with such courage, and with such regret.

In the dark hours before dawn, he woke to hear a single-engine Piper Cub go by overhead, and a little later a muffled explosion from the valley. There goes Greenfield, he thought, and saw him in his mind, a lonely speck in the black sky, over the Iraqi encampment.

"Good luck, Hyman," he said, and made a circle with his fingers in the air.

Below the parapet, a sentry girl was singing:

> "*Hineh ma tov*
> *Uma noim*
> *Shevet Acheem*
> *Gam yahad.*"

"Behold, how good and pleasant it is for brothers to dwell together as one."

CHAPTER

❧❧❧❧❧❧❧❧❧❧❧❧❧❧❧❧❧

2 1

THE TWO THOUSAND Iraqi troops in front of Kaukab el Hawa were part of a triple offensive designed to bring the Arab forces together in the form of a triangle at Nablus, Tulkarm, and Jenin, thus cutting off northern Galilee and securing a sweep to the south.

The Teggart Police Fort at Gesher was their first objective, but the main attack was launched at the heights of Kaukab el Hawa, whose capture would have made the Israeli positions around Gesher all but untenable.

Gesher itself, before which the Arabs had massed most of their artillery, was holding. It remained for Kaukab to hold also, until Carmel, with the pressure removed, could move on Jenin.

On both sides intelligence was faulty. Neither Brigadier Carmel nor Glubb of the Arab Legion had any knowledge of each other's plans, or the number of troops opposed to them. Had the Arabs known the truth about

Israel's few and ill-equipped forces, they would have attacked with confidence, driven forward on all sides, and cut Palestine in two. But the Arabs were far from being united either in plan or in purpose. The Arab states viewed one another with suspicion and with reserve; each wanted a private and personal victory for itself. Trans-Jordan's King Abdullah wanted Jerusalem; he had no intention of sacrificing his splendid Arab Legion to the designs of Syria or Egypt. The Arab Legion, which might elevate Abdullah to power, was as much a threat to Iraq and Lebanon as it was to Israel.

Nor were the Arab armies, whether Syrian or Egyptian, impelled by the same spirit which sustained and lifted up the ragged battalions of Israel. Arab fighters were violent, and excitable, but what were they fighting for? Between the Palestine Arabs of Haifa, of Lydda and Ramleh, and the soldiers of Naguib of Egypt, there was less in common than between the villagers of Abu Shusha and the colonists of Mishmar Haemek. The Irregulars of the ex-Mufti, Haj-Amin, and the cavalry of Glubb Pasha had no common cause; if they died, they died for their rulers, for the *effendis*, or for loot. The Jews who died, died for a better reason.

Volunteers kept arriving at Kaukab, a few at a time. They came from neighboring settlements, some even from as far away as Nazareth and Haifa. They came on donkeys, in lorries, or on foot, carrying with them food and whatever they had in the way of weapons, a gun, or even a pitchfork. One man, from Afule, brought along an accordion; the moment the first notes sounded in those crumbling walls, everyone began to smile.

Joseph talked to his mother in his mind. You never

really told me what music meant to us, he said to her, but then, you probably didn't know. To you it was always wealth, and glory; an honor, instead of what it really is: a way to speak to God. What was it David said? "Oh come, let us sing unto the Lord!" You see—I remember. But you'd have to be here with me, on a hill above Golan, to hear it.

He could imagine his mother's voice in answer, and he smiled at himself. *Do you have to make tsurus for me on a hill? Haven't I enough worries without you should get yourself shot?*

A hero he has to be!—for nothing.

On the twenty-third of May, the second day of Joseph's stay at the fortress, the Arabs mounted an assault on the cliff-face, which was their only way of taking Kaukab by storm. The tanks laid down a barrage behind which two Iraqui battalions started the attack, pushing upward from the valley floor, making a screen of the rocks, and covered by rifle, mortar, and machine-gun fire from below. The defenders waited quietly: Ben-Abba, keeping his forces hidden behind the walls until the shelling stopped, deployed them swiftly and suddenly onto the parapet, where, lying flat, they presented almost no target to the guns of the attackers, whom they proceeded to pick off one by one as they scrambled up the cliff.

Crouched behind the wall, Joseph listened to the sounds of the battle, with a beating heart and with a sense of unreality and high drama. He felt calm one minute, and the next he was overcome with anxiety for the Palmach, for the young men and women whom he had come to think of as his friends. He felt no overriding anxiety on his own account, just a cautiousness and coolness; his fear was for the others, and at the thought of their losing the battle. The cries of the attacking Arabs, the jarring report of rifles above him, the deadly chatter of the machine gun on the parapet, all flowed over him like a wave, drowning him in noise; but at the same time he wished that the Jews would shout a little, too; their silence frightened him.

He felt that he ought to be somewhere else, that he ought to be moving about, observing, taking notes; it was his first battle, and he was missing most of it, cowering behind a wall; but he didn't know where to go or what to do. He had a feeling that he'd be in the way; and besides, everything seemed to be happening around him in such a series of unrelated episodes, flickering on and off as in a dream. He saw Bonneau up on the parapet, grinding his camera at some unseen object; and Ben-Abba, pointing downward, and shouting something to a small group at his side. Slowly, with sickening clarity, he saw a girl fall from above and flop helplessly on the ground like a broken bird, and saw Dr. Feinberg run out to her and carry her, dangling in his arms, into a shelter. A dozen men scrambled past him, up the ladders to the ridge, and disappeared. An overpowering sadness seized him; he wanted suddenly to weep: for the broken girl, for her stillness and desolation, for man's fragile hold on life, the sudden end of laughter and singing, for man's forlorn and silent, desperate condition.

Someone went stumbling, slipping, and sliding down the ladder next to Joseph, blood running from his face; and Joseph closed his eyes and leaned back against the wall. A little later, Malvois came over to him, holding a brandy bottle. "Here," he said, "take some of this. False courage—but nevertheless."

"Hell," said Joseph. "I don't need it."

"Certainly not," Malvois agreed. "You are a brave one, who cannot keep from shaking."

Joseph took a big swallow of the brandy; it burned his throat and made him cough, but it warmed him, too, and he felt better. He realized that he had been shivering, although it was a hot day.

Malvois smiled at him amiably. "There is no cause to be ashamed," he said. "It is easily more agreeable to be fighting a battle than watching it."

"I keep thinking of the families," Joseph said in a surprised way. "I never thought of the families before. They have mothers and fathers; and they get killed so easily."

"It is very difficult for a newspaperman to make accommodation to this," said Malvois—"the fact of the unimportance of life. To understand that a strong young man, a beautiful young woman, can be crushed—*écrasés* —like a bug, in the twinkling of an eye! One asks oneself: where is the dignity of such a performance?—and one becomes mournful.

"However—after a while, one comes to accept; one comes not to think about it. One becomes inured, one becomes a hard case, and one keeps a bottle handy."

"I'll remember that," said Joseph.

"Also," said Malvois, "always remember to keep the head down, and so forth."

"Thanks," said Joseph. "I'll remember that, too."

Above them, on the parapet, the gunfire was dwindling; for a panic-moment, Joseph thought that the Israelis had been overrun. But when there were no more Arab cries, he realized that the Arab charge had been stopped, and that, for the time being, the Jews had beaten off the attack. Actually, as he later learned, the Arabs, seeing several of their number fallen among the boulders, had first wavered and then broken, and had run for it, leaving their dead behind.

O'Connor came around the corner, and clapped him on the shoulder. "How are you?" he inquired solicitously. "You look a bit green. Whatever did you stay outside for?"

"I'm all right," said Joseph. "How did we do?"

The Iraqi tanks had resumed their shelling, and the remainder of the Israelis came down from the parapet. Their losses were three killed and several wounded: Ben-Abba figured the Arab losses to have been ten times that number. But the odds were still weighted heavily against him. *"Tonnerre!"* said Bonneau. "Take ten from sixty, that is one-sixth; but take a hundred from two thousand, and that is only one-twentieth.

"Saperlipopette!"

They found Kastler leaning against the wall outside the dressing station; he looked pale, and his eyes seemed wet and slightly bloodshot. Bonneau went up to him and put his arm around his shoulders. *"Finie, la petite Deborah, n'est ce pas?"* he asked gently. "I saw it happen."

Kastler nodded his great head. *"Finie,"* he said.

And pointing to a spot between his eyes, he added:

"She got it there."

Joseph stared; it seemed impossible to imagine that young, warm, eager girl no longer young and warm, but cold and still, staring out with sightless eyes at nothing . . . all her courage, her sweet and subtle thoughts, memories, hopes, dreams, snuffed out like candle flames, suddenly and altogether gone, vanished as though they had never been . . . except as they might echo from time to time in someone's memory, always fainter and fainter. . . .

They comforted Kastler as best they could, and the

big man appeared grateful, though somewhat embarrassed. "I've seen a lot of people die," he said; "I don't know why this hit me. I didn't even know her very well. We were just talking around . . . you know . . . like a man and a woman. She had a lover in Yadin's Brigade."

"She was a nice girl, the little Deborah," said Bonneau.

"I guess that's what's so hard to get used to," said Joseph.

At the command post, where they went to get the official report of the action, they found an old Arab woman and a young Arab boy, whom the commotion of the attack and the rush and movement of the defense had flushed out of a cave in which, apparently, they had been hiding ever since the Palmach had taken over. Guarded by two soldiers with rifles, they stared around them at their captors, the woman small, wizened, half starved, looking— Joseph thought—like a trapped rat, and the boy frightened, too, but insolent and full of hate. To judge from their manner, they both expected to be killed out of hand; and when one of the soldiers offered the old woman a pepper, she first drew back and hid her face in her hands, and was persuaded to take the bit of food only after a great deal of patient coaxing.

Arieh, standing near, gazed at them with a veiled and bitter expression. Joseph knew what he was thinking: An eye for an eye and a tooth for a tooth. An old woman and a boy for Deborah.

The woman was little more than a filthy bundle of rags and bones, and the boy had an insufferable air of meanness and arrogance about him. Joseph turned away from them in distaste, and with a sense of overwhelming weariness. Could he hate these people? Was he to forgive them? For what? They hated him, with every fiber of their being. Arieh is right, he thought; I don't belong in this business.

And feeling suddenly very lonely, he went off and lay down on his mattress in the shade of the archway.

Lying there, he let himself think about Anna. He conjured up her image; he tried to remember everything he could about her. As long as he kept her face in front of him, he could keep the sadness and the bitterness out of his thoughts.

He wondered what she was doing; he imagined that he heard her speaking to him, and tried to remember the exact tone of her voice. "Someday we will make a wish together," she had said. "Joo," she had called him; and "*drágám.*"

"I miss my girl," he told O'Connor, when the Irishman came to join him later. Then, feeling embarrassed at having made such a confession, he smiled self-consciously.

"You don't mean Pat?" asked O'Connor. "Priscilla?"

"No—not Pat."

"I didn't think you did," said O'Connor, relieved. "It would be this woman Anna then, I take it."

"I want to marry her," said Joseph, for the first time.

O'Connor clucked sympathetically. "Well, now," he said. "Have you told her?"

"Yes," said Joseph, "I think so." But then he hesitated. "I don't know," he said.

"And the child? What's her name?—Mia?"

Joseph smiled dreamily at the stained and moss-covered stones above his head. "It's funny," he said; "I never thought about having a child. I wouldn't even know if I wanted one of my own. But Anna's child . . .

"I could love Anna's child, Kevin," he said.

. . .

They had allowed her to practice on the piano in the main room at Degania, and she was playing there now, in the hour allotted her for lunch—a time when she thought she would be least likely to disturb anyone. The children, who had already eaten, were playing outside on the grass of the playground; she could hear Mia's voice singing her little song and then suddenly rippling into laughter and squeals. The child is happy, Anna thought gratefully; already the memories are fading from her mind, as they are from mine. Except for Joseph . . .

Not that I had the choice of where to go; there was nowhere else. Though, perhaps—if I had met him sooner . . . before I was already committed to this course . . . But he might not have wanted me. It was only that on the ship . . . I did not make it very easy for him. . . .

She was playing Chopin, the C sharp minor Scherzo, Op. 39, playing it as well as she could, which was not nearly as well as she would have liked—a fact which made her toss her head in discouragement. She let her work-coarsened hands lie still for a moment in her lap, and stared out across the long room, hearing in her mind the way the cascading runs should have sounded, the way she had heard Hofmann play them once in Vienna. She could bear to remember it now, that world which seemed—looking back at it—to have been on the other side of the moon.

Now there was only Mia—and Joseph. He had said he would come; but the war . . .

Would it ever end? At Degania they said that there was serious fighting going on only a short distance away at Gesher, and at a tiny hilltop fortress called Kaukab el Hawa—Star in the Wind. The Palmach who were there needed volunteers, and Menasha had told her that he was going. She had begged him not to go, her friend—but he had answered her by saying that if he did not go the Arabs might break through to the west, and then there would be no friends anywhere, for her or for anyone else. "I am an old man," he had said; "my home is a green hill and a valley, and trees planted there by my own hands. It is all I have to leave behind me for those who come after. I am going to Kaukab, to keep it mine, and theirs."

He was leaving in a lorry the next day, with a dozen volunteers from the settlement. Degania's own defenses had been strengthened, and sentries watched from the watchtower of the kibbutz, and on the rooftops.

Anna sighed, and let her hands drift once more across the keys. The laughter of the children came in through the open window and mingled with the notes, with the rippling raindrops of the Scherzo, and with the sound of a plane somewhere in the sky.

Her thoughts slid off the edge of her mind, and she dreamed for a while as her fingers moved mechanically but a little clumsily up and down on the keyboard.

> "*Lánc lánc eszterlánc . . .*
> *Forduljon ki Marika*
> *Marikának lánca.*"

She dreamed, in a little island of quiet in a noisy world. How little that world had changed, over all the centuries; so, too, in Jerusalem, children had laughed and sung long ago, in the small time between the wars . . . before the chariots ground them under, and they went to weep by the waters of Babylon. And the young men, and the old, went to battle, and were killed, and the cities taken. Egypt, Nineveh, Rome, the Diaspora—Cologne, Frankfurt, Kiev, the camps—Dachau, Auschwitz, Buchenwald, Maidenek . . . she saw the history of her people in a great cloud through which the storms crashed and the lightning played, with moments when the heavens opened and the clear golden light shone through; with the rainbow and the rain, with thunder and bright winds. . . . She saw herself in Vienna, in Buda Pesth, with the sweetness of her own springtime all around her; she heard the shouts of *Anschluss,* the terrible *Sieg Heil;* she fled again at night across the borders, in the shadowy moonlight among the trees; she slept once again in the crowded hold of the *Teti.* . . .

History: she was part of it; she had lived in history, in days as bright and golden as those of Solomon, in times as dark and bitter as those of Jeremiah.

What now, Anna Muhlmann, born Czeffy of Buda Pesth?

Her hands, lifted from the keys, stayed suspended in midair. An inner sense told her that something was the matter; something was wrong, she could feel it. She didn't know what it was yet—but her heart was suddenly beating fast, and at the same time her whole body was still. There was a curious, breathless silence all around her, and it was quiet outside where the children had been playing. They weren't playing any longer, or if they were, it was some strange, unusual game. And the sound of the plane was too loud . . . much too loud. That was it—the sound of the plane. . . .

She heard the sudden shrill whistling dive of the bomb, and the house shook a little when it hit in the playground outside. The noise and the shock of the explosion deafened her for a moment. A little plaster dust fell from the walls.

She was still sitting with her face in her hands when the searchers found Mia's body.

CHAPTER

(((+(((+(((+(((+(((+(((+(((+(((+(((+(((+(((+(((+(((+(((+(((

22

THE LORRY from Degania reached Kaukab toward noon, having encountered no rifle fire at the spot where the Arabs had waylaid Joseph and his party. All during the journey, Anna leaned against Menasha, her eyes closed and her head bent, not looking up. What was there to see? She was going to Kaukab because she couldn't stay at Degania any longer. And because it made no difference to her whether she lived or died.

"Now I know there is no God," she had said, standing dry-eyed over Mia's grave. She had shed too many tears in the past; there were none left for the present.

It was Menasha who recited the Kaddish over the dead child: "*Yisgadal v'yiskadash sh'meh rabbo.*" But he did not praise God in his heart as he was supposed to. And he did not make the mistake of trying to offer Anna any consolation. What comfort can I give her? he thought. It is

275

true that she has been hunted down. Even this little was denied her: to leave one child behind in memory that she lived.

"If this is the way God loves His people," said Anna, "I will not ever speak of Him again. I will not go out any more to greet the Sabbath, or light the candles for the prayers. I will not be a witness for Him: if this is His universe, I renounce it, I will have no part in it."

"You have not been asked," said Menasha sternly. His heart ached for her, but he offered her no pity, for her own sake. She understood, and was grateful. Pity would not make her grief any more bearable.

The day was hot, and Anna was mortally weary. She had no thoughts in her head; her movements were mindless and automatic. At one point the lorry stopped to let a flock of sheep cross the road, and between its stopping and starting up again, she fell asleep with her head on Menasha's shoulder. For a moment or two, half sleeping and half waking, she thought that she was a child again, resting against her father.

She was scarcely aware of her arrival at the fortress, stumbling out of the lorry and following Menasha in a daze along the old stone walls and down rubbled alleys, to sink down at last onto a mattress under an archway, and there to lie with closed eyes, not caring, feeling nothing, sinking deeper and deeper into a blessed oblivion, all lost, all forgotten, washed away . . . only to hear, suddenly, through the peace and the forgetting, small and far away, a voice calling her name:

"Anna!"

It seemed like a voice in a dream; it took her a moment to place it, to remember whose voice it was . . . to tell herself that it couldn't be, to realize where she was, to rouse herself, to remember, to lift her head, to open her eyes . . . and find herself staring into Joseph's face as he bent over her.

In that moment of astonishment there was such a conflict within her, of delight and grief, of gratitude and anguish, of belief and disbelief, that she froze, unable to speak or even to move, her eyes wide and dark against the pallor of her face. She seemed to be staring at him almost in terror, before the warmth came back to her cheeks, and the color to her eyes, and her rigid body flowed once more into lines of softness and tenderness; and with a single cry of "Joo!" she threw herself upward into his arms.

Later, while he held her, she wept as she had done once before, and, as before, repeated over and over again:

"Why? Why?"

He had no answer. He wanted so much to comfort her, but there was no way.

She was no longer the Anna he had known in Tel Aviv. She had drawn back into herself again—but with this difference: that she loved him. And that only served to make her more vulnerable; it was the breach in her defenses through which pain could enter. "You are all I have," she said to him over and over; "you are all that is left me."

There was something about the way she surrendered to grief that almost frightened him. It was too much like the girl falling from the parapet and lying there, flopping a little, on the ground. She was stricken; she was like Deborah, for whom there was nothing to be done.

O'Connor, Malvois, and Bonneau gave up their mattresses and moved to another shelter, so that Anna and Joseph could be together. "He is very kind," she said; "your friend, this Mr. O'Connor."

"Yes," said Joseph, "he is kind." It hadn't occurred to him before.

That day the tanks shelled the fortress again, and a probing column tried an ascent at one edge of the cliff, but gave up on being fired on from the ridge. The volunteers from Degania were given rifles—those who hadn't brought weapons of their own—and posted to the Palmach units, all except Anna and Menasha; she was asked to help in the kitchens, and Menasha, being thought too old for actual battle, was given a donkey and a shovel and sent out to the back of the fortress to fill burlap sacks with sand. "I suppose I shouldn't complain," he said, "since I am helping with the fortifications, but I am a good shot —and my life could be more easily spared than that of some young person." "Grandfather," said Ben-Abba earnestly, "I am keeping you in reserve, in case things go wrong."

"Very well," said Menasha, "in that case. But remember: I was fighting Arabs before you were born." "They are all dead now," said Ben-Abba, "those Arabs you fought. These are their sons and grandsons."

"I will do the best I can," said Menasha, shouldering his shovel.

And Anna, too, said to Joseph: "I will do the best I can." But her mind was very tired, and she wanted only to sleep.

Yet in another moment she cried out: "I must fight; I must avenge myself. . . ."

Then, again, she buried her head in his shoulder. "There is already too much hate in the world," she murmured. "Forgive me."

After a while she said shakily: "I can at least make *Knaidlech* to put in the soup."

But when she went to the kitchen, she begged Joseph to go with her. "I am so frightened," she said, "of something which I do not know. For the first time I feel a malevolence in the world, coming to me not from men— but from God. My little Mia harmed no one; she did no one any harm."

"Don't, Anna," said Joseph. "Don't, my darling."

She looked at him with brimming eyes, and nodded gravely. "I will not think about it," she said. "But do not go very far away, please. . . ."

Joseph had no intention of leaving her; all he wanted was to be near her and to be able—somehow—to comfort her. She went so swiftly from one mood to another: from bitter grief to an almost childlike astonishment, from deepest despondency to a sort of muted joy. He knew that he couldn't make up to her for her loss; that his love, his presence, wasn't enough to comfort her. "I don't know what to do," he said to O'Connor. "I feel so helpless."

"Again?" asked O'Connor.

Again? Joseph didn't understand him at first. But then, as O'Connor's meaning sank in, he flushed, and turned away. "You mean Priscilla, don't you?" he said in a strained voice. "I wasn't very grown up in Rome.

"How do you grow up, Kevin?"

"It takes time," said O'Connor.

Anna and Joseph ate their supper on the parapet in the twilight, seeing the hills of Amman dark against the night which rolled up behind them like a cloud, and the campfires of the Iraqis in the valley below twinkling like fireflies in the dusk. The fires covered a large part of the valley, and Anna's eyes widened as she gazed down at them. "Can we really hold off such a great army," she breathed, "when we are no more than a handful?"

"If we get reinforcements," said Joseph, "we will hold."

"Where are they to come from?"

"Ben-Abba says they will come."

The night sank slowly down around them; above them the sky grew luminous and the stars appeared; the moon rode overhead. Anna looked up at the vast starry dome, as though she wanted to stare it down. "It is an empty sky," she said. "There is no one in heaven."

He put his arm around her, and felt her shivering. "It isn't empty, Anna," he said. "It is full of sound."

"Of weeping," said Anna. "That is empty enough."

"Hush," said Joseph. He sat rocking her gently, her head on his shoulder, her dark hair cascading over his jacket. Moonlight silvered them both.

It was a night in Palestine, like no other night that he had ever known. The heavens reached up over them in a great peaceful arc, over Israel, over the deserts and the valleys, over the hills; the stars seemed to glow with more than usual brightness, steel-silver and butter-gold. No one in heaven? No sound but weeping? The sky was a river of movement, chariots and archers sweeping across the heavens in shadowy tides of air; it was full of ghostly sounds: the ram's horn, the bugles of Nineveh, the drums of the Crusades—the bagpipes of Allenby. And Joseph, gazing down at Anna's dark head, thought with awe of the long, long years of history, of all who had loved and died and been swept away in this land, in Gilead, in Babylon, in Askelon, in Tyre . . . who had held one another under such a moon, murmuring as they were murmuring . . . promising, hoping, longing, whispering . . . before the spear was thrust, the arrow loosed, the knife driven home. Thousands of years, millions upon millions of hearts beating each to the other in delight and great plans . . . in heartbreak and despair. . . .

"*Behind us . . . just over the hill . . . lies Parthia. Do you see beyond those hills, the Gauls?*"

That had been in Rome—how long ago? Priscilla's world: the Gauls, the Teuton forests, the Saxons. . . . the cemetery at Marblehead. Strange to think of that now. . . . Well, this was his; it was his turn to feel the earth turning under his hand, carrying the centuries with it.

When he bent to kiss her, she returned his kiss briefly, and he felt again that withdrawal, that turning of her body away from him. "I am tired," she said. "Let us go to sleep."

He helped her down the ladder, and in the moonlight they found their mattresses in the recess of the archway. Joseph covered her with his own blanket, and she caught his hand and put it to her lips as she had done once before. "Thank you, dear Josef," she said, "for being good to me, and for being patient with me. I do not have much courage."

Bending his face to her, he kissed her hair. "You have enough," he said.

She fell asleep quickly, but Joseph lay awake for a long while, in a strange, disturbed state; he yearned toward her in pity and distress—and yet, there was so little he could do! He hated to feel so helpless. He tried to put his mind on other things, to think about his cameras, about tomorrow's fighting . . . instead, he lay there remembering . . . going back in his mind to Rome and beyond, to his years in Los Angeles with the orchestra, to his days in New York, to the debut, the concert that never was, the Conservatory, the butcher shop, the lonely child sawing away at his exercises. He had run away from it all—and it had all come to this, to this moment, in a beleaguered fortress above the river Jordan.

What strange paths one follows; and who knows where they lead, to what end? If he were to settle in Israel? It was not an impossibility. He gave himself over to a waking dream; he saw himself and Anna married, living in a city like Tel Aviv or Haifa, going back to music again —perhaps a quartet, a chamber-music group . . . or perhaps in a house on a hill looking out over the sea, the "blessed sea" which had brought them together. He imagined his mother coming to visit them all the way from Cleveland. "Mom," he would say, "this is Anna"; and Anna would call her "Mother." He would study Hebrew; their house would have a garden, with flowering trees and bushes, with olive trees and cypress, like in Italy. . . .

He was roused from his half-waking, half-dreaming by the sound of shots; and for a second he forgot where he was. Then he thought the fortress was under attack. A moment later he realized that the shots had come from inside the walls, and heard a bullet ricochet off stone near by. A group of men in Irgun caps, led by Arieh, raced past him, followed by Bonneau, who was putting on his jacket.

"What is it?" Joseph called out to him. "What has happened?"

"*Peste!*" cried Bonneau. "It is that accursed Arab boy, who has gotten hold of a gun."

By this time Anna, too, was awake; roused from deep slumber, she clung to Joseph in fright, not knowing what was happening. "It is nothing," he told her. "An incident: nothing. Go back to sleep."

"You are leaving me? No—stay with me."

"Only for a moment. It is nothing, truly."

With a sigh, still dazed with sleep, she let her arms fall to her side. "Only for a moment," she murmured; and slept again.

The Arab boy stood in an angle of the fortress, with a rifle in his hands. The men of the Irgun, taking cover along the walls, were creeping up on him; whenever one of them showed for a moment in the moonlight, the rifle was brought to bear on him. Keeping low, Joseph joined Bonneau, who was crouched behind a pile of rubble. "It is an uncomfortable situation," said Bonneau.

"How did he get the gun?" asked Joseph.

"He stole it," Bonneau declared indignantly. "The child has no honesty!"

They heard Arieh give a staccato order, and saw the Irgunists aim their rifles at the dark shadow where the boy stood. "Aha," said Bonneau, "they are going to shoot him finally."

"I'd rather not see it," said Joseph.

The Frenchman looked at him in surprise. "Why not?" he demanded. "After all, he did not care if he shot you."

Joseph didn't answer. He felt uncertain, and confused; the boy was just a child, and grown people didn't go around shooting children. But he was an Arab, and the Arabs had killed Mia, who was a child, too. . . .

"The hell with him," he said, and turned away.

But when there was no sound of rifle fire, he turned back again. An old man stood there now, between the Irgunists and the child. As the others watched, the old man walked slowly toward the boy. "Give me the gun," he said in Arabic.

It was Menasha. By way of answer, the boy spat at him, and fired. The bullet grazed Menasha's side, and spat-tered against the wall behind him. It did not stop his steady advance; going quietly up to the boy, he took the rifle out of his hands, and gave him a sharp cuff on the side of the head. "You do not even know how to shoot," he said disdainfully. "Your father was a dealer in mutton fat."

Weeping and muttering, the boy was led out to the waiting men. Now that he was among them, they didn't know what to do with him. But Arieh drew his knife.

Menasha placed the boy behind him. "Peace, Arieh," he said. "Sleep on this a little."

"You yourself are bleeding, old man," said Arieh roughly. "Others might have died."

"*Na*," said Menasha; "it is not the first time my blood has spilled. There is still plenty left."

"Then step aside," said Arieh, "and let me do what is to be done."

"What is that, my son?" asked Menasha quietly. "Are you one of Herod's men, to kill children? Or is this perhaps the King of Araby, this sniveling crust?

"Sleep on this thing, Arieh. He has already been shamed."

"I will sleep better when his throat is cut," said Arieh.

The two men faced each other: the young, black-bearded Irgunist and the white-haired farmer. Joseph could feel the silence close in around them, the moment drawn out like a fine, thin wire; and in his heart, too, the antagonists confronted each other, the light and the dark—Arieh with his anger, Menasha with his pity. Yet both were Israel, and each was Israel.

Before either one could move, Ben-Abba had pushed

his way between them. "Go back to your posts," he said
to the others. "Tomorrow we will talk about this."

Without a word—almost gratefully, Joseph thought—
the riflemen faded back into the moon-shadows, to resume
their watch on the campfires below. Ben-Abba turned to
Menasha. "Old man," he said gently, "I was perhaps
wrong in sending you out with the donkey.

"Go to the dressing station now, and let Dr. Feinberg
look at you."

To Arieh he said simply:

"Tie up that boy."

But Arieh did not move. "The Irgun does not take
orders from the Haganah," he said curtly.

"In Kaukab el Hawa," said Ben-Abba, "even the Irgun takes orders. Or the Irgun leaves. The road is open.

"Tie the boy," he said quietly, "and set someone to
guard him."

Slowly, unwillingly, Arieh put his knife back in his
belt. "Very well," he said at last, "if you order this thing.
On your head, Ben-Abba.

"I will tie him the way I would tie a pig."

"Tie him the way you would a goat," said Menasha.
"A young goat, with very small horns."

CHAPTER

23

SAMI, the Arab boy, and his grandmother were shipped out the next night in a lorry with the wounded, who were being evacuated to the settlements near Afule and Nazareth. During the day there had been two more assaults on the fortress, the Iraqis storming the cliff in waves behind a barrage from the tanks, only to be turned back each time at the crest by the thin, deadly line of rifles along the parapet. But the losses to the little garrison were heavy. The Blenheim came over twice and dropped its bombs, and once made a strafing run the full length of the fortress, raking the walls with machine-gun fire. In this attack alone, seven of the Palmach were wounded—a schoolteacher, two young farm helpers, a shoe salesman, and three girls from Mishmar Haemek.

To Joseph it was like being caught in a kaleidoscopic dream, a nightmare of jarring crashes and sudden shocks, of endless noise, of smoke and haze and the bitter taste of dust and gunpowder, of rocking waves of air, appearances and disappearances, and an endless thin sound of wailing which seemed to come from nowhere and everywhere.

But this time he wasn't crouched behind a wall; excited, confused, not quite sure where he ought to be or what he ought to be doing, he dashed from post to post with his camera, sometimes following Bonneau or O'Connor, sometimes finding himself alone. He heard bullets rip past him like flights of bees, but he didn't think about them; he paid no attention to them. It wasn't because he was brave, it was only that he was busy, and that after a while they seemed to have no connection with him.

Toward the end of the afternoon, Malvois caught a shell fragment in his shoulder, and was taken to the dressing station. "*Tonnerre de Dieu!*" exclaimed Bonneau, when he and Joseph went to see him. "Have you nothing better to offer history than that?"

Malvois, who was pale from loss of blood, smiled at him smugly. "Look," he said, waving his good arm around at the bare walls of the dressing station, "*tout confort moderne!* In addition, this little incident, which aches, will unquestionably take me back to Paris in time to see the last of the chestnut blossoms."

He sighed, and closed his eyes, suddenly weary and unhappy. "Damn," he said. "*Je suis foutu.*"

Anna was on the parapet. She had been helping Dr. Feinberg in the dressing station, but after the attack by the plane, she snatched up a rifle from one of the wounded girls and went out with it into the smoky, hot sunshine. She was lying close to Menasha when the second assault rolled up the hill.

Like Joseph, she felt no fear. But where he was keyed

up by excitement, Anna was quiet and almost detached. She knew, at one moment and another, that she might be killed, but it didn't seem to matter. She had no feeling of wanting to hold on to her life; if they wanted it, they could have it. They'd get what was left of it, and that wasn't much. She kept loading and firing almost mechanically; when she hit anyone, she felt a moment of reality, as though she had reached out and touched him.

On the ridge, watching the second wave of attackers reel backward down the hill, Ben-Abba wearily wiped his face and gave orders for the Palmach to take shelter once again. "Now the shelling begins," he said unhappily, looking around him at the wounded who were being helped or carried off the parapet. It was the cannon from the tanks which had done so much damage that day, and which continually tipped the scales in the enemy's favor by keeping the defenders pinned down during the start of each assault. The Arab aim wasn't good, but one shell exploding inside the walls could do a great deal of damage. And then, besides, there was the plane, against which the Israelis had no weapons except their rifles and one .30-caliber machine gun—too light to be of any use.

"If only we had a fifty," said Ben-Abba. "One heavy piece, to shoot that vulture out of the sky!"

At sunset the Arabs withdrew, leaving the day's dead strewn on the hill among the boulders; already the smell of death was in the air from the assaults of the day before. As the twilight deepened, Ben-Abba ordered out a detail to cover the bodies with earth, and lanterns and torches flickered for a while along the slope.

In the darkness of the recessed archway, Anna and Joseph lay beside each other without speaking. They were exhausted, physically and emotionally; and at the same time, they were unable to rest. It had been too much: battle, love, loss, and grief, all poured together into so small a time. I have killed, Anna thought over and over; I have killed.

She waited with closed eyes for a feeling of satisfaction, of regret, of revenge, of guilt—anything; but all she felt was emptiness, and an infinite weariness of body and spirit. And like Iago she thought:

Death is nothing.

As for Joseph, on the other hand, no matter how tightly he closed his eyes, he could still see the attack swirling around him. "Anna," he whispered at last, raising himself on one elbow, "are you awake?"

"Yes."

"I can't sleep."

"I cannot, either."

"There's no use lying here," he said. "I'm going to walk a little, back of the walls."

"I will go with you, then."

Hand in hand, they went out through the darkened fortress to the wide empty fields in back. The full moon, rising over the valley, made strange shadows around them, and threw a cold light on the old stone, the low walls, and the flat roofs. They could see the sentries standing silent and motionless on the parapet in the moonlight. A few lanterns glowed gold and yellow in the walls, where groups of men and women sat cleaning their rifles, laying out ammunition, talking, and resting. Somewhere an accordion was playing, and a man was singing.

> "*Ze dodi ze reie*
> *Benot Yerushalayem*
> *Ze dodi . . .*"

"This is my beloved, my friend.
O daughters of Jerusalem,
This is my beloved . . ."

The sweet tenor voice floated clear and small in the still night air. It was such a little sound in the vast silence, plaintive and tender; it seemed to come from far away in space and time, from courtyards long crumbled into dust, from hilltops receding, lost in the deepening night like waves at sea farther and farther out, dimmer and dimmer in the distance.

"If I forget thee, Jerusalem . . ."

The fields around them in the bright moonlight were like hillocks and hummocks of snow. All at once, Anna let go of Joseph's hand, and stood still. Lifting her arms to the sky, she gave a single cry.

The sound of it was like a blow: it froze him and shocked him. Frightened, he took hold of her arms and held them tight. "Anna," he cried, "don't!"

She was panting, her breath coming in little gasps, and she was glaring at him; in the darkness of her face, her eyes were black as obsidian. "Why must I not?" she demanded hoarsely. "I am an animal like any other. I am hunted and killed, my young are killed, and I, too, have killed . . ."

"Don't say such a thing!"

"It is true! It is true!"

He shook her, while her hair swirled about her face. "Stop it!" he cried. "Stop it!"

Suddenly she was at him, raging, twining herself around him, clutching at him with desperate hands, her mouth, cold as ice, on his; he could hear her moaning deep in her throat like a wild animal. His arms tightened about her, he was gripped by a sudden fury of desire and by an excess of terror; animal-like also, he exulted and trembled. Together they fell to the ground, their hands fumbling in the stiff khaki, unaware of the earth beneath them, the drenched grass, the bare night all around them. "Quickly," she whispered. "Oh, quickly!"

There was something ferocious about the way she gave herself to him, drenched and glowing, insistent, and yet isolated within herself like a stone, obdurate and hard. She was fire and ice; she replied to Joseph's passion, to his awkward haste, almost with desperation, as though she wanted to do violence to her own body. Her whispers were like a hissing of snakes.

And then suddenly it was over, and she was weeping—not the wild sobs of the night before, but good, salt, gentle tears, flowing from her heart.

They lay quietly together on the dew-wet grass, and the moon shone down on them; their thoughts were few and faint and far away; they seemed to have no thoughts. In the fortress a man was still singing:

"*Ze dodi*
Benot Yerushalayem . . ."

She nestled against him, lying warm on his breast. "I wish that I may die peacefully," she said. "Not in fright, and not in pain."

"You're not to die at all," said Joseph. "Not ever."

"Not ever?" she said gravely. "It must come sometime. When there is nothing left."

"Don't say that, Anna. Not any more."

"Dear Joo!" She reached up to stroke his face. "*Te vagy a szerelmem.* Someday you will leave me, too."

"No," he said stoutly, "no. We'll be together. Someday, somehow . . . you'll see. . . ."

He could tell from her voice that she was smiling sadly. "Someday," she said. "Somehow.

"Yes," she said, "it will be so."

"I swear it!" he said. *"If I forget thee, Jerusalem . . ."*

He had to believe it; he had to make her believe it. Otherwise . . .

Otherwise what was the good of love? And he did love her; he loved her with all his heart, with all the longing and the loneliness and the sorrow that was in him. She was his beloved, out of the days of his life; the one, the only one he would have loved in childhood as well as in youth, if they had met, if he had known her.

He drew a deep breath; he was aware of a sorrow, a heaviness of heart . . . what was it? Why should he have such a feeling, now of all times? He had possessed her at last, he had gone to the warm, secret core of her. . . .

The warm, secret core . . . ? He had gone in a rush, in a blind fury; he couldn't even remember, now, what he had wanted, or what he had received. Where was the mercy and the beauty, where were the things he had dreamed about, the soft, scented night, the slow unfolding, the long and tender rapture?

Anna's heart, too, was quiet and sad. She had no illusions. Her dream—which she had fought so long against dreaming—had died when Mia died. Someday, perhaps—somewhere—there would be a new dream for her . . . but not with Mia.

It had been Mia who had given her the will to live all through those desperate, bitter years. Nevermore with Mia.

It was not Joseph's fault; he had given her everything

he had to give: himself, and she blessed him for it. Perhaps someday . . . What was it Menasha had said? "God's love is like a lamp in the world."

There would be light again in the darkness.

They walked back together hand in hand as they had come, slowly and silently. When they got to the walls, Joseph stopped and took her face between his hands. She smiled up at him, steadily and bravely. "I will always love you," he said; and bent and kissed her.

Kastler, in yellow lantern light, with a half-empty bottle of vodka in front of him, was writing to his brother in Switzerland. "This is a small war," he wrote, "and for that reason perhaps a pathetic one. It touches the sensibilities. No great armies are involved; each death is personal, and not anonymous, as in Stalingrad or Africa. Here a young girl dies like a heroine with a rifle in her hand, and one weeps for her; ten thousand such deaths would leave a person unmoved.

"I am in a little fortress called Star in the Wind. Do you remember Musa Dagh? It is like that here, except that the stage is tiny, and the people Jewish. And besides, the ending will be different. It is wonderful to see how these people fight; the same ones who for two thousand years only offered their throats to the butcher. On their own soil, with their backs to the sea or the desert, they defy empires.

"There is a plane which comes over two or three times a day to drop its visiting cards on us; and, of course, we have no means of replying. Everything here is surplus, left behind by the great powers either on purpose or in secret, under the table. Except for what Avriel was able to

buy in Czechoslovakia. American armor, loaned or sold—
who knows?—to Britain, and handed over by her to the
Arabs, bombards us; we bind up our wounds with ban-
dages made in the U.S.A., for the American Navy. Meanwhile, the diplomats hem and haw at Lake Success, where
Milord Cadogan is waiting for an Arab success before
agreeing to a truce. He will not get it, and we shall have a
truce nevertheless, with Count Bernadotte marking the
play—and marking the cards, too, in London's favor.

"But I do not complain: life here is no worse than
anywhere else where one is being shot at. There are diver-
sions: people sing, and men and women enjoy one another's company; it becomes a family affair, like market
day in a village—with differences—

"When this is over, I am coming home, to write
novels. I have in mind the story of a young woman whose
lover is fighting in another brigade, somewhere in the
south; well, what do you think? She meets a handsome
war correspondent—"

Seeing O'Connor go by at that moment, Kastler put
his letter aside and motioned toward the vodka. "Come,"
he said, "keep me company awhile. Now that Malvois has
left us . . . well, what do you think of that? And the
devil only knows where that rascal Bonneau has disappeared to. . . ."

"He's gone off with Arieh," said O'Connor, "on some
devilish errand or other."

"And the young Joseph?"

"He is with Anna."

Kastler nodded his head. "Naturally," he said. "There
is more there than meets the eye?"

"It is a long story," said O'Connor, "and I don't know
the end of it."

The Arab supply depot was in a village somewhere to the right, well out of range of the fortress. At night the two Sherman tanks rested in the village, where the British officer in charge of the Arab armor maintained his headquarters. It was his voice which the girl at the field radio sometimes heard giving orders, half in English and half in Arabic, to the tank crews and to the plane which was based on an airstrip in Amman.

Arieh and six of his men, armed with Sten guns, knives, and sticks of dynamite, slipped down the hill and disappeared one by one into a wheatfield between the main Iraqi encampment and the Arab village. In the shadow of a cloud covering the moon, they reappeared at the edge of the village and advanced toward the two tanks which stood grim and silent in the night shadows, their crews asleep near by, wrapped in their djellabas. A sentry sat nodding before a small fire; quietly, himself a shadow in the night, Arieh stole up on him, and the knife flashed. The sleeping men were dispatched by the others.

Working swiftly, the Irgunists dismantled one of the .50-caliber machine guns from a turret, while Arieh placed sticks of dynamite between the cogs of the tracks of both tanks. One of the sticks of dynamite went off; there was a flash and a roar, and the crank floundered for a moment like a dying monster. Almost at once lights went on in the village, the alarm was sounded, and the entire Arab encampment was aroused; shots were fired, and the second tank blew up.

The Arabs converged on the burning armor like a swarm of angry hornets. By this time the raiders were already back in the wheat; but the cloud-cover was off the moon, and the night was bright. Arieh sent three men ahead with the machine gun, while he and three others covered their retreat; by firing rapidly in bursts, and moving from place to place, he hoped to give the impression of a considerable force. He knew he couldn't hold the Arabs back for very long, but he figured that all he needed was a few minutes. He had no fears for himself or the members of his tiny rear guard; they would slip away like foxes when they were ready. Meanwhile, the gun was on its way to Ben-Abba on the ridge.

Bonneau scrambled up the cliff-face in the white moonlight, his camera knocking—like his heart—against his ribs. He didn't know whether he'd gotten much footage or not; he'd have to wait to see what developed. He kept thinking about Kastler's vodka, and O'Connor's brandy: which was it to be? It wasn't very amusing, being shot at; he looked forward to getting just a little bit potted. Or, as he put it—*soulé*.

CHAPTER

24

ANNA lay on her mattress, her eyes closed; but she was not asleep; she was unable to sleep. She was confused and unhappy. Those terrible feelings she had been unable to control . . . they frightened her. Such a mixture of love and hate, of pain and violence! Like an animal, she thought; an animal. . . .

She thought of that day at Degania, when she had sat with Menasha under the tree above the lake. How sure she had felt then, how peaceful and simple everything seemed. They had talked about so many things: life, and death, and love. . . .

Oh, Menasha, she thought, my friend—there is still something to be said for the old ways. I do not know what to do. . . .

She talked to him, and she imagined that he answered, and it comforted her. What if I were to have a child? she asked him in her mind.

Do you want a child?

I do not think he wants one, Menasha. I would not wish to place such a burden upon him.

And if it should happen?

I do not know. My heart is still broken for Mia. I cannot think of another.

Then look to your defenses, Anna.

She sighed deeply. To love, she said, is to be defenseless. Whoever loves, goes *wehrlos* in the world.

In his sleep, Joseph heard her sigh, and it started a dream. He dreamed that he was running down a street, a familiar street dark and wet and lined with many fountains. It rose and fell like the sea; and the waves which were like hills, green and flowing, rolled slowly toward him and he ran from them, through caves and catacombs in which he could make out the white feet of skeletons. He ran easily, without fear, and with the knowledge that he was running toward something, as well as away from something; but what it was, he didn't know. And then he was standing at the foot of a wave, which was no longer a wave but a hill, and looking up he saw himself standing at the top of it. So that, then, was where he was going; or perhaps he had already gotten there.

The only trouble was, his visas weren't in order. They kept asking him for his nationality.

Anna was still awake when the raiders returned and, hearing the stir of excitement and the subdued jubilation, rose quietly from her bed and went to see what was going on. They were already setting up the machine gun in a nest of sandbags on the flat roof of one of the buildings, and she watched them working; she would have helped, but the sandbags were too heavy for her to lift. After a while she went to the kitchen and lit a fire, and heated some soup and some tea for the men.

By the time she had brought it out to them, the stars had paled and the first grayness was in the air; the dawn wind was coming in from the desert, fresh and cold as spring water, making her huddle in her jacket and rub her hands together to keep them warm.

She climbed the ladder to the parapet and looked out across the world. The east was already faintly rosy, the yellow light beginning to reach upward from below the horizon toward the paling sky. Far to the south the distance was all a pearly gray, while a blue mist still lay in the valley below, through which the dying fires cast an occasional reddish glow. Except for the sentries sitting cross-legged, wrapped in shawls and jackets, there was no one about.

Alone, facing the rising sun, Anna bowed her head. There was such a glory of light coming up behind the dark hills across the way; as the sky above her lifted like a sail and began to shine she felt suddenly lifted with it, tranquil, humble, and at peace. She remembered something Menasha had said to her: Ask God what He wants of Israel.

"I have done the best I could," she said, "and I accept the outcome. I do not ask to understand it."

She remembered something else, from her childhood, something she had not said for a long time:

> "Mi atyánk, ki vagy a menyekben
> Szenteltessék meg a te neved."

"Thy Kingdom come, Thy will be done."

And thinking of Joseph with tenderness, she told herself: I must not be a burden to him. He has another world to which he can return; if someday he comes for me, that, too, is God's will.

I was wrong in thinking myself *wehrlos*. Love does not make the spirit defenseless, for it opens the heart to earth's beauty. To leave the world with love is the best way, for it is the only thing, except hate, that one can carry as far as one goes . . . until the last breath.

Not the love taken, but the love given—to a child, to a lover, to the earth itself. That is what Menasha meant. And afterwards, perhaps, to be with God; who can say?

I, too, can make a little sound.

The rising sun gleamed in patches of gold on the fields behind the fortress, and Anna had a sudden wish— more than a wish: a desire, a longing—to walk in those golden fields, so clean and shining, where only a little while before she and Joseph had lain in darkness. Climbing down the ladder, she stopped in the kitchen long enough to take one of the flat thin loaves of bread from the top of a hot stone, and with her *pita* in her hand she went out between the walls.

There was no shelling from the valley that morning. A little later, Menasha took his shovel and, leading his donkey by a rope, started out for the place where he had been filling his sandbags.

It was a hot, cloudless morning, bright and glittering, and the sun cast long shadows on the ground. The plane that came over from the east had the sun behind it, and it was hard to see until it was almost on top of him. He threw himself to earth, and the shadow of the plane passed over him like a swift, dark cloud, and when it had passed him he lifted his head to watch it. There was a little rise of ground ahead of him, and he saw the plane veer upward, and bank, and come back, and heard the short, rapid barking of its guns as it dived and then zoomed upward and banked again and started back over the fortress.

The new, .50-caliber machine gun on the rooftop went into action behind him, in three short bursts, and the plane faltered, side-slipped, and started to fall; a wing came off, and it plummeted to earth, trailing black smoke, and writhing like a snake. But Menasha didn't see it. He was on his knees, beyond the little rise, staring down at Anna, whose jacket was soaked with blood. Her face was white, and in her eyes the colors of the sky were already fading. But she seemed to be in no pain, and smiled when she saw him. "Father," she whispered.

Her dimming eyes looked out over the fields for the last time. Faintly in her mind, she heard the last notes, the last sounds of earth.

"*Allüberall im ewig blauen Licht die Fernen.*"

"The fields were all golden," she said.

A fresh company of the Palmach had come to relieve the fortress, and in the valley the Iraqis were getting ready to pull out. The assault on Gesher had failed; Kaukab had held, and Abdullah needed the Iraqi brigade to help out at Jenin as the battle for Latrun developed.

Stony-faced and stony-hearted, Joseph stood with O'Connor and watched Anna's body being lowered into the ground. "*Yisga dal v'yiskadash sh'meh rab bo . . .*" "That His great name may be exalted." She has drawn the final loneliness around her, he thought. She will not answer me now, or ever.

There were so many things he wanted to say to her, so many things that he hadn't told her; he wanted to cry out to her: Wait! Wait! He could feel the tears forming in the back of his throat. I mustn't cry, he thought; but then he thought with a sudden sense of revelation: I am old enough to cry.

There were so many questions still to ask. But he knew that she had answered him already, and that the answer would be with him all the days of his life.

He imagined that he heard her voice, as he had heard it that night on shipboard, when he had found her at the dancing: "*I wondered where you were!*"

"I am here," he said.

Quietly and simply he put his gear together, and prepared to leave. Menasha had given him Anna's scarf, and he put it about his neck.

"*Lilah tov,*" he said. "Sleep well, my love."

"Will you be going back to Rome, do you think?" asked O'Connor as the station wagon wound its way back down the road to Tiberias, over which they had come less than a week before. "There's little we can do here now, with the truce coming, and us having to stay cooped up in Tel Aviv."

Joseph shook his head. "I wouldn't be happy in Rome," he said. For a moment he wondered wryly at his own choice of words. Happy? Would he ever be happy again?

But he was too old, now, for that sort of self-pity. Whether he was happy or unhappy, he would go on living, with what he had learned, with what he remembered. He knew that he wouldn't run away any more. That was a strong place in any man's life, a fortress to be defended.

There was nothing mystical about it; he had to learn to accept things as they were, as Menasha accepted them, as Anna had accepted them in the end. *Ewig, ewig . . .* So it had always been, and so it would always be. There were no small accidents; all that had happened to him had made him what he was, and what he would be. . . .

"I am committed, Kevin," he said.

The car rounded a turn, and looking back he saw, for a moment framed against the intense blue of the sky, the flag, the Star of David, blowing in the wind.

BOOKS BY

ROBERT NATHAN

NOVELS

A Star in the Wind   (1962)
The Wilderness-Stone   (1961)
The Color of Evening   (1960)
So Love Returns   (1958)
The Rancho of the Little Loves   (1956)
Sir Henry   (1955)
The Train in the Meadow   (1953)
The Innocent Eve   (1951)   The Married Look   (1950)
The Adventures of Tapiola   (1950)
(containing Journey of Tapiola, 1938, and
Tapiola's Brave Regiment, 1941)
The River Journey   (1949)
Long after Summer   (1948)
Mr. Whittle and the Morning Star   (1947)
But Gently Day   (1943)
The Sea-Gull Cry   (1942)
They Went On Together   (1941)
Portrait of Jennie   (1940)   Winter in April   (1938)
The Barly Fields   (1938)
(containing The Fiddler in Barly, 1926,
The Woodcutter's House, 1927,
The Bishop's Wife, 1928, The Orchid, 1931,
and There Is Another Heaven, 1929)

The Enchanted Voyage   (1936)
Road of Ages   (1935)
One More Spring   (1933)
Jonah   (1925)

POEMS
The Green Leaf   (1950)
The Darkening Meadows   (1945)
Morning in Iowa   (1944)
Dunkirk   (1941)
A Winter Tide   (1940)
Selected Poems   (1935)

THEATER
Jezebel's Husband & The Sleeping Beauty   (1953)

NON-FICTION
Journal for Josephine   (1943)

FOR YOUNG PEOPLE
The Snowflake and the Starfish   (1959)

ARCHAEOLOGY
The Weans   (1960)

These are BORZOI BOOKS, *published in New York
by* ALFRED A. KNOPF

ROBERT NATHAN *was born in New York City in 1894,* *and was educated at private schools in the United States and Switzerland. While attending Harvard University he was an editor of the* Harvard Monthly, *in which his first stories and poems appeared.*

Except for two short periods during which he was a solicitor for a New York advertising firm and a teacher in the School of Journalism of New York University, Mr. Nathan has devoted his time exclusively to writing. He is the author of over forty volumes of poetry and prose, and from this body of distinguished work he has acquired a reputation as a master of satiric fantasy unique in American letters. He lives now in California with his wife, who was Miss Helen Shirley Kneeland of Salem, Massachusetts.

January 1962

A NOTE ON THE TYPE

THIS BOOK is set in ELECTRA, a Linotype face designed by the late W. A. Dwiggins (1880-1956). This face cannot be classified as either modern or old-style. It is not based on any historical model, nor does it echo any particular period or style. It avoids the extreme contrasts between thick and thin elements that mark most modern faces, and attempts to give a feeling of fluidity, power, and speed.

Composed, printed, and bound by
H. Wolff, New York.
Paper manufactured by
P. H. Glatfelter Co., Spring Grove, Pa.
Typography by Vincent Torre